# THE LITTLE FLOWERS

# THE LITTLE FLOWERS

## Nicola Thorne

This first world edition published in Great Britain 2004 by
SEVERN HOUSE PUBLISHERS LTD of
9–15 High Street, Sutton, Surrey SM1 1DF.
This first world edition published in the USA 2004 by
SEVERN HOUSE PUBLISHERS INC of
595 Madison Avenue, New York, N.Y. 10022.

British Library Cataloguing in Publication Data

Thorne,   Nicola
    The little flowers
    1.   Catholic schools - Fiction
    2.   Convents - Fiction
    I.   Title
    823.9'14 [F]

    ISBN 0-7278-6128-X

Except where actual historical events and characters are being
described for the storyline of this novel, all situations in this
publication are fictitious and any resemblance to living persons
is purely coincidental.

Typeset by Palimpsest Book Production Ltd.,
Polmont, Stirlingshire, Scotland.
Printed and bound in Great Britain by
MPG Books Ltd., Bodmin, Cornwall.

Dedicated to the memory of
June Burger Finch
Wonderful doctor, counsellor, friend

# Foreword

This novel has rather a curious history, and it has been suggested I should write an introduction to put it in context as it is unlike most recent Nicola Thorne novels, being not exactly historical, but set in the past. I rather baulked at this idea at first but decided to fall in with it as it is an interesting story in itself, with a touch, perhaps, of melodrama. The novel has in fact languished unpublished for over thirty years in the flotsam and jetsam I have carried about with me as I moved house, completely forgotten and finally discovered as I rummaged through boxes in my garage a few months ago intent on a good clear out.

Its genus is as follows: my first novel, *The Girls*, was published in 1967. It did rather well, especially in paperback, in numbers which today would be considered astronomical. The subject of five girls living in a London boarding house was considered rather scandalous for its day, and maybe as a contrast I decided to write a much gentler, nostalgic sort of novel about girls growing up in a convent boarding school during the war. This, however, did not find favour with my then publishers, and it was put on the back burner and ultimately forgotten.

At the time it was a big setback in my burgeoning career as a novelist and for several years I abandoned writing and concentrated on my 'day job' as a book editor and publisher. Eventually I began to write again, achieved some success, and since that early hiatus nearly fifty of my novels have been published.

However, in 2002 I was seriously injured in a car accident that threatened not only my life but also my career, and because of my injuries I have since been unable to compose an original work of fiction.

To keep my name before the public Severn House has reissued some of my backlist in the last couple of years and now, finally, an original novel. *The Little Flowers*, so lovingly written all those years ago but completely forgotten, seems somehow determined after a long hibernation to see the light of day. Re-reading it I was quite amazed to find that it had weathered so well. However, you learn a lot in the course of writing fifty novels and it did need some fairly drastic cutting and light revision, but apart from that it has scarcely been touched.

Naturally I hope my readers will enjoy it and think it a worthwhile undertaking.

Nicola Thorne
Chideock, Bridport, Dorset
Spring 2004

# PART ONE

Governed by Bells

*1942–1944*

# One

In the early evening of a day in late September Mother St John stood at the top of the steps vigorously ringing her little bell to summon the boarders up from the playground. According to the way she rang it the girls knew what sort of mood she was in, whether they could dawdle or had to run. On this particular day the bell was protracted, insistent, and a concerted effort was made by the netball players to return the balls to the games house, don cardigans and be first up the steps.

From her position at the top Mother St John viewed with approval the effect of her summons. Even then she singled out one or two stragglers, and resolved to make things unpleasant for them when they reached the top.

Mother St John was mistress of the boarders, and quietly or violently dictatorial according to mood. A woman of power. She could make the lives of her charges easy or difficult merely by the expression on her face or the way she walked or rang her bell. She stood back, clasping her little bell tightly to her flat black bosom, and pursed her lips as the first girls reached the top.

'Good evening, Mother,' they chorused, bowing nervously as they passed her, and then they bunched themselves into the cloakroom and whispered anxiously among themselves.

'She's in a mood! She's in a mood!'

The last two up the steps wilted as they saw their way blocked by Mother St John.

'Good evening, Mother.'

Bows, squirms; but only silence from the nun, who stared at them with her pale blue eyes.

'Go to bed early,' she said. 'Straight after supper. You are lazy, disobedient girls.'

'But Mother . . .'

'And don't answer back.'

Mother St John followed her brood into the cloakroom, and stood in the doorway looking for trouble.

'Cynthia! I have told you to hang your gym tunic on a hanger, not on the peg.'

'Yes, Mother.'

'Gertrude! Yours has dropped on the floor!'

'Yes, Mother. Sorry, Mother.'

Then, changed and groomed, hair neatly combed, her charges shuffled expertly into line in the playroom waiting for the next command.

'Straight into the study, girls, and no talking.'

The line marched with the precision of well-trained cadets, the youngest first, the eldest at the back. Mother St John darted back into the cloakroom and sentenced a few more stragglers to early bed; then she brought up the rear of the line still clutching her little bell, still pressing her thin lips into an unpleasant and menacing grimace.

The Convent of the Blessed Apostles stood in the working-class part of the grey northern town. There were four hundred day girls and seventy boarders. There were a dozen weekly boarders, but they were frowned upon and any increase in their numbers was not encouraged. Besides, they were mainly Protestants.

The boarders came from all over the country, some from the same town, and some from the south. One or two came from Scotland, and several were Irish, but there were no real foreigners. The convent was but one of a number in England and on the Continent belonging to the Order, which had been founded in France in the middle of the nineteenth century by the Venerable Françoise-Marie Bechaud for the teaching and improvement of young Catholic girls.

In the town the convent was a respected institution. All families aspired to sending their girls there in the hope that an education amid such refinement would give them if not intelligence, at least a better start in life. Although the nuns considered that education was of secondary importance to the knowledge and practice of the Faith and the acquisition of gentility and good manners, they nevertheless turned out girls who were not wholly deficient in the elements of scholarship, and one or two who even aspired to university.

Mother St John had very pale blue eyes, a peculiarly white skin that puckered by the nose and chin, and blond eyebrows. It was difficult to know her age. To the young she seemed very old, but was probably not more than forty, maybe younger. The only part of the nuns' habit that was not black was the white wimple at the forehead, and Mother St John's always seemed rather tight, pressing on her forehead and crumpling her skin. The effect was to give her an almost permanently discontented expression, making her seem hard to please. This stood her in good stead in the role she had to perform, a responsible and sometimes onerous one. However, when she smiled her expression was transformed and she looked almost benign.

She had joined the Order when she was eighteen, having set out from Ireland on the big adventure to the mother house in the south of England. Her education had been rudimentary but there was enough of it to make her into a choir nun, and spare her the menial tasks of the lay sisters, who polished and cooked and saw to the material wants of those in the convents. She taught religious studies for several years after her profession, and had then been sent to the northern town in the early 1930s as mistress of the boarders, then numbering only a few.

She had thus almost grown up with her job, and, in fact, she did it quite well. She was an extrovert and a pragmatist and she did not look too closely into the meaning of things. She was obedient to her superiors, and expected discipline in turn from those in her charge. She could be demanding and bad tempered, but also playful and compassionate. There were girls whom she favoured or punished more than others, but on the whole she administered a kind of rough justice that was endurable.

She was in such a mood this particular evening because she had received a summons from Reverend Mother, of whom she was in awe. As well as being her superior in religion, Reverend Mother was capricious, and could start off being very nice about something and finish the interview by being absolutely horrible about something else. One never knew where one was with Reverend Mother, hence the reason for her power. In another age she would have made a magnificent and formidable abbess of some medieval foundation because she could be alternatively confiding yet suspicious, trustful yet accusing, forceful yet weak, gay yet vengeful. She ruled the convent like a domain from her room next to the chapel, and everyone, nun or girl, watched their step as they passed it, fearful of a summons.

On this occasion Mother St John feared that the interview would surely cover the fact that the previous night several girls in the dormitory of the Immaculate Conception had been found having an improvised midnight feast of an assortment of goodies, smuggled in from outside. Mother St John was in charge of this dormitory, but because it was so large she was assisted by a rather frightened, weak-willed nun called Mother Euphrasia, who loved to tell tales about the girls to Reverend Mother.

Mother Euphrasia had reported the midnight feast to Mother St John, and they had both agreed on a punishment for the girls and to say nothing to Reverend Mother. But Mother St John knew that Mother Euphrasia could be trusted to keep nothing to herself, and she was sure that by this time the news of the disaster had reached Reverend Mother.

Mother St John positively debased herself in the presence of Reverend Mother. Whereas most of the nuns were dignified, respectful and deferential to their superior, Mother St John tossed off any restraint and became a pitiful creature of cunning, humility and guile.

Thus she knocked timidly on Reverend Mother's door at exactly five thirty in the afternoon and slithered before the presence smiling a smile that only Reverend Mother and the better class parents of the children ever saw. And there, behold, chatting away to Reverend Mother, positively lolling in a chair, was a young girl with long golden hair, fine fiery eyes surmounted by dark brows and a dress that only just covered her knee. Reverend Mother kept Mother St John waiting a moment or two and then turned to her with a smile.

'There you are, Mother St John. I want to introduce you to one of your new charges. Andrea Mackintosh, Mother St John, who is in charge of the boarders.'

The golden girl took her time about rising to her feet, bestowed on Mother St John a smile of unforced brilliance and took her hand.

'How do you do, Mother St John?'

Mother St John was all confusion. How like Reverend not to have warned her; not even to have discussed the matter with her. Not a word; and there she had been all prepared to do battle over the consumption of the midnight feast. However, she quickly recovered and composed herself, giving the newcomer her most ingratiating smile.

'How do you do, Andrea?'

Andrea smiled back, and gave up her chair to Mother St John, drawing up another which she placed near to Reverend Mother, with whom she had already established a rapport.

'Andrea is the daughter of a great friend of my brother. Her father is a diplomat and is to be sent to the United States of America. So Andrea is to come to us as a boarder. I only knew of it today, Mother, so I did not have the chance to consult you. The whole thing has been arranged rather hurriedly. Andrea has no mother, but an aunt lives nearby and her father thought it would be nice for the aunt to keep an eye on her, and also that she should be under my charge as he knows my brother so well.

'I know term has already commenced,' Reverend Mother went on, 'but Andrea has been at a very good day school in London. She will be in the Lower Fifth and will have no difficulty in keeping up with her class. Her headmistress has

7

sent Mother Michael a glowing report of her work. She will come to us next week after her father has returned to London. Mother St John will look after you, Andrea, and see that you have all you want.'

'Thank you, Reverend Mother.' Andrea got languidly to her feet, carefully observed by Mother St John. No nerves about her, she thought; she was used to rather more deference from new girls. However, she gave her another of her toothsome smiles, resolving that she would soon reduce her to quaking conformity with the rest.

'Daddy is calling back for me at six. I'll go and wait for him. Next week, then, Reverend Mother?'

'Yes, dear child.' Reverend Mother did not rise. She never did when addressing the young or her inferiors. She pressed the bell, which summoned a lay sister, whom she asked to take Andrea to the parlour where she could wait for her father.

Mother St John did get up, and trotted outside with her new charge, clasping her arm. Then she shook her hand warmly and echoed Reverend Mother's sentiments that Andrea should be happy in the convent and make lots of nice friends.

As Andrea was escorted away Mother St John went more boldly back into Reverend Mother's room feeling happy and relaxed.

'Such a charming girl, Mother. We must make her very happy here. Such good class.'

'Of course, Mother.' Mother St John fluttered her hands and looked ingratiating.

'You must think of some very nice friends for her. There is one tiny thing. Andrea is a Protestant, and her father is most anxious that she does not change her religion.'

Mother St John and Reverend Mother exchanged knowing looks. What was a Protestant if not a challenge? Why, a soul crying out for the Faith.

'Of course, that does not mean that if the dear girl is convinced in time of the truths of our religion she will not persuade her father to change his mind. But it must be tactful and subtle, do you understand, Mother? Andrea will stay with us until she is eighteen. Her father is anxious for her to go to university, and we have already discussed this with Mother Michael. Now, who shall we choose to help her settle down?'

'Anne Hollings, Mother? A most delightful girl. She has not been in trouble all this term.'

'I'm not surprised. I can think of few people so dull as Anne Hollings. It must be someone with spirit, as Andrea has spirit. She is a very spirited girl.'

Mother St John grimaced. She did not like spirited girls one little bit.

'Now how about Clare Bingley?'

Mother St John's face darkened.

'Clare, Mother . . .'

'All right, I know. Clare is not the best girl in the school, but she has class. She has style. Also, her father is a doctor and this will be more the social level of our dear Andrea.'

'Clare is bold, Mother.'

Bold was about the worst term Mother St John could apply to anyone.

'I do not share your opinion of Clare, Mother, though I know she is a trial to you. Clare will do very well to show Andrea round,' Reverend Mother said firmly.

'But Clare's best friend is Lucy Potts, Mother, and her father is a plumber.'

Despite her own feelings about class, feelings that she did her best to conceal, Reverend Mother would not take blatant class attitudes from anyone else; certainly not from Mother St John.

'Our Lord was a carpenter, Mother,' she chided her. 'Would you have disapproved of that? Besides, he is a very good plumber and has his own business. No, I can think of no one better than Clare, and if we have to have Lucy too then we have to. Besides, Lucy is very devout and her simple piety may work wonders on Andrea. Clare has no piety at all. She was reading John Buchan during Holy Hour in the chapel the other night.'

'That's what I mean, Mother. She is bold. No other girl

9

would read John Buchan in chapel. However, if it is your wish . . .'

Reverend Mother nodded, and seemed to indicate that the interview was at an end. Mother St John's timid heart stopped its wild beating. Reverend Mother had not heard about the midnight feast after all. She began to back towards the door like a Chinese coolie in a melodrama.

Reverend Mother was diminutive in size, not more than five foot one or two. She had a good complexion, not the dreadful whiteness of so many nuns, and dark almost violet eyes. She could sometimes look really beautiful, and sometimes she looked very stern. Her moods changed almost without warning. She beckoned to the retreating mistress of the boarders with a gesture that was almost regal, not forbidding at all.

'There is another thing before you go, Mother. A matter, rather grave, that has been brought to my attention, I shall not say how. It concerns several girls in your dormitory who were indulging in a riot of feasting last night. Can you explain it, Mother?'

Mother St John was immediately reduced to quivering flesh.

'We have taken action, Mother.'

'I dare say. But prevention is better than cure, is it not? How did the girls come to have food in the dormitory and who brought it?'

'The day girls, Mother.' Mother St John spoke derisively of that large majority, as though they were another species. 'There would only have been cakes, maybe cordial . . .' Mother St John trailed off, looking vague. 'Certainly no alcohol.'

'I should think not, the idea is preposterous!' Reverend Mother looked shocked. 'I suggest,' she went on sternly, 'that Julia Beck, whom I understand was the ring leader, is put into St Imelda's dormitory, where better care will be taken of her.'

'Yes, Mother, I . . .'

'It is disgraceful, Mother. Your charge of the girls is a

sacred trust, to their parents as well as Our Lord. Do not abuse this trust, Mother, and let the girls misbehave.'

'No, Mother. The girls will not be allowed their sweet ration next week.'

Reverend Mother looked sadly at her victim.

'Mother, how could you? In these hard times of war, deprive the young girls of their sweets? They get little nourishment enough as it is. I am surprised at you, Mother, for thinking such a thing.'

'But I didn't, Mother . . .'

'But you did.' Reverend Mother's insistence was very gentle. 'You did, Mother. The children must have their sweets and eat them in the playroom. Not in the study, the chapel or the dormitories. If that is clear to you now, Mother, you may go back to your charges.'

Reverend Mother picked up a book from the table by her side to signify dismissal. In fact it was the volume of John Buchan that she had caused to be confiscated from Clare Bingley, and she was enjoying *Greenmantle* enormously. Clare, who had style, was one of her pets, and she approved of her choice of literature but not, as she had gently pointed out, for Holy Hour in the chapel.

As Reverend Mother started her reading Mother St John stumbled towards the door. She recovered herself outside, and made straight for the study to see what pickings she could glean from those who had spoken during the study hour while supposed to be on their honour. In fact, she made the rest of the evening very unpleasant for the boarders, who, for once, were glad to get to their beds, where the more wilful of them lay sticking pins in little mental images of Mother St John before they could get to sleep.

Clare Bingley was furious at being singled out to look after the new girl. Mother St John had assured her that the idea was Reverend Mother's, because anything she thought of was sure to be opposed by Clare.

Clare had come to the convent at the age of seven, and

11

from the day of her transition to the senior school at eleven she and Mother St John had failed to understand each other. Apart from 'bold', the other word most used by Mother St John to describe Clare was 'wilful'. This was a term of abuse too. Clare was bold and she was wilful. Mother St John was disturbed by anything she could not understand, anything which did not fit exactly into the pattern of order and regularity required by the convent rule. Many girls were more naughty than Clare; it wasn't naughtiness at all, in fact. It was simply that Clare went her own way in her own time, and invariably did just what she wanted.

On the whole Clare was popular in the school. But some did dislike her very much because, besides her boldness and wilfulness, she was clever at her studies, good at games, attractive to look at and generally scornful in her attitude to others. The most timid and masochistic among the girls thought she was marvellous, but others were genuinely afraid of her. She was clever with words, and could hurt in subtle as well as more obvious ways.

Clare was Mother St John's cross, and she was sure that one day the girl would come to a bad end. Piety did not allow her actually to hope this, and she often examined her conscience on account of her, and prayed for her frequently.

From time to time throughout her school life, Clare would adopt one of her admirers for the role of 'best friend'. The function of this minion was to be a victim of Clare's whims, tantrums and spite. The best friend always suffered a lot, but most of the chosen seemed to enjoy this masochistic role and wept bitterly when they were discarded for another, like Louis XIV swapping his court favourites.

Besides her capacity to receive abuse, the best friend was, above all, required to listen to the current of comments and confidences that poured out of Clare in a monosyllabic diffusion. Clare enjoyed the sound of her own voice, liked to hear it often, and was frequently among the ranks of the prolific talkers who lined the study walls doing penance.

\*     \*     \*

12

Lucy was hovering in the corridor outside the study when Clare emerged from her conference with Mother St John about Andrea. Lucy had been Clare's best friend for two terms by this time, and was proving a success mainly because of her own lack of words and almost limitless capacity for self-abnegation.

Clare, in her temper, just strode past Lucy as though she hadn't seen her. Unabashed, Lucy, used quite well to this kind of treatment, jogged along after her friend, giving little runs in order to try and catch her up.

'Clare, Clare,' she called. 'Tell. Oh, Clare.'

Clare ignored her and marched down to the refectory, where the others at her table tried placatingly to establish what had happened. They wondered if Mother St John had heard about the secret society that Clare had formed called the Bloody Hand, of which a requisite for membership was that an initiate had to draw blood from the fleshy part of her palm and mingle it with one of the others. Clare was rather old for secret societies, but she had been forming them for years simply because they were forbidden and it was a way of protesting. Now the younger girls mainly asked her to be their leader and think of a name, and she let them get on with the blood mingling by themselves. The Bloody Hand had been formed as a final act of defiance before she went into the Lower Fifth and became a senior girl.

The girls did not sit in forms in the refectory, but were mixed in ascending order of seniority, about eight or ten to a table. 'What is it?' they hissed when Mother St John had banged the gong for talking. 'Is it the Bloody Hand?'

Clare gave them a look of unimaginable scorn, carefully buttered her bread, put jam on it and began to discuss the composition of the netball team for Saturday's away game against another convent.

Lucy, at a separate table, brooded about her friend, kept giving her back little hurt reproachful glances, and was so upset that she only had one slice of bread and no jam. This was not the first time that Lucy had been put off her food by Clare, who always had a good appetite and was now enjoying a hearty tea.

After study, chapel and supper those who had not been sent to bed early would gather in the gym, split into groups and chat or play the gramophone. Some danced a sedate tango or waltz with one another.

Clare came late into the gym because she had had a meeting with the members of the netball team, presided over by Mother Mary David, whose sole claim to athletic prowess was that she had once organized chess for the others in her novitiate ten years before. As soon as she saw Clare, Lucy ran eagerly up to her.

'What *is* it Clare?'

Clare looked at Lucy as though still undecided about whether to snub her or not; but she was bursting with indignation and simply dying to speak about it all.

'I have to look after a new girl who is coming at the end of the week. Fancy asking me!'

'What a cheek.' Lucy felt restored to grace. 'Why *you*?'

'Because Johnny hates me.'

'Perhaps it won't be too bad. I'll help.'

'Of course you'll help. I shan't do a thing. I'll leave it all to you.'

Lucy smiled gratefully. 'Oh thank you, Clare. Shall we have a dance?'

Clare scorned dancing with girls. She said, 'Don't be absurd,' and went to talk to someone else. Lucy watched Clare, sighing sadly. She was afraid that Clare was getting tired of her. Perhaps scorn for the new girl would help to bring them together.

When Mother St John came in tinkling her bell for the end of recreation the girls formed before the statue of Our Lady, sang 'Hail Queen of Heaven' with great fervour and went up to their various dormitories. Washing and going to bed was one of the times for keeping silent; in fact, the last words, except for prayers, were supposed to have been spoken in the gym. But after lights out and the final 'praise be to Jesus's' were said Clare made her way along the back

14

of the cubicles, carrying for Lucy a two-day-old cream cake that one of the day girls had smuggled in for her. Clare often made conciliatory gestures of this kind after she had been especially beastly to her friend.

They shared the cake amidst whispers until they heard Mother St John come in from the nuns' night prayers. Nervously they held their breath because Mother St John had a habit of moving quietly along the cubicles to see if she could hear any talking. But tonight she went straight to her own cubicle at the end of the dormitory, and those who were nearest to her could hear the soft jangle of her rosary beads and the swirl of her clothes as she undressed.

'You're not cross with me, are you, Clare?' Lucy said, brushing the crumbs from her lap into her tooth mug.

'Of course I'm not, silly. I'm cross with that beastly old nun. Surely she knows I am too busy and important to have time for some stupid new girl?'

'Perhaps she thinks you'll do it best.'

'She said the Rev chose me. But she tells lies, of course. Why should Rev choose me?'

'Because she likes you. Perhaps it's some very special new girl.'

'She's a Protestant.'

'Well that will be it then.' Lucy always wanted to try and make everyone happy; the feud between Clare and Mother St John made her nervous in case it involved her.

'What do you mean, "That will be it?" What a daft thing to say.'

'Sorry, Clare. I meant that with your tact, and . . .'

'Piety?'

'Yes, that too of course, you would be the very best person to show the new girl round.'

'I am not at all pious, and you know it. I think religion is soppy.'

'Clare!'

'You know I do.'

'But you mustn't *say* it Clare. You must never say a thing

15

like that.' Lucy started to tremble, and looked fearfully at the curtain in case the Devil walked in.

'I'll say what I like. I THINK RELIGION IS SOPPY.' Clare said the words very loudly and slowly as though there were some kind of natural pause between each one.

'Clare, Clare. Shhh!'

'You are silly.'

Without another word Clare got off the bed, put her crumbs in Lucy's tooth mug and peered out of the curtain.

'I shall never bring you a cream cake again,' she said to Lucy as a parting shot, and made her way back to her cubicle.

Not for the first time she wished her best friend had a little more to her. She got into bed without saying her prayers and lay looking at the ceiling, listening to the little noises of people settling to sleep. The awful drip next to her said the rosary in bed every night and she listened contemptuously to the beads clanking away, then said, 'Shhh!' very sharply and hit the curtain between them.

Although Clare spoke so boldly about religion she was sure there was a heaven and a hell, and she knew whose side she would be on when the time came to go. As with much else, Clare's attitude towards religion was bravado, and she didn't really believe what she said. But she did scorn open religious practices like the rosary, which she thought boring and dull. She only said it during Lent for a penance, and then never in bed.

Clare got herself to sleep by telling herself marvellous stories about what life would be like when she grew up. She would go to London and the university. She might have a boyfriend, and would know lots of sophisticated people. Clare was not really happy at school, which was why she was so irritable with people. She regarded it as a time of waiting and suspension until womanhood emerged, which was frightening and mysterious. She had a very vivid imagination, which seemed frustrated and contained by the narrow world of the convent, and the small town further north where her parents lived. She knew that bursting to get out was this great potential for living, and she could not wait to grow up.

After thinking for some time she knew she would not sleep, so she got her torch out of her locker and retrieved a Catholic Truth Society pamphlet that she had hidden up her knicker leg and brought from the study. She pulled the sheets well over her head leaving only a small gap for breathing. The girls were given the pamphlets by Mother Euphrasia in an effort to try, vainly, to gain their favour even more than by telling them nasty things about Mother St John. They were supposed only to read them in the gym or in study after homework was finished. They were published in Dublin and were stories with a strong religious theme. They were not in the same class as John Buchan or Wilkie Collins, but these were too heavy to be concealed in one's knickers. Even so Clare enjoyed the pamphlets because they were about life outside the convent. She had never been further south than Manchester in her life. She also enjoyed the fact that she was breaking the rules by reading in bed while the other silly girls said their rosaries or fidgeted with the things on their lockers. Clare did her best to adapt the rules of the convent to her own convenience or to ignore them altogether.

The convent day was divided into parts with almost liturgical regularity. Mass was at 7.00, breakfast at 7.45. Bed-making afterwards, and school at 9.00. Recreation in the playroom or grounds from 12.30 to 1.00, and after lunch forty minutes in the playground, regardless of weather unless it was pouring. School from 2.00 to 4.00, free time until tea, and then study and games or piano practice from 5.00 until chapel at 7.00. Supper at 7.30 and then forty minutes recreation, except for the bad ones, who had been sent straight to bed, or those whose weekly bath night it was. Lights out at 8.45, winter and summer alike, except for the more senior girls, who slept in the dormitory of the Holy Ghost and whose hours were more flexible because of their studies.

The rule of the Order was based on that founded by St Benedict for his monks in the sixth century so that, by frugality, contemplation and work, his followers might shun earthly attachments and grow closer to God. To expect girls from the ages of seven to eighteen to follow this kind of discipline in the twentieth century was doubtless asking too much of them. It was, of course, not as severe as monastic life or even that of the nuns, who got up at 5.30 in the morning, and spent more of the day on their devotions. But if one began it early enough one grew up with it, and if one came to it later one adapted to it. Convent girls were expected to be modest, decorous and be able to endure long periods of silence. This was the way of perfection. But, as girls, they had to learn these things, how to control themselves, how to enjoy themselves and even how to protect themselves.

Reverend Mother, in the little homilies she sometimes delivered to the boarders, was fond of quoting Ecclesiastes to them: 'For everything, girls,' she would say, ' "there is a season, and a time for every matter under heaven: a time to be born and a time to die; a time to weep and a time to laugh; a time to mourn and a time to dance". Above all, dear girls, there is "a time to keep silence and a time to speak". This is in the Bible, children, and we must remember it all our lives. It is the way of perfection.'

The girls found this passage from Ecclesiastes very uplifting. Even the number of times Reverend Mother quoted it to them did not dim their appreciation of the beauty and nobility of the sentiments. But some of the more imaginative would adapt it to express the very monotony and drabness of the routine, and would bowdlerize it by intoning, in an imitation of the cultured voice of Reverend Mother:

'A time to get up and a time to go to bed; a time to get dressed and a time to get undressed; a time to eat and a time to swallow; a time to brush your teeth and a time to do your hair.'

The varieties of this were, of course, endless, and some of them were quite rude.

The only way Clare could live was not to conform: to be as unlike anyone else as possible. But like anyone else she disliked punishments, especially as most of them deprived her of a chance to talk. So she had become skilful in her deceit, and a most practised liar. She didn't think this was wrong, because if the convent made one this way it had only itself to blame. Clare felt responsible for no one and nothing; her only concern, the only object of her devotion and admiration, was herself.

# Two

A ndrea Mackintosh was one who, despite her youth, had long ago learned to conceal emotion and make the best of situations that she regarded as inevitable. The idea of going to a convent in the north of England was a notion at first quite shattering. Her father did not discuss it with her, he merely informed her of his decision. He could not help his postings in the foreign service and he wanted to do nothing to impede his career by deferring promotion. It was out of the question to take his daughter abroad in war time, and she would be safer in the north than in London, where they had already lived through the Blitz together.

Once the decision was made, no time was lost in its execution. The London house was shut up; Andrea said tearless goodbyes to her friends and travelled up with her father to the aunt she hardly knew.

Andrea was appalled as her aunt now drove her through the narrow little streets of the northern town that was to be her home. The late-afternoon sun shone insipidly on the rows of brown terraced houses, and there was no colour in the children who played hoop-la on the pavements or in the mangy dogs who attempted to play with them. She cheered up as they drove through the convent gates and she saw the park about her and the buildings before her.

The buildings and grounds were in harmony with the lofty aspirations of the Order. They were elegant, beautiful and well kept. There was the main residential block, which was L-shaped, consisting of quarters for the nuns and boarders, a chapel and an infirmary. This had once been the grand mansion of one of the rich cotton merchants who had contributed to the wealth of the town in the nineteenth century. Linked to it by a covered passage was the new modern school building, which was higher than the rest.

At the front was a paved drive and forecourt, formal lawns and gardens, and then a gentle undulating few acres of field sweeping down to the lake. On the far side of the lake were fields and woodland that climbed up a slope to meet the surrounding wall, which intervened between the privileged few who were in the convent and the majority of the towns-people.

Inside the floors were parquet and richly polished. The walls were white and hung with pictures depicting noble religious subjects like the martyrdom of St Sebastian, his body covered with arrows and bleeding profusely, or the ascension of the Virgin into heaven. Most of the pictures were intended to raise the mind towards heaven, where God lived in splendour with his saints. But some of them were meant as a warning: they depicted scenes of hell, that frightful place of the afterlife where those who had not done God's will on earth suffered the torments they deserved. Pictures like this were usually strategically placed outside the chapel, refectory or study, where the girls formed in lines, sometimes waiting, and thus could spend time in a fearful contemplation of the fruits of misbehaviour.

After some ringing the door was opened by the same nun who had seen Andrea out the week before, Sister Angela. She was a hearty Irish nun with a face like a friendly bargee, and she knew all about the fears of little girls because she had been admitting them and seeing them out for years. She bustled about chattering all the time while she fetched Andrea's two cases from the boot of the car. Then she took them to the parlour and told them she would bring them some tea while they waited for the end of Benediction.

''Tis the feast of St Michael,' she explained. 'So there's an extra bit of fuss today.'

'Why?' Aunt wanted to know.

'Because he is the patron saint of Mother Michael, the

21

headmistress. The girls always have a special treat on this day.'

'Do they?' said Aunt, unimpressed. 'How very interesting. But we have already taken tea, thank you. We shall just wait.'

She sat herself in the most comfortable seat and lit a cigarette, which she fastened in a long holder. Then she looked about her.

The best parlour had honey parquet flooring, which Sister Angela polished twice a day, a huge oval walnut table where the priest had breakfast after Mass each morning, and several fine pieces of furniture. A bow window looked on to the park, and there was a view of the rose beds and the tops of the tall trees.

'Well, I expected a dump,' Aunt murmured. 'In fact, it's quite elegant, Andrea.'

'It's *beautiful*, Aunt. I thought so when I was here before, though I came the back way and did not really have a good chance to see it properly. It cheers me up. I was depressed.'

'Were you?' Aunt looked curiously at her niece. 'What a very odd emotion.'

'Are you never depressed, Aunt?'

'Never. I am too busy. I am still not sure your father was wise to bring you to this place. You would have been better off in London.' She paused for some moments, gazing about her. 'Just look at that clock. It is Empire and must have cost a fortune. Of course these Catholics have money. It comes from the Vatican.'

'Does it, Aunt? All of it?'

'Don't be sarcastic, Andrea. The Vatican helps the Catholic Church in all the countries of the world because its main object is world domination. I told this to your father, but he laughed. You must be careful not to attend any of the religious services and to ignore the mumbo-jumbo they will undoubtedly try to instil into you. Look at those preposterous paintings. Superstition, that's all it is.'

Andrea looked. Over the mantel was a fine reproduction of the Virgin with St John and St Jerome of the Quattrocentro Italian school, and on the far wall was an Andrea del Sarto

Madonna and child. A long tryptich after Cimabue ran along the wall by the door.

'I think they're rather nice, Aunt. They are probably reproductions of old masters.'

'They are superstitious rubbish,' Aunt said, drawing on her cigarette. 'Where are these wretched nuns?'

Andrea gazed at the paintings. She had visited most of the European art galleries during her holidays abroad. Her father was a connoisseur of art, and he and Andrea had shared some of their happiest moments together in the Uffizi and the Louvre, but not the Prado, because of the civil war in Spain.

Andrea scarcely knew her aunt, who had been left a large estate and wealth by her husband, who had died after only two years of marriage. Accordingly she had been too long cut off from human warmth and had never known the company of the young. She felt very put upon by this imposition of her brother's, and only a sense of family duty had made her agree. Her hobbies were bridge and blood sports, and when she was doing neither of these things she looked after her estate and husbanded her wealth.

Aunt did not rise to greet Reverend Mother, who came in at last, with Mother St John a respectful step behind. Aunt did not believe in standing up for women, nuns or not, and she just stretched out a languid hand and took Reverend Mother's firm one in an insipid clasp. Reverend Mother turned and opened her arms to embrace Andrea.

'My dear little girl!' she cried. 'Welcome.'

Andrea had never been kissed by a lady with a complicated helmet affair obscuring most of her face, but she responded with the warmth and ease of one who had been doing it all her life and pressed her cheek to Reverend Mother's mouth. She was quite determined that she and Reverend Mother would get on. Mother St John, diffident about kissing someone who had just been kissed by Reverend Mother, clumsily seized Andrea and pressed her to her breast. Then Sister Angela came in carrying a large tray with tea cups, dainty sandwiches and little orange cakes.

'We have already taken tea, Reverend Mother, thank you,' Aunt said politely.

'But you will surely be persuaded to have another cup?' Reverend Mother insisted gently. 'I will pour it myself.'

Aunt grimaced and accepted the cup with bad grace, refusing the sandwiches.

'And how is our dear Andrea?'

'Very well, thank you, Reverend Mother.'

'And looking forward to being with us?'

'Yes, of course.'

'She is a darling child,' Reverend Mother said to Aunt. 'You will miss her.'

'I shall,' Aunt said briefly, not caring to elaborate too much upon the untruth of this statement.

'We have a nice friend for her who will help her to settle down. Mother, will you fetch Clare?'

Mother St John nearly fell over backwards on the slippery floor in her anxiety to execute Reverend Mother's wishes immediately, and while she was gone Reverend Mother poured tea and pressed a small orange cake on a reluctant Andrea, who was by now feeling rather sick with the strain of Aunt being awkward, and the two gushing nuns. It was a horribly artificial situation.

'Andrea has no uniform, Reverend Mother. My brother said you would buy what she needs and send me the account.'

'Of course. She will have everything she needs. You may come and visit her on alternate Saturday afternoons if you wish.'

'Well, I don't know that I will always be able to do that. I hunt at weekends.'

'Really? How civilized of you. I have not hunted since I was a young girl. In fact, I did not realize people still hunted, because of the war.'

'The war?' Aunt gestured vaguely as though hearing the news of hostilities for the first time.

'Never mind if you can't come; the older girls will look after Andrea. And here *is* Clare.'

Clare stood at the door on the other side of Mother St

John. The resistance she had felt to the new girl had mounted so much inside her that it had etched its mark on her features, which registered remoteness, almost disdain.

Andrea, turning to greet her, sensed it, and looked boldly into her eyes as they shook hands.

'Hello, Clare.'

'Hello, Andrea.'

Clare dropped her gaze. The new girl was unexpected. Her glance had disturbed her. Andrea was still looking at Clare when she raised her eyes, and she felt the rise of something warm and confused inside her, and looked away again.

Andrea was amused by the change in Clare, in that fractional moment, and knew she had made an impression, as she invariably did on people meeting her for the first time. She turned away to press her advantage home with Reverend Mother. Mother St John was pacing about in an excited way, making little clucking noises like a hen answering the call to mate.

Then it was time for Aunt to go, and she was seen to her car and waved off with more enthusiasm than sincerity. Andrea was glad to see Aunt go, but as she turned and faced the door she had a sudden feeling of strangeness and fright. Everything up to now had been acting, but here she was, quite alone and with new people. She was going to live here.

'We want you to be happy here, Andrea,' Reverend Mother was saying. 'Very happy.'

'I'm sure I will be, Reverend Mother.'

Then Reverend Mother went away, and with Clare on one side and Mother St John on the other Andrea waited to be initiated into her new life.

'We want you to be happy here.'

The expressions on the faces of the girls in the study, mostly, were not altogether welcoming. Yet nor were they hostile. They were curious; they were measuring. The main thing was that the advent of the newcomer gave them a chance to stop work and chat, and after the great inquisitive silence

25

that greeted Andrea murmurings and whispers broke out. Not about her, just about anything.

Clare, Andrea and Mother St John formed a little procession that paced carefully down the study to the fourth row of desks, by the window.

The study was a long, low room running half the length of the old building, directly under the chapel, and was in essence the home of the boarders. There each had a desk where she kept her books, missal, black veil for chapel and such small personal possessions as were allowed. Diaries, for instance, were forbidden, and so were novels, sweets and chocolates, and, of course, cosmetics.

'This is your desk, Andrea. You are just in front of Clare. Here you keep all your small things. Here you work and spend time at weekends. It is like your home.'

Andrea inspected her home, and saw that it was empty except for a few large ink stains and bits of dust in the corners inside. The hinged top section was worked with small holes and deep lines engraved in the wood by some past occupant, no doubt while toiling with the rigours of composition, calculation or simply boredom. This was her home.

'It's very nice,' she said woodenly. 'What a lovely room.'

The windows of the study were high up so that the girls should not be distracted by too frequent a contemplation of the grounds. But there were many windows and the room was light. There were glass cases full of books, and a small library at the end with open shelves. On one side of the high nun's desk was a painting of the Sacred Heart with the names underneath of those who had enrolled themselves in a special fellowship of love. On the other side was a brightly painted statue of the Virgin Mary with her arms stretched towards the girls who sat before her. A little blue altar light flickered in front of her and there was a bowl of large yellow and white chrysanthemums. At this end of the study there were two doors, one leading to the new school building, the other to the laboratory, which ran the length of the study on the street side of the building.

Clare watched Andrea's reactions, and she envied her. Here

she was seeing something new; but even when the newness went and became accustomed and stale, it could not last for very long. For Clare, it was eight years old already. Andrea was very composed and smiled all the time; she did not seem afraid at all.

Mother St John walked up and down wielding authority with a frown or muffled sharp word here and there, or smiling grotesquely at Andrea every time she came near her. As she walked Mother St John's habit swished; her long rosary jangled by her side and she folded her arms in her sleeves across her waist. She was feeling nervous but slightly triumphant, because she was sure she had already made a very good impression on the new girl.

'Show Andrea her bed in the dormitory, and then you may take her on an introductory tour of the school, Clare. You will bring Andrea down for supper.'

'Yes, Mother.'

Clare looked away with impatience. The cloying sweetness of Mother St John contrasting with her customary illtemper nauseated her. She didn't try to hide her contempt and her replies were monosyllabic and sullen.

As they walked from the study Clare noticed that Andrea sauntered. Her gait was easy and unhurried, very leisured. After a time in the convent the girls tended to walk as though they were always in a mad hurry to get somewhere, which in a sense they were, their lives being governed by bells.

The nuns were always pulling the girls up for the way they scurried along, squelching on the polished floors in their rubber-soled shoes. Clare admired the way Andrea sauntered, and tried to adapt her pace. She was conscious of Andrea as they walked. They were about the same height but Andrea had long golden hair, loose about her shoulders, and Clare's was black and curly round her head. She was not jealous of the pink jumper and skirt that Andrea wore, because she thought she looked rather smart in her navy school dress, with the light blue ribbon of Child of Mary around her neck, fastened at the back with a pin and ending in the front with the silver medal.

Most of the girls in the convent belonged to the sodalities, which started for the young with the Infant Jesus and worked through the Holy Angels, St Philomena and St Aloysius to Child of Mary. The sodalities were pious associations, the basis of which was prayer and acts of self-sacrifice. But, really, the fact was that the ribbons looked so smart on one's uniform – pink, green, yellow, red and blue in ascending order.

Had Mother St John had her way, Clare would still be applying for the medal of the Holy Angels; but Mother St John had nothing to do with the sodalities, which were under the overall charge of Reverend Mother. Clare's rise had been untroubled and swift; she had never been referred back a degree, despite Mother St John's efforts, and had become a Child of Mary in the Lower Fifth, which was unusual. Because most of the nuns and staff knew about Mother St John's obsessional dislike of Clare they tended to protect her, and thus she got away with much that she would otherwise not have done.

The dormitory of the Immaculate Conception was on the far side of the house, furthest from the chapel and overlooking the steps that led to the playground. Each girl had a bed, a locker, a chair and a strip of carpet. Each bed was curtained, but during the day these were drawn back and secured by blue ribbons. At night they were drawn round for the sake of modesty, rather than privacy. The curtains were white and were changed once a term. A perpetual talker was soon exposed because her curtain was finger stained by the head of her bed, where she had drawn it aside to chat to her neighbour. No girl was supposed to go into the cubicle of another at night. The older girls, or the ones whose bosoms had developed prematurely, washed in their cubicles. They got hot water from the bathroom in a porcelain jug and took it to the porcelain basins on their lockers. Each girl, regardless of swell of bosom or lack of it, was expected to drape a towel round her shoulders when she washed, and was never allowed to strip completely, so the lower parts only got washed on bath night, once a week.

Andrea's bed was on the window side of the dormitory, near the end and almost opposite the larger cubicle of Mother St John. On one side of her was Clare, who had been moved across the dormitory especially for this, and on the other the head of the dormitory, a sixth-form girl called Mavis Myers who had a nervous disposition and suffered from painful periods and bad dreams. Mavis was afraid of Clare, even though she was two forms below her and two years her junior. She was glad that Clare's bed was not next to hers.

Andrea slowly moved round the dormitory touching things. 'It's quite charming,' she said.

Clare thought 'charming' was an unusual word, quite sophisticated in its context, and dwelled on it. She and Andrea had hardly spoken at all. The process of communication was difficult between two who were not only strangers, but who had so far failed to establish a rapport. Clare was on her dignity, yet wanting to show off a bit, and Andrea was unsure and feeling her way, but pretending nonchalance. Clare was anxious to impress Andrea rather than please her, and yet this came over badly because she was ill at ease. She could sense a detachment behind the smile of the new girl and she could not understand it at all.

Andrea sat on her white-counterpaned bed.

'Do you like it here?'

'It's all right.'

'How long have you been here?'

'Since I was seven.'

'Goodness. I have been to about six different schools since I was seven; one in Belgrade.'

'Really?'

Clare decided the new girl was a snob.

'I'm not a Catholic, you know.'

'I know.'

'Are there many non-Catholics here?'

'A few. We don't have much to do with them.'

'What a funny thing to say.'

Andrea got up and drifted up the dormitory to the long chest of drawers at the end, on which were small mirrors

29

where the girls brushed their hair. Clare blushed, and went after her slowly.

'I'm sorry, I didn't mean you. The Protestants are usually weekly boarders and they don't really fit in.'

'That's all right, you can say what you like. I don't mind.'

Andrea smiled in a distant way, and walked back to her cubicle looking at it. She felt depressed again. This hostile, superior girl was hardly worth making an effort for.

'I suppose I'd better unpack. You can go if you like.'

'Mother St John said I was to show you round.'

'What's she like?'

'Mother St John? Awful. We don't get on. She's jealous of me, I think, that's why.'

Andrea laughed. 'Why ever should she be jealous of you?'

'I'm good at things. I'm top of the form, and captain of netball. The Rev adores me. See, I'm a Child of Mary.' She pointed to her ribbon.

'And what does that mean?'

'It's the highest you can get. I'm rather young to be a Child of Mary.'

'How clever of you. Well, I'm sure I'll never be a Child of Mary. I've left it a bit late, haven't I?'

'You can't anyway. It's only for Catholics.'

'My aunt thinks Catholics want to take over the world.'

Clare thought this was a trap. 'Well, only in a spiritual way. They want everyone to be saved and go to God.'

'Can you not go to God unless you are a Catholic?'

'Not really.'

'Poor me,' Andrea said. 'Well you had better show me round then.'

The new girl drifted towards the door and Clare trailed after her, feeling angry with herself. She envied Andrea her poise, and knew she had not really been impressed by her boasting. The new girl had style, such style, the way she sauntered and was remote, not really seeming to care. Here was someone at last of her own standard, and yet she could not get at her. Clare flushed, feeling anxious. She was trying to make a good impression and not succeeding very well.

She wanted Andrea to like her, maybe even be her friend. She was doing everything wrong.

Andrea, oblivious of her disturbing and unsettling effect on her companion, wandered casually out of the dormitory, Clare walking quickly behind her, the rubber soles of her shoes squelching upon the highly polished parquet floor.

The greenhouse was built on to the convent, next to the infirmary block. It was very large and provided most of the flowers and shrubs that were needed for the adornment of altars and the chapel on feast days.

Because of her piety Lucy Potts had a special charge in the convent, which was to assist Mother Monica, who was the sacristan and also taught pianoforte to the girls. Mother Monica had bunched arthritic fingers, so that she did not teach the pianoforte very well; but she had a good command of theory, and beat time with her poor painful fingers, assisted by the steady clicking of the metronome.

In overall charge of the greenhouse and the garden was Sister Mary Benedict, who was a farmer's daughter, and loved everything that grew and came from the soil. Onions and sprouts and potatoes were cared for just as lovingly as the waxy camellias and stern arum lilies which grew in the greenhouse at a special temperature, or the velvety roses which were such a feature of the formal gardens in front.

Lucy loved to work with Sister Benedict, tending the young plants, potting the seedlings, and watching them burgeon and grow. There was a variety of shrubs of all shapes and sizes, big and small, as well as forsythia, azalea and fuchsia. There were gladioli, iris, hyacinths, agapanthus, lilies of all kinds, geraniums, camellias and hibiscus.

Lucy especially loved the hibiscus flower, which she grew in the summer. It was so beautiful, the way it budded and then burst into splendour like a flame, and burned and died. Lucy would nurse each bud, and glory in it for the brief time in which it bloomed; and sadly it would fold into itself and wither.

'Why does the flower only bloom for such a short time?'

31

Lucy would ask Sister Benedict. 'It lasts for a night and a day.'

'That is the way of the flower,' Sister Benedict would reply. 'All flowers and plants have their ways, and only the Lord knows why.'

Sister Benedict had a patch outside the greenhouse where she fed the birds that flocked there from the trees in the park, and the pigeons that gathered from the convent buildings or the roofs of the houses in the town. The pigeons would strut up and down and chase the other birds away, gobbling everything up. Then Sister Benedict would wait in the greenhouse until the fat greedy pigeons flew off in search of more elsewhere, when she would emerge stealthily and give a little call for the blackbirds, thrushes and tits. As if knowing the game, they would fly down and have a good tuck in before the pigeons, realizing that they had been evilly misled, flew in again complaining loudly to Sister Benedict.

This was a grand game and could have gone on all day. But Sister Benedict, new to the Order, and yet to take her final vows, was a diligent and hard-working nun. She was a chubby friendly person with the red cheeks of the country girl, and she loved life very much and especially her vocation to serve God in this way by growing flowers and making the house more beautiful. She and Lucy were a good pair because Sister Benedict was a great chatterer and Lucy did not have much to say but was a good listener.

On feast days the girls would help to carry the plants from the greenhouse to the chapel, or to adorn altars and statues through the house. They would put overalls over their dresses and form a kind of chain. This was a very popular activity because it was done during study time. On days like this Lucy would come into her own, and would give instructions about where each shrub or plant should go.

Lucy had been very religious ever since the time of her first communion, when she was sure she'd had a vision of Our Lady, just as she was about to receive the host. She had been quite certain about this, but had kept it to herself because she didn't want people to laugh. Ever since, she had kept a careful look-out but had never seen her again. When she read about the children at Fatima or Lourdes she knew that she had seen Our Lady, too, and wondered why God had singled her out in this way.

At fifteen Lucy had mouse-coloured hair that got greasy very quickly, steel-framed spectacles with thick lenses that made her eyes seem very small, and a tendency to eczema. She thought slowly but she spoke in the short staccato sentences of uncertainty. She had been selected as Clare's best friend as the perfect foil, because the contrast between them enhanced the brilliance of Clare. Lucy worshipped Clare, and suffered much on account of her.

During the weeks following Andrea's arrival at the convent Lucy had spent a lot of time in the greenhouse, to console herself. Clare was so taken up with her new charge that she hardly ever addressed herself to Lucy at all; she had never even introduced them properly. And to think what she'd said about her before! Lucy was terribly hurt, and wondered if Andrea knew what she was doing to the special relationship that they had shared. She saw how the girls reacted to Andrea, with a kind of awe, but she reacted the other way. She thought her hateful and snobbish and, above all, she had stolen something which did not belong to her: Clare.

Lucy and Clare were now on different sides of the dormitory, and the bliss of those nocturnal visits was in the past. Clare never came near her, and when she did stop to talk to her it was in a very distant kind of way: polite, not chummy and intimate at all.

It was terribly wounding. Lucy brooded over her plants in the greenhouse, and thought this was the most difficult trial that God had ever sent her. Perhaps that was why she'd had the vision all those years ago: to strengthen her for this terrible ordeal by rejection.

Mother St John and Mother Euphrasia had taken Andrea to the school's outfitters in the town to buy her uniform. The nuns wore an extra veil and a cloak when they went out, black knitted gloves and a long black reticule made of cloth which swung at their sides. Andrea felt slightly ridiculous in the middle of this penguin-like pair and wished they could have gone by car instead of bus.

They bought for Andrea two blue dresses, one to be kept as best for Sunday; six starched white collars; two scapular-like overalls; a tunic for gym and games; a blue serge coat, double-breasted; a felt hat with the convent badge and a long scarf in the school colours. There were, in addition, four woollen vests, four pairs of linings, two pairs of thick blue knickers, four pairs of lisle stockings and two pairs of black lace-up shoes.

With her uniform Andrea became a pupil of the Convent of the Blessed Apostles, and as she put away her pink twin-set and skirt she also put away one mentality and donned another. She was introduced to the nuns and mistresses who would teach her, and given a desk in the Lower Fifth, on the top floor of the school building, next to Clare.

Under the friendly eye of Mother David she learned netball, showed Mother Monica that she was already skilled at the pianoforte, and astonished Miss Larkin, who taught singing throughout the school, with the range and clarity of her soprano voice. She impressed everyone except Mother Veronica with her scholarship (she was not good at maths); overawed the junior girls by her remoteness and the seniors by her diffidence that yet was not obsequious. The nuns were ecstatic over her gentility and good manners, by the way she opened doors for them or stood back to let them pass in the corridors. Everyone agreed that she did not push herself forward, nor was she awkward and shy.

She was knowledgeable, respectful, well mannered and charming. Yet she was anything but happy. For Andrea this was a new feeling. She thought she had guaranteed herself happiness by her skill at adaptation, by the way people instinctively took to her. Happiness for her had never been a very positive kind of thing; it had simply been the absence of distress or sadness. But the complete change in her life had taken away her freedom. She had never known that every minute of one's time could and should be accounted for.

She was sought after by the girls because she was such good fun, and told stories about places they had only read about in their geography books. Yet she never seemed to swank about it, but mixed skilfully with both nuns and girls. She never talked in the study, never had to stand out, was never late from the playground or slow to bed. Everything she did seemed natural to her, so that no one resented her. Among all these smiling helpful people she was lonely, an experience she had never had even when she had been alone for hours in the past. At night she gazed at the dormitory ceiling, watching it fade into darkness, and little tears of pent-up frustration and despair would gather in the corners of her eyes and trickle on to her cheeks. She felt completely disorientated, and she longed for her father and her familiar home.

The fact was that she had no intimates at all, not even Clare, who tried so hard.

One day she went into the greenhouse to help carry plants for the feast of All Saints on the first day in November. There she discovered Lucy lovingly tending the huge bowls of chrysanthemums, which she had grown in white and brown specially for the feast. Lucy was watering them as Andrea came in before the others and stood watching her. 'They're lovely. Did you grow them?'

Lucy paused and turned very red when she saw who it was.

'Yes.'

'Are you in charge of the greenhouse?' Andrea sat on an upturned bucket and cupped her chin in her hands.

'Oh no. That is Sister Benedict. She's ever so sweet. She lets me help her because I love flowers. She even lets me order some of them from a catalogue. We work out the feasts in advance and then plan for them. I do that mostly.'

Andrea smiled a genuinely warm smile. How this plain little girl with the steamy glasses changed when she talked about her job. She seemed to open, just like her flowers.

'You must be very clever.'

35

Lucy looked at the ground.

'I am *not* clever at all.'

'Which form are you in?'

The painful red returned to her face.

'In your form. I sit at the back near the wall.'

Andrea felt awful. She started to go red too.

'I'm terribly sorry. I'm new, you know, and faces are still strange to me.'

'That's all right. I don't show up. I don't want to.'

'People only notice me because I'm new. Otherwise they wouldn't.' Andrea knew she was talking nonsense, but she was upset at hurting the girl. Her wish for prominence did not include crushing other people, and here she was very different from Clare.

'They would notice you, they would,' Lucy said. 'You are pretty and you show up so. It is obvious that you are clever, and Miss Clark cast you for the part of Henry V in the form reading of the play because you have such a nice voice. You have no accent,' she said accusingly.

'I think accents are very nice.'

'Miss Clark doesn't. I'm sure she will give you a part in the school play.'

'When is that?'

'Quite soon. It's ever so important. It's a great thing to be in it. I never have.'

'What a pity. I'm sure you'd be very good.'

'I wouldn't. I can't act.'

Lucy stared at Andrea, suddenly remembering the reason for her hostility. 'Clare is always in the school play. *She* is very good.'

'I'm sure she would be.'

'She is.' Lucy turned her back and slowly started her watering. 'She used to be my best friend.'

'And isn't she now?'

Lucy went to the end of the row with the watering can, and slowly came back again to where Andrea still sat on the bucket.

'I don't know. It's since you came.'

'Me! But I haven't stopped you being best friends. All she had to do was show me round.'

'That's why. She's been too busy. I never see her at all.'

'Well she isn't busy now. I'm fine on my own.'

'I think she would like to be your best friend.'

'*My* best friend? But I haven't one. Clare certainly isn't my best friend.'

'But she likes you. It's so obvious.'

'Don't be silly.'

'She admires you.'

Andrea became thoughtful. Clare had never mentioned best friendship to her.

'I'll talk to her if you like.' Andrea examined a chrysanthemum bud.

'Oh you must never do that. Clare would be *furious*. She is so clever. I admire her enormously, don't you?'

'Well, since you ask me, not particularly.'

'Oh! You can't feel like that about Clare!'

'Well, it should show you that I don't want to be her best friend. I mean it. Why don't *you* talk to her . . .?'

The door of the greenhouse opened and Sister Benedict came in with a throng of girls behind.

'Andrea! Trust you to be here first. You are such a thoughtful girl. Has Lucy been showing you what to do?'

'Yes, thank you, Sister. She has been very helpful.' Andrea gave Lucy another special smile, and turned away to join the others, who were carrying the plants to the chapel for the great feast.

# Three

In the convent on the feast of All Saints the altars and statues throughout the house were decked with flowers and shrubs, candles and little coloured lights. In the refectory there were blue and gold paper streamers down the middle of the tables, which were joined together as though for a banquet. Delicious things were had to eat that day; there was icing on the cakes and hundreds and thousands on the trifles, which were laced with plenty of cooking sherry.

The feast of All Saints was in honour of all the blessed in heaven. The following day was devoted to praying for the souls in purgatory; it was a mournful occasion and the food was suitably austere as though to empathize with the suffering souls. But for All Saints everyone felt very joyful, and the atmosphere was jolly and gay with no school because it was a Holiday of Obligation.

The convent made a lot of great feast days, there were several of them throughout the year. Reverend Mother's feast day – the feast of St Teresa of Lisieux – was kept with all the pomp of a queen's birthday. Everyone looked forward to these occasions as especially nice interruptions to the routine of community life.

In the morning of All Saints Andrea joined the others to help carry the rest of the plants from the greenhouse to bedeck the altars and the chapel. Later in the morning there would be a procession through the house. Andrea was trotting along the hall carrying a tall conifer when she was stopped by Mother St John, who instantly relieved her of the pot.

'No, Andrea, no.'

'But, Mother—'

'You must not carry plants, child.'

'I like it, Mother. I love the greenhouse and all the flowers.'

Mother St John smiled sympathetically, nursing the plant in her arm. Then she peremptorily stopped a small junior who was wending her way cautiously past the obstacle presented by the nun, and thrust the pot into her hand.

'Grace, take this to the altar of St Jude in the new building.'

Grace clasped the pot and made off obediently. Mother St John rearranged her features, and put an arm protectively round Andrea's shoulder.

'My dear, we have given an undertaking to your father that you should take no part in religious ceremonies.'

'Carrying plants is not a ceremony, Mother.'

'In a way it is. Later we are going to process through the school to pay honour to all the saints whose statues these plants adorn. I think you could say it was religious.'

'Very well, Mother. If you say so.'

Mother St John's stony old heart turned right over with tender compassion for the child, who, she was sure, was inspired by an innate love of Christ and his saints to carry plants in their honour. She made a point to remember to tell the nuns this edifying story later in the common room during recreation.

'I know how you feel, Andrea. But we must keep our promises, mustn't we?'

'Yes, Mother.'

'Good girl. We must pray that your father will change his mind quite soon.'

'How do you mean, Mother?'

'And let you carry plants.'

'But I'm sure he would now.'

'Then you must write and ask him. Now, Andrea, would you take your books from the study into your classroom as the study will be used during the procession. You can read or do anything you like up there.'

Andrea felt this was punitive. She would have wept, but she had to remember her image. The face-saving part had to come first. This was the act of the brave girl, punished most

39

cruelly and unfairly. She gave a stoical smile, and while the girls got their black veils and formed for the procession she took her books up to the classroom. She was the only Protestant to be excluded, as all the others regarded processions as a good form of junketing, with some lusty hymn singing while the gifted and volatile Mother Mary Paul pounded her harmonium. It was rather like the Salvation Army, without the brass band.

Mother Mary Paul, who taught music throughout the school, had been born in France of an English mother and a French father, and spoke with a rather studied broken accent. It was rumoured, wrongly, that she was a countess who had entered the Order after an unhappy love affair, and despite whatever anyone said to the contrary the story stuck. She was regarded with interest by the girls as a person of undoubted mystery who, somehow, had mistaken her vocation and should not have been in the convent in the first place. She communicated abysmally with her students as though her mind were constantly somewhere else, as if dwelling on higher thoughts. Her vague, affected air, her detachment, added to her remoteness. But there was no doubt about her musicianship and her passion for Gregorian chant.

Few of the parents of the Protestants cared about the religious activities of their children, or else they would not have sent them to a convent in the first place. The Protestants were not obliged to go to Mass or any of the services if they didn't want to, but many of them did, except when they were tired and felt like a lie-in in the mornings.

In the classroom Andrea idled over her work. She alternated between sitting and standing by the window overlooking the trees, which were nearly bare, and the swans sailing unperturbed on the lake ruffled by the November wind. The playground and the tennis courts on the far side of the lake were covered with stiff brown leaves.

Andrea liked to be alone; she wished she could be by herself more often. But today the thin strains of hymn-singing filtering through the building seemed to accentuate her isolation. She wished almost that she could be with them, and this was a very curious thing. The idea that she should want to be like everyone else was unusual. It was nothing to do with religion, but to be away from the group was even more lonely than being with it.

Andrea realized, then, that she was beginning to enjoy her life in the convent. What had initially seemed an impossible monotony, a series of meaningless silly little events, now appeared to have a harmony that was relevant to everyday life. It seemed almost logical to stand up or sit down, speak or be silent, according to the command of a tinkling bell. Why, after all, should one not move about in lines, and be hoarded in places all at the same time and all together?

She had seen herself as an actress playing to a varied and enthusiastic audience, aware all the time of herself as Andrea. Now she wanted to be one of them; not in the sense that they accepted her, because they did already, but that she accepted them. It was like the beginning of love: to give to people as well as to take.

Only she didn't realize this all at once. It was just a notion in the mind, a possible explanation for her unease. She waited impatiently for the procession to end, and then went cheerfully to join them.

It was part of the convent discipline that most of each meal was eaten in silence. During this time there was usually a reading from some edifying work, the lives of the saints or the *Imitation of Christ*. If Mother St John was in a bad mood there was hardly any talking at all, sometimes none. If she was feeling good humoured she would bang her gong quite soon after they sat down, for talking to begin. On feast days there was no religious reading, and talking was allowed all the time.

At the end of lunch Mother St John banged her gong for grace, but first she had an announcement.

'This afternoon,' she said importantly, 'Miss Clark is coming in to cast the school play. I have a list of those she wants to see . . .' There was a rush of excited chattering, and Mother St John banged her gong again.

'That does not mean that each girl will automatically have a part in the play. Some will be asked to help with staging and props.'

Then she read out a list, and among those selected were Andrea Mackintosh and Clare Bingley. As she heard her name called Andrea sat up with interest. The school play! She rolled her clean cutlery up in her napkin, bound it with a ring and suppressed the little smile that wanted to break on her lips. It would never do for anyone to see how much she cared.

The school play that year was a free dramatization of *A Christmas Carol*. Free, that is to say, in the sense that some of the trickier haunting bits were omitted, or put at the beginning to provide more background for Scrooge's meanness. Clare was cast as Scrooge, Andrea as Marley's Ghost and Lucy was given the job of drawing half a front curtain at each performance, in addition to her usual task of arranging the plants for parents' day.

Neither Clare nor Andrea was particularly pleased with her casting or, indeed, with the choice of play. Scrooge and Marley's Ghost were hardly romantic parts. The previous year the school had done an adaptation of *The Scarlet Pimpernel*, and this was fine because of the number of dashing roles, and the gorgeous costumes that had been hired from London. Clare had had only a minor part as one of the Scarlet Pimpernel's adventurous band, but there had been plenty of shouting and sword drawing, and she had worn a moustache that curled over on to her cheeks. Clare coveted glamorous male roles, but the idea of Scrooge did not satisfy her at all. Old, decrepit *Scrooge*? No fine clothes to wear or moustaches to twirl? However, as it was the lead and obviously required much skill, she threw herself into its execution with enthusiasm.

The play had a large cast because of all the festive scenes that Scrooge witnessed with the ghosts, and the number of little children who were required to plague the mean old miser as he ambled along the streets muttering 'humbug' every two seconds. The free adaptation had been made by Miss Clark, who taught English and rather fancied herself as a writer. Miss Clark was in her early thirties and had been with the school since her graduation from Manchester University. Ten years before she had been an attractive, fresh-faced girl, very optimistic about the good things with which she was sure life would provide her. She knew, of course, that you had to make compromises and that you had to give. She was not an extrovert, nor was she morbidly inward looking. She dressed nicely, was sociable and lived with her parents outside the town. Everyone had thought how lucky Jennifer Clark was to get such a good job so near home.

Jennifer Clark had been sure she would marry. In the casual way that people plan their lives, when they are still young enough to think that they can affect their own destiny, she had decided that twenty-five or twenty-six would be a very suitable age. But at thirty-two she was no nearer being married than ten years earlier and the idea, though not abandoned completely, had nevertheless begun to recede. It was simply that one did not meet men. There were none available; perhaps they were all at the war. There had been men at the tennis club and church social and so on, but she had not, all those years ago, thought them worth a glance, so imminent did the arrival seem of some young Lochinvar who would ride out of the west.

Miss Clark was of a very romantic disposition and was prone to illustrate her thoughts, especially the sad ones, from some of the more familiar classics that she taught in school, or the works of T. S. Eliot when they seemed apposite. The beginning of 'Burnt Norton', the footfalls echoing in the memory, always seemed to express exactly what she felt about the lover she had not yet had. She thought it was so lovely, mysterious yet quite explicit. It made one's involuntary sacrifice seem noble, and it also gave one hope.

Miss Clark was a gentle creature, and popular with the girls. But she could be stern, irrational, and she could get

43

quite besotted with those girls she selected to be her favourites. No doubt it was her passionate nature, unwillingly suppressed, but not altogether sublimated, that made her get so stuck on her special girls that she would weave little dreams about them and have quite a frisson when they came near.

The girls did not necessarily have to be clever, but they had to be attractive and possessed of a certain *je ne sais quoi*. Andrea was clever, attractive and oozing *je ne sais quoi*, so that Miss Clark fell for her as soon as she saw her. She was so fine, with that blond hair, and those lovely clear, evasive – slightly haunted perhaps? – eyes. Miss Clark had immediately given her the role of Henry V in the form reading of the play, so that she could watch her without it seeming in any way odd.

Despite her obsession Miss Clark was not stupid, and knew that she must not obviously appear to favour Andrea, because she was a new girl and had not proved herself, even though she read Henry V so well. So she cast her in the role of Marley's Ghost because, of course, she could not bear to have Andrea *not* in the play, and it was a good strong part that would need plenty of rehearsal. She even wrote in an extra scene right at the beginning, which showed Jacob Marley still alive and arguing with Scrooge about money. This would enable Andrea to appear twice; but Miss Clark justified it to herself by thinking it logical to show how Scrooge deteriorated after the death of his partner.

Unlike most of the staff Miss Clark had never favoured Clare Bingley, but there was no doubt that she had talent as an actress, and from her junior days she had always been fitted into the school play.

The importance of the school play in the lives of the girls lay in the fact that it was not only a chance to show off, but also a break in the monotony of the daily routine. The casting was done early in November, and the players performed in the middle of January. For over two months this much sought after, different kind of life was lived by those fortunate enough to be selected. Rehearsals were called every evening, and nearer the time they were held at weekends. Those who were in the school play could be late, could plead it as an excuse for not doing homework, or could use it to explain eccentric or erratic behaviour. Mother St John always found the time of the play a time of trial, because of the difficulty she had in getting the players to fit in with the others.

Andrea realized that Marley's Ghost was a key role and intended to do it well. But more than this, it meant that she was now 'in' something, and this suited her new attitude as one who wanted to be involved rather than set apart.

It threw her and Clare together once again in a more positive way, and she quietly reappraised her attitude towards her, without attempting to take an initiative. But Clare was standoffish towards Andrea. She had begun to regard her as a rival more than a soulmate. and Andrea's success in such a short time had rather annoyed her, so that she tried more vigorously to shine at everything. Having the lead in the school play seemed to establish her pre-eminence.

Andrea decided that Clare was intolerable, boastful and pushing, and she cast her off in her mind as a possible best friend.

However, the excitement of the play and the preliminary readings, the effort of games and work, seemed to eclipse the nuances of the personal relationships among the girls and if nothing stood still, nothing changed either.

It was the practice in the boarders' refectory that each week certain girls were detailed to help clear and wash up after meals. This was known as 'helping', and helpers were drawn from all forms except the sixth. It was an unpopular chore, because it meant missing recreation unless one were very quick indeed, and Sister Mary Francis, the refectorian, was usually careful to see that one were not by inspecting the tables and the clean plates with irritating and deliberate slowness.

Sister Mary Francis saw life only as a preliminary to heaven. She didn't think there was any joy to be had from being on earth, and the only merit was to be gained by suffering as much as possible. Working all day in the gloomy refectory, which was a semi-basement, and the even gloomier scullery next door would have instilled in few people a really happy disposition were they not inclined to overcome all obstacles in an attitude of spiritual joy, and laugh at them. Sister Mary Francis firmly was not. She declined all aids to levity, and suffered with enthusiasm.

She was addicted to the recitation of the rosary and encouraged her various squads of helpers as well as the kitchen staff to participate, several times a day, and to dwell on the joyful, sorrowful and glorious mysteries that were its essence.

As soon as the squad of helpers began to clear, the rosary would begin, and a chorus of 'Holy Mary Mother of God' could be heard from the kitchen by obedient voices trained to enter, in almost contrapuntal fashion, after Sister Francis had intoned the first part.

One evening the school play set had come down late for supper, and were lounging, in the manner of actors and artistic people, over their bread and margarine and cocoa. The main course had been macaroni cheese, which was a euphemism for a congealed and gluey substance with a strong taste of Jeyes fluid. The nuns who did the cooking were young and untrained, they had never been taught to cook in bulk. The nun who did the washing up of plates in the kitchen was a believer in strong antiseptics and abrasives. It was amazing that the combination of bad cooking and disinfectant had not yet killed anyone.

The play set were chatting, and the Hail Marys were droning away in the scullery, with Sister Francis's voice dominating the rest. If they were inclined to hurry, she always came in a bit more slowly and made them start again. At the table, in addition to Clare and Andrea, were Virginia Clearwater, a rather sophisticated girl from the Lower Sixth, who played Bob Cratchit; Martha Oldwhistle from the Fourth Form, who played the Ghost of Christmas Past; Judith

Lynch from the Lower Fifth, who was the Ghost of Christmas Yet to Come and Anne Wedgewood, also of the Lower Fifth, who was Mrs Cratchit. They had been rehearsing the haunting scenes, and it had been quite an exhilarating evening. The other parts were mainly played by day girls.

Lucy Potts was on helping duty this particular night, and she scuttled timorously round the tables sweeping the crumbs into a tray and trying to catch some of the precious words that came from the play table in the corner. Then Sister Francis clattered in, interrupting the artistic conversation, which was in full spate.

'It is time,' she boomed, 'that you girls were gone. We can't clear up.'

'We have been rehearsing, Sister,' explained Virginia, the most senior of those present.

'I know that. I don't want any of your airs, Miss Clearwater. You're the same as everyone else. Stop talking and finish your supper. Lucy, start to clear that table. Hail Mary Full of Grace . . .' And Sister Francis, who always had recourse to prayer to forestall argument, stomped back to the scullery.

Lucy went pink and walked timidly up to the table.

'I'm awfully sorry. I'll just take the things you've finished with.' She put out a hand for Clare's plate, which, like everyone else's, was hardly touched. 'Have you finished, Clare?' She began to ease the plate away from Clare's place.

'No I haven't.' Clare put a hand firmly on the rim of the plate.

'But your knife and fork are together, Clare.'

'Please leave it, Lucy. Can't you see we're busy?'

Lucy was so confused that she left the table altogether and went to another. Clare gave an annoyed look in Lucy's direction, raised her eyes heavenwards as though to imply how stupid Lucy was, and resumed her discourse on the interpretation of *The Christmas Carol* as a social commentary on life in nineteenth-century England. However, the girls were rather stunned by Clare's outburst, and looked uncomfortably over at Lucy.

'You see, at the one end of the scale you had all that wealth, and at the other—'

'Clare,' Judith interrupted quietly, 'weren't you rather horrid to Lucy?'

Clare flushed. 'Of course I wasn't. If she wasn't so anxious to please, she wouldn't get hurt. Mother St John said we could take what time we wanted for supper.'

'But you could have been more gentle with her,' Anne said. 'And you *had* finished.'

'Oh, what the heck does it matter? Aren't you interested in what I'm saying?'

'Yes, but—'

'Well, then. Where was I? Oh yes, at the other end of the scale you had this dreadful poverty, which is absolutely unbelievable if. . .'

She stopped as Andrea got up from the table and started collecting the plates.

'What are you doing, Andrea?'

'Helping to clear. It's time we went, or the helpers will get no recreation.' She removed Clare's plate without even glancing at her.

'But it's not your turn to help. Do sit down; we've got bags of time.'

Andrea didn't reply, just collected the plates and went with them to the scullery. When she came back Sister Francis was with her, and Andrea looked upset.

'Lucy!' Sister called savagely. 'Come over here, miss!'

Lucy crept from the far corner, brush and pan in her hand. 'Yes, Sister?'

'I thought I told *you* to clear away?'

'You did, Sister, but—'

'No buts, miss, no buts. I told you and I meant you. Instead you can't do what you are told and Andrea here has to do it for you.'

'Sister, *no*,' Andrea said. 'I told you I only offered to help.'

'But it is not your turn to help, Andrea, is it? You were

just being very nice about it, weren't you? If Lucy was not so lazy she would have done it, wouldn't she? And quicker, eh? I shall report you, Lucy.'

Virginia Clearwater rose from the table, a set expression on her face.

'It was not at all Lucy's fault, Sister Francis. She did try to clear but we said we hadn't finished.'

'So why did Andrea do it?'

'Because, by that time. . .'

Now Clare strolled over towards the group.

'It was *my* fault, Sister. Lucy tried to take my plate and I said I hadn't finished. Well, I hadn't.'

'You had,' Virginia said.

'I had not.'

'It's no use you taking the blame, Clare, in this generous way,' Sister Francis said fulsomely. 'Neither you nor Andrea is at fault. It is *Lucy* and her laziness who is to blame. Go to bed, Lucy. You should have been in the scullery helping to dry ages ago, instead of skulking away in here.'

Lucy had started to tremble, nervously rubbing the brush and pan together.

'I'll finish here, Sister.'

'You will go straight to bed, and report to Mother St John that I sent you.'

Lucy looked desperately for somewhere to put the pan. She tried at the same time to take off her overall, and dropped the pan and brush. She burst into tears. Andrea rushed up to her.

'Lucy, it wasn't your fault. Don't cry.'

'Andrea,' Sister Francis said carefully, 'you are a sweet thoughtful girl; but Lucy is very naughty. She must be punished. She takes twice as long to clear as anyone else. *Twice* as long.'

'Sister, it honestly was not her fault.' Virginia looked angrily at Clare. 'She did what she could.'

'Don't answer me back, miss, with your airs and graces. I'm in charge here, under God and Reverend Mother, of course. I don't want any of your back answers. Go to bed, Lucy; you can see what trouble you've caused.'

Andrea helped Lucy off with her overall, picked up the brush and pan for her and squeezed her shoulder. She whispered to her:

'You'd better go. I'll come and see you later.'

After Lucy had trailed off, still weeping, all the girls started to argue with Sister Francis. But she defended herself by lifting her head and intoning with the rosary chorus still coming from the scullery, 'Pray for us sinners, now and at the hour of our death.' Then she clanked back, victorious.

Another girl came from the scullery and started rapidly to clear, while the players walked uncertainly up towards the gym for recreation.

'You were beastly to Lucy,' Judith said to Clare on their way up the stairs. Clare stopped, hands on her hips.

'I was beastly! I like that. Can I help it if she is a timid little mouse?'

'Yes, you can. You hurt her very much.'

'It's none of your business, anyway.'

'Andrea shouldn't have taken the plates in,' Anne said. 'It just showed Lucy up.'

Andrea was very upset by the incident. It was not the first time she had seen a nun behaving in an absurdly illogical way, and she never ceased to be disconcerted by it. Instead of being kind towards the weak, they were always picking on them, rather as large animals attacked those unable to protect themselves.

'I didn't know that, did I?' she said mildly. 'I was really trying to be helpful. Clare, I do think you should apologize to Lucy.'

'I *apologize*? You must be mad.' Clare stopped in amazement.

'I am not mad,' Andrea said heatedly. Then she suddenly left the group and ran back down the hall and up the stairs to the dormitory. She didn't know where Lucy slept, and asked one of the girls, who was carrying a large jug of hot water carefully to her cubicle.

'She sleeps over there,' she said, nodding her head.

Andrea found Lucy still dressed and lying face downwards

on her bed, her thin little shoulders shaking. Andrea patted her back.

'It's silly to cry about it. It wasn't your fault.'

Lucy turned over, kneading her knuckles into her swollen eyes. She reached for her glasses from the locker, stuck them on her nose and examined Andrea carefully, her expression one of hostility.

'*You* are the cause of all my misfortune,' she said. 'Clare is horrid to me because of you.'

Andrea felt this was unfair.

'Don't blame me,' she said. 'I can't help it.'

'You c-c-can. You're so p-p-perfect.' Lucy removed her glasses and started to cry again.

'I'll talk to Clare,' Andrea said firmly.

Lucy put her glasses on again.

'No you won't. You mustn't. She'd hate me even more.' Her face puckered, like a seasoned pomegranate. 'Go away. I hate you.'

'No talking in the dormitory, girls,' Mother St John intoned. Her habit swished to a stop outside Lucy's cubicle, and she sharply drew the curtains apart. 'Andrea! What are you doing here? Lucy! You are lying on your bed with your shoes on! Get up, miss. Get up at once!'

'Lucy is upset, Mother. Something happened in the refectory. I'm just trying to tell her that it wasn't her fault.'

'But it was her fault,' Mother St John said, pulling Lucy's feet. 'Get up, Lucy. Sister Francis has just made a full report to me. Lucy was lazy and refused to clear away, so you had to.' She finished dragging Lucy until she was upright. 'Stand out, miss. Away from the cubicle. If anyone should cry it is Andrea, who had to do *your* work.'

Her anger gathering momentum, Mother St John tugged at Lucy's arm and drew her into the passage between the rows of cubicles. The firm clasp of her fingers pinched hard on Lucy's arm and left a red mark. Lucy hated to be touched; certainly to be dragged out of her cubicle in this brutal fashion.

She jerked her arm free from Mother St John's grasp and

51

pushed her in the chest. Mother St John lost her footing on the polished floor, fell against Andrea, who almost lost her balance too, but managed to retain the nun upright.

By this time almost all those who were in the dormitory had gathered at a safe distance to observe this fascinating fracas. The spectacle of Andrea, pushed against the bed, clasping Mother St John round the waist and watched by a distraught Lucy was better sport than they had had for a long time.

'Lucy!' Mother St John bawled. 'You are a monster!' Whereupon Lucy turned and fled from the dormitory.

Mother St John and Andrea regained an upright position, trying to recover their shattered dignity staring after the retreating girl, for whom the dormitory ranks had parted like the waters of the Red Sea.

'Go after her,' Mother St John squawked. 'Get her back! She will be expelled.'

Andrea recovered herself and brushed her clothes.

'Leave her, Mother. I'll go and look for her in a minute. She's very upset.'

'*She*'s upset? I have never had an experience like this in my life!'

'Listen, Mother. Listen to what happened.' Andrea helped Mother St John to a chair and told her the whole story from the beginning, finishing: 'That's why she acted like that, Mother. I'm sure she didn't mean to push you.'

'But she did, Andrea. She did. It was deliberate. She pushed a sacred, consecrated nun. I have been consecrated to God, you know. To attack me is a sort of violation. It *is* a violation.' Mother St John brooded on the word for a while, liked what she heard, and repeated it. 'Violation,' she said again.

'She acted outside herself, Mother. After all, you did pull her rather roughly.'

'I never touched her.'

'Is everything all right, Mother?' Mavis Myers peered round the curtains. 'I just came up to see, because you haven't been to ring the bell for the end of recreation.'

'Everything is *not* all right,' Mother St John said. 'Go and ring the bell. Ring it hard. And if you see Lucy Potts on the way bring her straight to me. I am going to see Reverend Mother.'

'I'll go and look for her too.' Andrea followed Mavis out of the dormitory. Mother St John muttered to herself for a while and then turned sharply on the girls who were standing around and ordered them to bed. Of course, she was not in the least minded to see Reverend Mother; the less that nun heard about this the better. Then she put the girls on their honour, and went out.

Andrea looked for Lucy in all the obvious places: the classroom, study, playroom and gym. She went to the end of the house, where the music rooms and infirmary were. She did not think Lucy would have gone out, because it was a very wet night, so she went back through the house and climbed the stairs to the chapel. Opposite the chapel was a corridor that was out of bounds to the girls. It was called the nuns' passage, and led to the nuns' quarters. But no girl was ever allowed to use it, unless she became unwell in chapel or there was some dire contingency of that nature. Andrea knew about the nuns' passage, and knew that Lucy would not be there. She had hardly ever been to this landing before, except for her interview with Reverend Mother and when she was taken to inspect the school. She had never been into the chapel.

Now she was curious to see inside, and quietly opened the door. At once she knew the origin of that very special smell which permeated the convent; it was a compound of sweetish must, snuffed candles and polished floors. It was intense as she opened the door, and swirled up her nostrils. Inside the chapel the only lights were from the sanctuary lamp, and the candles in front of the altars to Our Lady and St Joseph on either side of the high altar.

The sanctuary lamp gleamed on the golden doors of the tabernacle, which were bare because it was the season of Advent. The altar had a plain purple cloth on it, and tall brass sconces with high wax candles stood on either side of the tabernacle. The sanctuary lamp hung from a hook in the ceiling, and Mother Monica, the sacristan, would lower it, trim the wick, fill it with oil and then gently release it so that it hung before the altar again.

The nuns went to bed after their night prayers, very soon after the children. They did not say or sing the great offices of the Church, because they were essentially working and not contemplative nuns. But they did spend a lot of time in the chapel engaged in the various kinds of prayer or in meditation.

Andrea absorbed the aroma of the chapel, and its atmosphere by sense rather than sight; it was too dim to see anything except vague outlines and she was afraid to look for the light switch. As her eyes adjusted to the gloom, she could see that the pews stretched back from the sanctuary on each side of a central aisle, and that the tall windows were recessed.

Rapt as she was, breathing in, half frightened by it all, she thought there was something magical and remote about this place. Her first reaction to it was that it was like one of the great European art galleries, full of precious things. They too had this mysterious, sacred quality that made breathing more difficult, so that one had to do it more often in order to do it at all.

She sighed and wandered down the central aisle, letting her hands trail along the high, carved ends of the polished pews. The pungency of the smell seemed to grow more definite and pervasive as she moved nearer to the altar, which, because of the absence of light, was in shadow. In front of the altar a white cloth had been put over the rails for communion the next morning, and a long velvet kneeler stretched from one side of the chapel to the other. Andrea knelt on the cushion and folded her hands along the top of the rails ahead of her, trying to make out the details of the sanctuary.

When she moved it was because of a movement behind her. She started, and the calm left her; she became aware of a terrible dread, almost as though she were going to die.

Afterwards when she thought about this feeling, about the dread, because the movement had quite a rational explanation, she decided it was because the discovery of the chapel was like exploring one of those rich, unexpected places of the mind that are frightening because one did not know they were there. This was the case with her time in the convent; all the while she had been moving round this centre of mystery, without ever knowing about it.

The movement came from Lucy Potts, who had been crouching on a bench near the front asking God to console her. When she saw Andrea she tried to disappear beneath the pew, hoping she would go away.

'Lucy!' Andrea called, getting up and crossing the floor. 'Lucy. Is it you?'

'Ssh!' Lucy hissed, knowing that one must not talk in the chapel. 'Ssh!'

'Lucy, I have been looking everywhere for you.'

'Ssh!' Lucy hissed again.

Andrea came and sat on the bench in front of her.

'I—'

'You must not talk in the chapel,' Lucy said, primly.

'Well, come outside,' Andrea whispered.

'No. I don't want to. I feel safe here.'

'You are safe with me.'

'Hm!' Lucy snorted.

Andrea began to despair.

'Mother St John will be cross with you if you don't come out.'

'She is cross with me already. I am going to run away. Ssh!' Lucy added, remembering where she was.

'Don't be silly. I'll stick up for you.'

But any voluntary move on Lucy's part was forestalled by Reverend Mother, who opened the chapel door with a flourish and switched on all the lights. Behind her on the threshold was Mother St John, her bonnet slightly askew, clutching and unclutching her rosary beads with anguish.

'Lucy! Come here this instant!' Reverend Mother called imperiously.

Lucy got up, followed by Andrea.

'Andrea!' Mother St John exclaimed. 'What are you doing in the chapel?'

'I came to look for Lucy.'

'But—'

'Don't worry. I didn't say any prayers.'

'Andrea, that is cheeky.'

It was the first time Mother St John had ever reproved Andrea, and they both stared at each other as though aware of the significance of the occasion. Behind Reverend Mother and Mother St John were Clare and Virginia, who having been apprised of the situation in the dormitory had hastened to take advantage of it.

Reverend Mother gently drew Lucy outside, and Mother St John switched off the lights and closed the chapel door. She had been found by Reverend Mother sneaking along the nuns' passage, and had been forced to confess everything.

Reverend Mother took them all into her room next to the chapel and sat at her desk. She did not ask anyone else to sit down, and they formed a decidedly disconsolate group. Mother St John twitched and Lucy hung her head.

'Am I to understand you struck a *nun*, Lucy Potts?'

'I didn't mean to, Reverend Mother. She pinched my arm. It hurt.'

'I saw her,' Andrea said. 'She didn't mean it.'

'Nevertheless,' Reverend Mother reproved, 'nuns must not be struck. They are consecrated.'

'I was violated.' Mother St John delighted once again in the use of that expressive word.

Reverend Mother looked sharply at her, and Clare and Virginia, well versed in worldly parlance, understood the innuendo and exchanged furtive little smiles with each other.

'I am sure that is not the right word, Mother St John,' Reverend Mother said briskly, having caught and correctly interpreted the exchange of smiles. 'You were merely subject to an unpleasant experience. Quite rightly, it is to be deplored.'

'Deplored,' Mother St John echoed. 'Deplorable, Reverend Mother.'

'I am very sorry,' Lucy said humbly. 'I was provoked.'

'You were not provoked. You were a very naughty—'

'Mother St John, Mother St John,' Reverend Mother wafted her hands round in a placatory gesture, 'let us not be heated. May I have the whole story, please. From Andrea, seeing that she seems to have witnessed it all. Begin in the refectory.'

By the time Andrea had finished Mother St John was twitching even more, Lucy was quietly sobbing and Virginia and Clare were bored. At the end Reverend Mother folded her hands neatly before her and surveyed them with an authoritative air.

'Girls, one must never strike a nun, however provoked. I am inclined to believe that Lucy was a victim of a mistake in the refectory, on the part of that good and holy nun, Sister Francis. However, Lucy then lost control of herself. Girls, we must maintain control of ourselves at all times. Now if Clare will apologize to Lucy and Lucy to Mother St John we may all go to bed. There must never be an occurrence like this again.'

'The play set always causes trouble,' Mother St John murmured plaintively. 'I'm sure it is the artistic temperament, Mother.'

Reverend Mother smiled sarcastically. 'Clare?'

'I'm very sorry, Lucy,' Clare said stiffly. 'I didn't mean to cause trouble.'

Lucy shook and trembled all over at the notion that her idol was apologizing to her.

'That's all right Clare. It was *my* fault.'

'For heaven's sake, Lucy!' Virginia said, provoked, now, more than she could bear. 'We've just agreed it was not your fault.'

'Virginia, please. Control. Control. Lucy?'

Reverend Mother's impatience was beginning to show.

'I am very sorry, Mother St John, I did not mean to push you.'

'Strike,' Mother St John said, with an unusual insistence on the facts.

'Strike, Mother.'

'Now you may all go to bed,' Reverend Mother said, looking at her watch. 'Goodness, it is very late. Well after nine o'clock.'

# Four

What now transpired was a kind of triangular situation whereby Andrea wanted to draw Lucy out and protect her, seeing her as a sad little victim of forces that were ruthless and too strong for her, but Lucy did not want to be protected by Andrea, whom she regarded as the cause of her recent trouble and her break with Clare. She was unique among the girls in that she really disliked Andrea, and although aware of her charm was impervious to it. Clare, however, refused to have anything to do with Lucy. As someone seriously in love still yearns for the beloved, despite quarrels and misunderstandings, Clare yearned for Andrea's approval yet she was remote and abrupt with her, and despised herself for her weakness.

The three formed a little maelstrom, of whose currents and eddies their companions could not but be aware. They became a centre of interest in the Lower Fifth and among the play set, who observed them more closely. It was in this way that Lucy slowly and imperceptibly became a personality in her own right; people were suddenly aware of her. After all, she had struck Mother St John, and this in itself was a noticeable achievement. Despite the apology, Mother St John picked on Lucy more than ever, but nothing really serious happened until the Feast of the Immaculate Conception in December, which was a day of special devotion. This was another occasion for celebration with a procession through the school, coloured streamers on the table and, of course, plants to be carried and arranged round the altars dedicated to Our Lady in her various manifestations.

Lucy spent hours in the greenhouse on the days before the

feast tending her plants and helping Sister Benedict to prepare the lilies, chrysanthemums and other flowers and plants that had been nurtured through the autumn months.

For weeks, too, the girls had been carefully rehearsed in the singing for the Mass by Mother Mary Paul, who seemed to come into her own on these feast days.

Andrea was particularly upset at being excluded from the chapel choir. But she had been selected for the school choir by Miss Larkin, who had planned a beautiful four-part rendering of 'Sound the Trumpet', from Purcell's Birthday Ode, which would be sung in school at prayers the day before, as the feast day itself was a holiday.

Since she had been in the school play Andrea had come to feel more established and secure. It was a gradual thing, nothing that she had noticed as it was happening, except that she no longer wept in bed at night or longed for her home. She had also formed a sophisticated relationship with Virginia Clearwater, this rather grand girl in the Lower Sixth, whose father was a chartered accountant in Manchester and took her to London in the holidays when he went to see his mistress. So Virginia had travelled. She knew a lot about life, and had detected a similar quality of 'knowing' in Andrea, though it wasn't really done to fraternize with girls in lower forms. However, the school play, in which Virginia played Bob Cratchit, drew them together and they would hole up in some corner discussing life, while awaiting the call to rehearse; or they would saunter casually along the corridor discoursing about this thing or that.

The night before the Feast of the Immaculate Conception, Scrooge and the Cratchits were in the classroom of the Lower Sixth, which was in the old building off the hall, having an intensive rehearsal of one of the scenes that had been causing trouble. This was the scene when the Ghost of Christmas Present takes Scrooge to visit the home of the Cratchits, so also present was Gloria Smith, the day girl who played the ghost, and Judith and Martha, who played the other two spirits, in case more of the haunting scenes were to be rehearsed. Andrea was sitting in on the session acting as prompter; the day girl who played Tiny Tim was there, and also Miss Clark, looking positively bohemian in a brown pinafore dress with a scarlet silk bolero with flowing sleeves and a cravat.

Miss Clark, since she had begun to give up hopes of marriage, still took the same care over her appearance, but had adopted a severer style for her hair. It was brushed straight off the brow, swept up at the back in a chignon, secured by a small net and some pins. When she had still been hopeful of marriage, she had worn it loose and flowing, in the style of Veronica Lake the film actress, who was very much in vogue.

Rehearsals had started directly after tea, and the part with the Cratchits was over by six. The Ghost of Christmas Present went home along with Tiny Tim and others of the Cratchit family. Miss Clark was flushed, but pleased with her efforts. She looked at her watch.

'Now, girls, I think we just have time to run through Scrooge's journey with the Ghost of Christmas Past. Any other parts I will read myself for the moment. On stage please, Scrooge and Ghost.'

Clare and Martha Oldwhistle went and stood self-consciously in the space cleared in the middle of the small classroom. Miss Clark always used real theatrical terms like 'on stage' in the interest of verisimilitude; besides being an elegant thing to do, she considered that it gave the players a more intensive feeling for their parts.

Clare sat by an imaginary fire rubbing her hands and muttering a lot of 'arr's and 'urrm's to indicate how cold it was, as it was considered impracticable to have a real bed on the stage. Martha entered and Scrooge looked up.

'Are you the Spirit, sir, whose coming was foretold to me?'

'I am!' wailed Martha in the ghostliest voice she could conjure up.

'Firmer, Martha. Scrooge is the one to be frightened, not you. "I *am*!"'

'I *am*!' Martha shouted.

'Not so loud, Martha!'

'I am!' Martha's voice dropped.

They stopped and gazed at Miss Clark, who was looking at the ceiling in a grotesque and exaggerated imitation of despair.

'Never mind. Take it from there, girls.'

'Who and what are you?' asked Scrooge of the spirit.

Miss Clark went to the back of the classroom and sat next to Andrea, giving her her special smile. Then she leaned back and let an arm rest languidly round the back of Andrea's chair. Andrea privately thought Miss Clark just the slightest bit odd, but she also liked her so she kept her thoughts to herself, being, at the same time, careful to keep her distance. She had the script on her knee, and sat there idly turning the pages. From time to time Miss Clark would read in the part of Mr Fezziwig, or the young Scrooge. Occasionally she would stand to show a movement or give some direction, mostly so that Andrea would be more aware of her presence than she appeared to be. By activating the air thus, Andrea could not but be disturbed enough to look at her, at her fine figure or her nice clothes, and she used her arms a lot in a really theatrical way. Needless to say, Andrea hardly looked at her at all, and just flicked over the pages or gave little yawns to show she was rather bored.

Just at the end of the sequence, when Scrooge was saying in a broken voice, 'Spirit, remove me from this place!' the classroom door opened and Lucy Potts staggered in, half obscured by a large fir tree. This she plonked in front of the altar to Our Lady, and nearly collapsed on top of it.

'Oops,' she said, 'that was heavy.'

Miss Clark cared not whether the pot was heavy or light. She did care a great deal about her play and, in particular, the success of the haunting scenes. So she turned on Lucy rather sharply and asked her what on earth she thought she was doing.

'Preparing the altars for the feast tomorrow, miss.'

'Not "miss". Miss Clark.'

'Miss Clark. It is the Feast of the Immaculate Conception.'

'I am quite aware of what feast it is, Lucy. Pray, why

do you prepare your altars in the middle of my play rehearsal?'

'I'm sorry, miss . . . Miss Clark. I had no idea you would be here. I thought you would be in the gym or upstairs. This is one of the altars for the procession.'

'It is of no importance what you *thought*, Lucy. The fact is that we are here. You should at least have knocked before you came in and interrupted a crucial moment.'

'I'm sorry, miss. The pot was heavy.' Lucy gave an exaggerated sigh.

It was forbidden in the school to call the mistresses simply 'Miss'. It was considered extremely common, and, of course, only those of a vulgar disposition would consider such an appellation. This was quite different from that other informal practice, whereby the nuns would address the girls as 'miss' as a form of disapproval. 'Stand out, miss' was much worse than saying 'Stand out, Jane'; it implied an added reprimand. To many of the day girls and to boarders like Lucy whose backgrounds were rather humble, reminders about the correct form of address unhappily occurred rather often. These were usually made in public so that the humiliation the offender would surely feel would reinforce her sense of remorse. However, at the present time, Lucy's perturbation at seeing whom she had interrupted drove thoughts about niceties of address from her mind. She became flushed and confused, and she backed hastily out of the room, leaving her plant awkwardly in front of the statue. Miss Clark glanced at her watch and called after her:

'Lucy, we shall be gone in a few minutes. Come back and arrange your plants then.'

'Yes, miss,' Lucy mumbled and fell out of the door. Clare was smiling, but Andrea was concerned as she had watched Lucy's embarrassed performance. The two met each other's eyes and looked away.

'Such an awkward little thing,' Miss Clark said. 'So gauche. Now, girls, I have to go. I teach a class in English literature at the Tech on Thursdays, and I shall be late. You may continue to rehearse on your own, if you like, but don't be late for supper.'

She gave them an indulgent smile, as if to say that she knew quite well they would be late but it didn't matter on account of their being so artistic. Then she left, with Martha Oldwhistle carrying her books because she had a crush on Miss Clark; but Miss Clark did not have a crush on her and regretted casting Martha in the important role of the Ghost of Christmas Past.

Judith Lynch shut the door behind them, made a rude face at it, and then advanced stealthily back into the room, her hands above her head, fingers outstretched.

'I am the ghost of Jennifer Clark. I teach a class in English literature at the Tech on Thursday evenings, and I try and teach English literature throughout the school to the girls of the Convent of the Blessed Apostles. God help me, and them.'

'Don't be cruel,' Virginia said laughing. 'She's all right.'

'She has a bender for Andrea,' Clare said. 'She's always snuggling up to her.'

'Don't be silly,' Andrea said crossly.

'She does, she does.'

'It's true, she seems very fond of you,' Judith said slyly.

'Clarkie always has crushes,' Virginia said. 'Poor thing. She once had one on me. She couldn't keep her hands off me. What she needs is a man. She is frustrated.'

The girls looked at Virginia with respect.

'What does frustrated mean?' Anne Wedgewood asked. She always felt rather grand, but a bit frightened, in this exalted company.

'It means you are starved of sex. All the teachers here are sex starved. They are frustrated spinster women with no men in their lives. I intend to have a man,' Virginia stretched herself and patted her hair, 'as soon as I leave school.'

'But you're going to a teacher training college. There are no men there.'

'I'll find one. They mix with the students at the university. I don't intend to be like Clarkie and the others. Don't you worry.'

'I'm not worried,' Clare said nastily. 'I'd just like to see it, that's all.'

'But the teachers are all right,' Anne said quickly, fearing a scene between Clare and Virginia. Anne was a simple girl, pious and diligent over her work. This did her little good, however, because her application was all wrong and she was usually near the bottom of the class. She was very thrilled at being given the small role of Mrs Cratchit in the school play, and had taken on airs. 'Besides, what does "frustrated" do to a person?'

'It shrivels them up,' Virginia said. 'They do not experience life to the full.'

'I don't see how you can know.'

'I know.'

'I don't like the idea of sex at all,' Judith said. She was a very precise girl, tall and self-contained. She was a good mimic, was trouble-prone and indulged in daydreaming. Next to Clare she was one of the most accomplished liars in the school, and had also been there since she was seven. She had actually only the haziest notion about the facts of life, as biology lessons were taken by a very withdrawn mistress called Miss Parker, and it was a matter of some discussion among the senior girls whether she knew the facts of life herself. Lessons on reproduction were confined to tadpoles or the fertilization of flowers, the pollen being carried by the wind.

'Why don't you like the idea?' Virginia said. 'What idea is it you don't like?'

Judith blushed. 'I don't know.'

'You don't *know*, that's the trouble. You don't actually *know*, do you?'

'Don't be mean, Virginia.' Andrea was always on the side of the weak. 'You're getting at her.'

'I'm not. I merely say that she doesn't like the idea of something she knows nothing about.'

Clare, whose own knowledge was sketchy, said defensively, 'Well, what do you know?'

'I know everything. I read a book.'

'You shouldn't read those kind of books,' Anne said primly.

'Why not?'

'Because you're too young. Mother St John says that "that sort of thing" can "wait until you are grown up".'

'I am almost grown up.'

'Weren't you shocked?' Clare said.

'Of course I wasn't shocked. It's natural. Mothers and fathers do it.'

'I'm sure mine don't,' Anne said. 'Whatever it is they do.'

'They must have done to have had you.'

'Well, I'm sure they don't now.'

'I thought sex was disgusting when I first knew about it.' Andrea had been listening to the conversation with amusement. 'I'm not sure that I've changed my mind. A man and a woman have to lie together with no clothes on.'

Now most of the girls were blushing, except Virginia. Little frissons went through them at the thought of discussing something so exciting that it was forbidden. Even Andrea was a little pink cheeked at the frankness of the conversation, and though her last remark was meant to shock, she had almost shocked herself. Andrea was not curious about her body, and the romantic ideas she had about love in storybooks and literature was as a very pure, metaphysical kind of abstraction. But this was a phase that was almost over, her ideas would change and she would become very interested in the body indeed.

'They lie together with no clothes on?' Anne said in amazement. 'How absolutely terrible. I should hate that.'

'That's not *all* they do,' Clare said darkly.

'What do they do then?'

Clare hedged.

'It's worse than just lying side by side.' Virginia regarded all this talk as something of a challenge. She was also a bit uncomfortable, because the book had not been all that explicit, and there had been rather a confusing diagram. But she was sure she had the basic idea. 'They lie on top of one another,' she went on, and then gave a little gasp, because she had never said such a frank thing before.

'Lie on *top* . . .' Anne began.

'Really!' Andrea expostulated. 'This is all a bit silly. I'm

66

just not that interested.' She gave a big yawn in order to demonstrate the extent of her lack of interest.

'I'm not interested either.' Judith started busily to get her books together.

'It's worse than I thought,' Anne said shakily. 'Much worse.'

'It's something you have to face up to.' Virginia was more confident now that the actual moment of danger seemed to have passed, and no exact descriptions were required. 'It can't be too bad, or people wouldn't do it.'

'Men want it,' Clare said. 'I think that's what it is. Men want it, but women don't.'

'That is the most awful rubbish,' Virginia said loftily. 'Women want it too, otherwise they wouldn't get sex starved. They need a man. My father once told me that, and he is very knowledgeable.'

'Perhaps they need a man to look after them?' Anne said helpfully.

'No, not only *that*! It is a biological urge. We don't feel it because we are not fully mature. But we will.'

'I won't,' Anne said firmly. 'If that's what it is.'

'How does the feeling take one, I wonder?' Judith was always interested in facts to provide material for her daydreams. 'I mean, how does one feel exactly?' Her next daydream would be devoted to imagining sex feelings.

But no one, not even Virginia, could help her with this at all.

'I know I won't feel it,' Anne said.

'But don't you want to get married?'

'Of course.'

'Then you have to have that feeling. It's for sex.'

'Marriage is not sex!'

'It is, you silly chump. That's why people marry, for sex. Whatever did you think it was for?'

Anne was thinking of the beautiful Christian teaching about marriage: how it was like the love of Christ for his Church. Nowhere at all was sex mentioned.

'It is not for sex,' she said firmly. The thought of her gently pious parents lying on top of one another was outrageous.

'It is because people love each other in a very beautiful way. Like Christ and the Church.'

'That is only a symbol. How do you imagine people have children? Sex, that's how.'

Virginia was not quite so sure about things as she sounded. She took refuge behind her air of sophistication to try and conceal so much that she thought was frightening about life. She never felt anything for anyone very much, and she never had crushes like the other girls. She was always rather cruel towards anyone who had a crush on her.

When she went to London with her father in the holidays she spent a lot of time alone in the hotel room, or walking by herself in Kensington Gardens nearby. She knew her father was with this very pretty woman who wore furs and smelled like a flower garden in the height of summer. Sometimes they took her out too, but mostly they left her alone. On one occasion she had gone to her father's room in the morning and found he was not there. His covers had not even been disturbed, and his pyjamas were still on top of them, spread out by the maid, waiting to be worn. She had rushed down to the reception in a terrible state and said her father must have had an accident. The man at the desk had given a knowing little smile and said her father was perfectly all right.

Her father had come in at nine, and he was not even shaved. His shirt was the same one he had worn the day before. But he was very fond and affectionate with her, and she didn't ask him where he had been or tell him about the scare. Soon after that he had given her a book that he'd told her she ought to read. It was very general, about people loving one another, and how they expressed themselves in this physical way. Then there was the diagram, which seemed to be about inner parts, and which was confusing. But she began to understand about Daddy, and why he saw this pretty lady. When she got back to school the following term she felt rather knowledgeable, but also rather scared. She and Daddy had never talked about the book. She only knew he was bad tempered when they got back home. She suspected it was because he missed the lady with the furs.

But nothing had reconciled Virginia to the fact that her mother had gone away and left her, just before the war. She had simply gone, and Daddy had said it was because she did not love him any more, but someone else. If only it could have been explained to her why Mummy had gone without saying goodbye. That was the terribly hurtful part; she couldn't understand that at all. Daddy said Mummy did love her and had not wanted to hurt her by going away. She had gone away to America with someone else and would never come back.

Daddy had told her how much he loved her and wanted to have her with him. But he was very busy with his work, which was something important to do with the war. He was in what was called a reserved occupation, and had sent her to the convent in the hope that the nuns would take the place of her mother. But all the time she had this feeling that she could not really trust anyone again. She did not want to respond to affection, in case that person went away too.

She decided that men were more reliable, because they did not go away and, because she loved her father, she liked the company of men. If she had any feeling for anyone it was for the convent chaplain, Father Vincent, who lived in the presbytery that served the large parish of which the convent was only a part.

Father Vincent was dark and good looking, with little distinguished patches of grey at the temples. Some of the girls used to mob Father Vincent when he came in, but Virginia stood at a distance and waited for him to look over at her and smile. She always took a long time with her confession to Father Vincent, and thought him the most understanding man that she knew; more so than Daddy. He called her by her Christian name, and was a very consoling sort of person.

'Sex is not a beautiful thing,' Andrea said quite suddenly. 'It is quite cruel and causes people pain. My father said so.'

'Did he say anything else?'

'No, that's all he said; but he knows because he has travelled round the world. That's all he ever said about it. That is the emotional part, of course. The physical part is quite simple.'

There was an anticipatory silence.

'Then you *know*?' Judith said at last.

'About sex? Of course I know. I just put two and two together. Men have those things in front that we don't have. They are to do with sex.'

Now even Virginia looked abashed.

'How did you see?' she whispered.

'Good heavens, haven't you ever seen statues, or men on the beach? There is a hump there; you can tell they are not like us. It is called the penis.'

There was a shocked silence.

'And it is to do with sex?' Anne said, trembling a little.

'Emphatically. It goes into the woman when they are lying together with no clothes on.'

'I just can't believe it.' Anne sat down, clutching her books.

The meaning of the diagram suddenly became clear to Virginia.

'Of course it does,' she said scornfully. 'Everyone knows *that*!'

'I didn't,' Judith said. 'My brothers have them, but they use them for going to the lavatory.'

'Well that too, of course. But when they grow up they will use them for sex.'

A whole range of experience was suddenly revealed to the girls; even to Virginia, who had no brothers.

'Well, well,' Clare said. 'Now we know.'

'Tell you what. Next holidays I will bring that book my father gave me. It will explain everything.'

Virginia tried to be helpful. But Anne was troubled.

'Mother St John said, it was only for when we grow up. It might be a mortal sin to read the book. In fact, I wonder if this conversation is a mortal sin. The sixth commandment says you must not talk or read about impure

70

things. I think we should mention this conversation in confession.'

'I think we should too,' Judith said, regretting it all.

'I'm not. What rubbish.' Virginia could not bear the thought of talking about this to Father Vincent, that good pure man. They only discussed little sins, like being late for meals or rude to the nuns. She thought Father Vincent might be shocked, and the idea distressed her.

'I think we should go,' Clare said, getting up. 'They'll all be in chapel, and it's nearly supper time.' She was rather worried about the conversation too. Fancy Andrea *knowing*. Trust her. Even though her father was a doctor, Clare and her brothers and sisters had never been instructed in these matters. Like Anne, they had been told there was time enough when they grew up. They were always being taught the virtues of purity, without knowing exactly what purity was, except that it was rather a negative kind of thing. 'The rehearsal has gone well, I think. Except Martha is lousy as the ghost.'

'Anyone believe in ghosts?' Andrea said conversationally. 'I do. I believe in the occult.'

'Is that the same as life after death?' Judith asked, being concerned for facts.

'Not really. Spirits come back because they are unhappy. Or they have a purpose, like in the play.'

'That is not true,' Judith said. 'People go to heaven, hell or limbo. They do not remain in the world.'

'I think they do,' Andrea said. 'If they are unquiet spirits, they haunt you. There's a lot of evidence for it. My aunt thinks so too.'

'Then she is wrong,' Virginia said. 'Because she is not a Catholic. We know they do not come back.'

'It is an article of faith.' Anne was glad that the sex talk was over and they were on to a more normal subject.

'Let's prove it then.' Andrea was suddenly animated. 'We can have a seance. You call people back. I know how.'

'How?' Several excited voices at once.

'I'll show you. All we need is a glass and a piece of paper.'

71

'Oh that!'

'No, honestly. The glass moves, and this shows there is a spirit who wants to communicate with those on earth. The glass moves.'

'Let's do it,' Clare said.

Virginia was doubtful.

'Now I do think that *might* be sinful.'

'Oh rot. Let's do it now. I'll show you.'

'I don't mind,' Clare said, thinking that to back Andrea might be a step towards reconciliation. 'Let's do it. I'm game.'

'We haven't a glass.'

'After supper,' Anne squeaked. Goodness, the sophistication of these people. First sex and now the spirit world. 'We'll smuggle a glass and come back here.'

'That's it. We'll say we have to rehearse.'

'OK.' Virginia was reluctant, but curiosity overrode thoughts of mortal sin. Besides, it would be something to talk to Father Vincent about, not nearly as dangerous as sex.

'After supper,' Andrea said in her composed way, not so obviously as excited as the others, 'we shall do it. You will see then that there are very definitely unquiet spirits abroad in the world.'

The play group did not linger over supper that night. Judith, being the tallest, pushed a tumbler up the leg of her elasticized knickers and walked giggling out of the refectory, flanked by the others.

There was, however, one small snag, which they realized as soon as they were in the classroom, with the curtains drawn and the door shut behind them.

'There is no table,' Andrea said. 'We can't do without a table.'

True; there were fifteen desks for the sixth formers and a raised desk for the teacher.

'We can push the desks up perhaps?' Anne said hopefully.

'No, it must be a table. Can we get one from somewhere?'

'The parlour,' Virginia said. 'The parlour is the only place with a table.'

'That would be marvellous,' Andrea agreed. 'The table there would be just the thing.'

'We can't possibly go into the parlour!' Judith whispered because of the enormity of the suggestion.

'Why ever not?'

'It's not allowed.'

'No one will know. The nuns are at supper, and the girls are having recreation in the gym.'

'No,' Virginia said. 'I am inclined to agree we should not risk the parlour. For a seance of all things!'

'I'm game,' Clare said. 'Look, the corridor is practically in darkness. The parlour is only next door. There is no one about. Go on. It will be a lot of fun.'

Gradually the scruples of the others evaporated at the thought of what an adventure it would be. There was something extremely attractive in the very idea of the parlour; that special place reserved only for guests or priests. Virginia was the last to capitulate, because she was, after all, the senior girl, and to hold a seance in the parlour was the next worst thing to having it in the chapel, which would have been unthinkable.

'We will put the light out first,' Andrea said, pleased with her success in getting the others to conform, 'then creep along into the parlour. If anyone comes just go straight on as if you were going to the study.'

The girls filed singly along the corridor, keeping close to the wall. All over Europe at that time operations by stealth were taking place. The girls were cut off from the war, tucked away in their convent in that remote northern town, and, because they never read papers or went to the cinema or heard news broadcasts, the war was not part of their lives. But there they were, the brave five of them, stalking along, hearts beating fast, breaths held, just as though they were creeping up on an unsuspecting enemy and life was at stake.

Mother St John was always hanging over staircases and balconies, or perching in positions of advantage so that she

73

could spy on people unobserved. Those experienced ones who were on the alert could usually discern the black bulk of her habit lurking in the shadows, but for the unwary this was a very effective disguise. The dormitory window was a favourite spot, so was the top of the stairs, the rosary walk above the tennis courts and the balcony outside the chapel, which ran across the hall, rather like a gallery. It overlooked the hall and the parlour, which the girls were now approaching. It was also a favourite spying place for Reverend Mother because it was so near her room.

Fortunately for the girls Mother St John, in a mood for trouble, had just left the balcony from which she had been watching the girls go into recreation. Nothing had happened for which punitive measures were required, so she had gone in to have her supper. Had she seen the five members of the play set creeping in the dark towards that holy of holies she would have had a bonus catch, and would no doubt have enjoyed her supper more as a result.

Virginia, the last into the parlour, closed the door and Andrea put the light on. She did not touch the main light, which was a powerful glittering glass chandelier, but put on a side light that stood on a small coffee table in the corner. Clare quietly drew the heavy brocade curtains.

'This is ideal,' Andrea said, smiling with excitement. 'The round table is just perfect. Now get the chairs and we can begin.'

The girls drew the chairs round the table and sat down with pleasurable little shudders of fear. Andrea, clearly in charge, was the last to sit after placing a large sheet of paper, which she had brought from the classroom, in the middle.

'The glass please, Judith.'

Judith carefully drew the glass from her knicker leg and put in on the table.

'It's warm,' she said. 'Hope the spirits don't mind.'

'Don't make a joke of it,' Andrea said severely. 'This is very serious.'

'How about the light?'

'We can keep it on, it's so dim. Or we could cover it with

something. It depends, you see, on the level of concentration. Now, I want each of you to put both hands on the table, with the tips of your fingers touching the paper, like this. Will you do that, please?'

Five pairs of hands bunched together obediently on the paper.

'Now, you must all shut your eyes and concentrate.'

'What must we concentrate on?' Anne enquired, being the least quick witted of the group.

'Why, on summoning the spirits.'

'I see.' Anne screwed up her eyes tightly. She thought of Mummy and Daddy, and how cross they would be if they knew what she was doing. Then she thought of them lying on top of each other, and tried desperately to concentrate on spirits instead.

'Now,' Andrea said quietly, 'open your eyes, and look at the paper. Careful not to touch one another with your hands.' She got up and adjusted the paper so that it was even. She put the glass right in the centre, away from the fingertips. Then she took her cardigan and draped it over the light in the corner. The room was now almost dark, and the ticking of the huge clock on the mantel made it suitably eerie for summoning up the spirits. Now there was not a single girl who was not fearful and wishing it could all be over.

Andrea joined her fingers to the others on the table.

'Close your eyes,' she whispered, 'and concentrate.'

'What will happen?' It was a little squeak from Judith.

'Once we get the spirits, the glass will move; then we can ask them questions. Anne, your hand is trembling; it will shake the glass. Don't be silly.'

'I'm scared.'

'There is nothing to be scared of. The spirits are quite benign.'

'What is benign?'

'Friendly, silly.'

'What sort of questions will we ask them?'

'We shall wait and see if they are here first. They will not come unless you will them to, hard. Now shut your eyes, and will *hard*. Then you can open them, but leave your hands where they are. No one must touch the glass. Will, *hard.*'

'I still don't see how the glass can speak,' Anne said, anxious to postpone the crucial moment. 'So how can we ask it questions?'

'Anne, if you say anything more we shan't go on.'

'Sorry, Andrea.'

'Now shut your eyes and will; will very hard.'

For several moments the girls sat there, all willing hard that spirits should appear. Then Andrea said, 'Open,' and they opened their eyes and stared at the tall refectory glass.

'Are you there, spirits?' Andrea intoned solemnly. 'If you are, please move the glass.'

Nothing happened. Anne was about to speak but Virginia gave her a threatening look.

Then, almost before it could be noticed, the glass slid over in the direction of Clare. Anne gave a cry.

'Ssh!' Virginia hissed.

'Judith, you touched it,' Clare said.

'I did not. I never moved my hand.'

'She didn't,' Anne said. 'It moved itself. Oh, it moved itself. I want to stop.'

'Quiet!' Andrea commanded. 'Spirit, we shall ask you questions, and if the answer is "yes" please move the glass. If it is "no" don't move. If we ask you something about anyone here, move in their direction.'

'How will you know if it has heard if it doesn't move?' Anne asked timorously.

'Because we know it is here, in this room with us,' Andrea said gravely. 'I feel it is here; besides, it has just given us a sign. Now concentrate, concentrate hard. Virginia, will you ask the first question?'

'Spirit, are you from heaven or hell?'

'That's not the right form. It can only answer yes or no. Ask it again.'

'Spirit, is there really hell?' Virginia said, while Anne gave a sharp intake of breath at the audacity of such a question.

76

All gazed at the glass. The glass didn't move. Virginia asked the question again. Still the glass was stationary.

'Of course there is hell,' Judith said. 'Perhaps it didn't hear.'

All the girls, except Andrea, were puzzled too, because the existence of hell was taken for granted. They learned it from the catechism from their most tender years.

'It did hear,' Andrea said. 'Obviously there is no hell. Next question. Judith?'

'Well, is there heaven then?' Judith said. Again the glass didn't move.

'Something must be wrong,' Virginia said. 'Because we know quite well there is heaven and hell. Judith, are you sure you didn't touch it the first time?'

'Sure.'

Then the glass suddenly slid over towards Andrea.

'Now what does that mean?' asked Clare. 'We didn't even ask a question.'

'You are all talking too much,' Andrea said sternly. 'You will confuse the spirit. Now I will ask the question. Spirit, are you troubled? Is that why you are still in the world?'

Still nothing.

'Are you happy then, spirit?' Andrea was feeling a bit desperate.

Then the glass slid slowly over towards her, until it almost touched her fingers.

'There!'

'You pushed it, Andrea,' Anne said.

'I did not. How could I have pushed it towards me?'

'I saw you move your finger.'

'I didn't.'

'I think this is silly,' Virginia opined.

'Let's give it one more try. I want to ask a question.' Clare closed her eyes tightly in the effort of concentration. 'Spirit, will you move the glass towards the first of us who is going to die?'

'No!' Anne said sharply; and then suddenly the glass slid straight over towards her. 'No, no, no! That is a horrible question. I don't want to do this any more.' Anne pushed her chair back and started to cry. 'This is a *horrible*, silly game.'

'It was a very silly question,' Andrea said, also upset.

'You pushed it over to Anne.' Clare was desperate to defend herself. 'I saw you move your finger.'

'I never did.'

'I saw you.'

'You didn't. I would never do such a mean thing, or ask such a nasty question. Trust you!'

It was at this point, when nerves were taut and angry and on the point of breaking, that the door opened to admit a thin stream of light from the hall, and Lucy Potts stood on the threshold clasping the inevitable plant in her hand. She stood still, peering into the gloom. When she saw the figures at the table she gave a shriek and dropped the pot, which fell to the parquet floor and broke, spilling out the soil. Then a bell rang, and suddenly there was the sound of many steps in the corridor as the girls came away from recreation. Lucy fled into the corridor and fell into the arms of Mother St John, who was walking along with Sister Benedict.

'Mother, Mother,' Lucy sobbed. 'There is something awful happening in there.'

Mother St John gave Lucy to Sister Benedict and looked into the room, which was by this time in confusion. All the girls had got up, and Andrea was trying unsuccessfully to take her cardigan off the lamp shade. She pulled too hard, and the lamp toppled over and went out. As Mother St John switched on the main light the brilliant chandelier laid bare the disorder and chaos in the room.

'Girls! Girls! What are you doing here?' Mother St John's voice contained a distinct note of hysteria. 'What is going on? Anne, you are crying. What have they done to you?' A vision of awful tortures, unnatural goings-on, flashed across Mother St John's overworked imagination. Behind her, several interested faces peered curiously into the parlour. A gabble of sound had broken out in the corridor, above which Lucy's shrieks could still be heard. Mother St John began to panic. The noise would reach Reverend Mother's room. She

78

tried to shut the door, when Reverend Mother's voice came booming over the balcony, and all talking stopped – except for the noise made by Lucy, which was unstoppable.

'Girls! Is there a fire? What is happening? Stay there, all of you. Do not move.'

Sister Benedict had edged nearer, still clutching a sobbing Lucy in her arms, and Mother St John was vainly trying to shut the door. Anne had seized the opportunity to fall into a neat little heap on the parlour floor. Andrea was picking up the pieces of broken light bulb, and Virginia, Clare and Judith presented a tableau of the most extreme form of despair, hanging their heads.

'Shut the door, shut the door!' Mother St John cried, as she pushed on one side to shut it while Reverend Mother was pushing as firmly on the other side to keep it open.

'Mother St John!' Reverend Mother called. 'Kindly open this door and let me in.'

Mother St John fell back several steps into the room and gasped, 'Mother!'

Reverend Mother carefully looked about her, and when she began to speak the tone of her voice was not at its most friendly.

'Please explain what is happening here, Mother. Why are these girls in the parlour? Why is Anne on the floor? Who broke the lamp? Anne, get up.'

But Anne did not get up, for the reason that she had quietly fainted; or perhaps psychological trauma would be a more accurate description of what had caused her collapse. She was fully conscious and could hear everything, but she felt incapable of movement and her eyes were closed. The situation by now having exceeded her control Mother St John merely gave a limp gesture, as though she, too, would gladly join the others in their attitudes of desolation.

'Mother, I have no idea what has happened. I am trying to find out.'

Reverend Mother turned back into the corridor.

'Girls, go to bed. Go quietly to bed, and do not talk on the way.'

Then she saw Lucy still clinging to Sister Benedict. They had retreated to the fringe of the crowd, away from the parlour door. Sister Benedict's large hands were performing a kind of stroking movement on Lucy's back.

'Sister, who have you got there?'

'Lucy Potts, Mother.'

'Glory be to God,' Reverend Mother said. 'Trust her to be in this somewhere. Bring her over here.' Reverend Mother made an imperious sweeping gesture with her hand.

Sister Benedict more or less dragged Lucy into the parlour, and Reverend Mother shut the door.

'Now, Virginia Clearwater, I single you out as the most senior girl here. Please explain the situation.'

'We were in the parlour, Reverend Mother.'

'That I can see. Why were you in the parlour? You and who else?' She gestured to the others, to Lucy sobbing against Sister Benedict's bosom and to Anne Wedgewood, whose head now lay in Mother St John's lap.

'Lucy wasn't here, Mother. She just came in as we were . . .' Virginia faltered.

'You were what exactly Virginia?'

'Rehearsing the play,' Clare said quickly.

'But you may not rehearse in the parlour. Who gave you permission?'

'No one, Reverend Mother.'

'We thought Lucy would be doing the altar in the classroom, Reverend Mother, so we came here.'

Virginia and Clare now shared the narrative between them, having agreed by a process of divination on the line to take.

'Without permission? In the parlour? I never in my life heard of such a thing. So how is Anne on the floor?'

'She fell. It was part of the play.'

'And is she still acting?'

'I don't think so, Reverend Mother.'

Reverend Mother thoughtfully stirred Anne with her foot.

'She seems to be unconscious. Is this part of the play? What role does Anne take?'

'Mrs Cratchit, Reverend Mother.'

'Mrs Cratchit! Not a very dramatic role, if my memory is correct.'

'No, Reverend Mother.'

'So why does she come to be on the floor?'

'She just fell.'

'She slipped, you mean?'

'Yes, in the process of rehearsing.'

'And why is the lamp broken?'

'It was an accident.'

'Yet you did not move the table back for your rehearsal?'

'We just moved it back now.'

Reverend Mother gazed at the girls, and for several moments she did not speak. Then she folded her arms in her sleeves and said slowly, 'You girls are lying to me. And I will not move from here until I have the truth. Does Anne need a doctor, Mother?'

'I think she is coming round, Mother,' Mother St John said.

'I am going to die,' Anne said clearly.

'Don't be ridiculous,' Reverend Mother said.

'I am, the spirit said so.'

'Spirit? Spirit?'

'She means the spirit in the play, Reverend Mother, the Ghost of Christmas Yet to Come. We were rehearsing it tonight.'

'And the spirit tells Mrs Cratchit she is to die?'

Clare faltered for the first time. 'No . . . Scrooge is to die. The spirit tells him.'

'And who plays Scrooge?'

'I do, Reverend Mother.'

'Yet you are not lying on the floor?'

'No, Reverend Mother.'

Anne raised her head and looked feebly round the room. 'I am going to die first, the spirit says so.'

'She is delirious, Mother,' Mother St John said.

'Perhaps she has had a fit?' Judith proffered hopefully.

'Did you see her having a fit?'

'Oh, no, no. She just fell.'

'I am going to die first,' Anne said again in a firmer tone. 'The spirit moved the glass over towards me.'

It was then that Reverend Mother walked over to the table and inspected the glass and paper still lying in the middle.

'Girls, may I have the truth please?' She looked at Andrea, hopeful that, as a Protestant, she would be more willing to tell the truth. By this time Andrea had already perceived that the truth would have to be told.

'We were having a seance, Reverend Mother.'

Reverend Mother uttered a long 'ahh' sound, and sat neatly down on a chair.

'A *seance*?'

'Yes.'

'*Here?* In this room?'

'Yes. It was only in fun, Reverend Mother.'

'It was not fun. It was very very wicked. So that is how poor Anne got her notion about spirits. Whose idea was this?'

'Mine, Reverend Mother.'

'Andrea! How you disappoint me.'

The hurt tones of Reverend Mother did more to affect Andrea than any amount of shouting.

'I'm terribly sorry, Reverend Mother. It really was only a game. We didn't mean to summon up spirits. It was only that Clare asked who would die first and the glass somehow slipped over towards Anne. At that moment Lucy came in with the plant and must have got a fright.'

Lucy was calmer by now and no longer plucked compulsively at Sister Benedict's full bosom.

'I had a shock. I just saw these vague figures, Reverend Mother.'

'I am sure you had a shock, Lucy. It is not at all what one would have expected. For once I do not think you are to blame.'

'I am going to die,' Anne said, wondering if she was losing the limelight. She was by now fully in control of her faculties, and starting to enjoy the occasion. She thought that maybe she had, after all, the makings of a fine dramatic actress.

'You are not going to die, Anne,' Reverend Mother said firmly 'Not at this moment, anyway. Get up.'

'I can't,' Anne said. 'The spirit said I was to die first.'

'I think the poor girl is out of her mind, Reverend Mother,' Mother St John said sorrowfully. 'Her wits have gone.'

Anne thought this not quite so flattering, so she said nothing more but still lay on the floor staring up at the chandelier.

Now arrived Sister Matilda, who was the infirmarian. Her main qualification for having remained so long in this responsible office was that, although prior to her appointment she did not even know the fundamentals of first aid, had never staunched a flow of blood, applied a bandage or given medication, she had after twenty years of trial and error – more error than trial – become proficient at her job. At least she could carry out simple instructions given by the doctor, and she employed a kind of folksy medicine of her own invention, which comprised alternating attitudes of sweetness and terror, assisted by aspirin tablets and castor oil. It worked quite well. She terrorized someone until she had ascertained that they were really sick, on the assumption that no one could possibly want to come into the infirmary unless they had to. She was right. Only those too desperately ill to care were admitted, after which they got excellent, even loving, care and treatment, and quickly recovered.

Mother Euphrasia had been told by one of the excited girls coming into the dormitory about the accident, and had sent for Sister Matilda.

Anne had not thought things would go so far, and tried quickly to rise to her feet when she saw Sister Matilda, being extremely loath to go to the infirmary, with good reason.

However, that unsentimental and brusque nun scooped her up from the lap of Mother St John, and half carried, half dragged her out of the door.

'Thank you, Sister,' Reverend Mother called after Sister Matilda. 'Such an efficient nun,' she commented to no one in particular. 'Anne will soon be well.'

'Or dead,' Clare murmured. But the words did not reach

Reverend Mother, only Judith, who felt slightly hysterical but disguised her paroxysm by pretending to cough.

Reverend Mother got up, looking at the watch she carried in a little leather pouch on her waistband.

'You will all go to bed now, girls. It is late. Andrea, will you stay behind with Mother St John? The rest of you come to me in my room after breakfast tomorrow.'

The girls trooped out, stepping carefully over the young fir, which still lay where it had fallen on the floor. Sister Benedict went out too, her arm round Lucy.

Reverend Mother composed her features into an expression of infinite sadness tinged with mercy.

'Andrea, my dear child, I hardly know what to say to you. Because you are not of our Faith I have no doubt that you are unaware of the enormity of what you have done. We Catholics do not believe in the spirit world. That is, we do but we know they do not roam in the world, and cannot be summoned by a group of young girls gazing at a glass.'

Andrea cast her eyes to the ground.

'No, Reverend Mother.'

'Do you really believe this, child? Has your family any, er, spiritual inclinations?'

'No, Reverend Mother.'

'But did you believe it yourself?'

'Well, we did this at my last school, and the glass does seem to move.'

'Because people push it, of course. You see, Andrea, to introduce this kind of practice into a convent simply cannot be tolerated. After death souls go to heaven, hell, purgatory or, if unbaptized, to limbo. They do not remain in the world. Such manifestations or apparitions as we have, and are accepted by our church, come only from God; as when the saints appear or Our Blessed Lady. Do you understand this, Andrea?'

'Yes, Reverend Mother. I am terribly sorry. I will never do it again.'

'I am glad to hear this, Andrea. Because, if it does happen again, or anything like it, we should be unable to keep you

in our school. Had one of our Catholic girls initiated something like this I should have had no hesitation in sending for
her parents and asking them to take her away. But you are
a special case; and I do not see how I can ask your aunt to
take you away. You would not like that, would you?'

'Oh no, Reverend Mother. It was not meant to be wicked;
it was only a silly game.'

Mother St John, who had been standing on one side
listening quietly, moved forward and put a hand on Andrea's
shoulder.

'I am sure Andrea will never do anything like this again,
Mother. She has been a very good girl, until now.'

'Until now, Mother, that is the point. Ordinary naughtiness is one thing; it can be tolerated. But something like this
– never!'

'Quite so, Mother.'

'It will never happen again, Reverend Mother. I am beginning to be happy here. I should hate to go.' Andrea bowed
her head, as if close to tears.

Reverend Mother's pious heart was moved by the sight of
the young sinner doing penance.

'I am glad you are settling down, Andrea, and I only have
very good reports of you.'

'Do you think I could take part in the procession tomorrow,
Reverend Mother?'

Mother St John and Reverend Mother exchanged glances.
Here indeed was someone in whose heart lurked the seeds
of repentance and belief.

'Alas, dear child, I have given my word to your father.
However, you may watch the procession from the balcony
over the hall. Then in the Christmas holidays you should
mention your feelings to your aunt and see what she says.'

'I have felt terribly left out, Reverend Mother, being a
Protestant. The play has made me feel I belonged more.'

Andrea felt she was doing rather well; there was nothing
quite like capitalizing on an unfortunate situation to turn it
to one's own advantage. She thought she would emerge from
this stronger than before. She wondered if she should shed

a few tears, just to turn a good job into a triumph. However, she was not practised in the art and all she could manage were a few sniffs and a wobble of the chin.

'Do not cry, child. You are quite forgiven. We all love you, Andrea, and want you to be happy. Now go away and forget the incident.'

Reverend Mother nodded to Mother St John, who, still with her hand on Andrea's shoulder, led her from the room. She was an emotional, even sentimental woman and her heart was full because it was just like the parable of the lost sheep in the New Testament; and in such small ways did grace work and transform the soul.

# Five

From the balcony in the hall Andrea watched the procession passing underneath. Because of the importance of the Feast of the Immaculate Conception the girls wore white veils with their dresses, but not white dresses, because it was too cold. These were only worn once a year, in the summer time, for the great Corpus Christi procession, which was held out of doors.

The procession this day was only for the boarders, and was confined to the school. It started in the playroom, next to the refectory, and continued through the hall and study, into the gym. It finished in the chapel with Benediction. There were four special altars to Our Lady, by each of which the procession gathered, sang a hymn and recited a decade of the rosary led by Father Vincent and Reverend Mother.

Below Andrea the procession formed round the altar outside the sixth-form classroom, where the rehearsal had been the night before.

Andrea was moved by its majesty, its beauty, as she looked down on the white heads, the black-robed nuns standing behind the girls. The singing, led with great forcefulness by Mother Mary Paul, who always got very excited on such occasions, dropping her intrinsic reserve and waving her arms about as though she were conducting a large choir, had the thin reedy quality of youthful voices, backed by the deeper tones of those nuns who could sing. Mother Euphrasia could sing, but not in tune, and the off-key note of her sonorous contralto was like a descant; no one minded, they were used to it. The only times Mother Euphrasia was forbidden to sing were during solemn Masses in the chapel, because here the

87

descant became a discord and seriously interfered with the three- or four-part harmonies so carefully arranged by Mother Mary Paul. Mother St John could not sing a note, and never attempted to unless she thought the eyes of Reverend Mother were on her, whereupon she would pretend to sing by opening and closing her mouth.

Andrea tried to pick out the girls she knew, but the faces were hidden by their veils. Everyone had rapt expressions, intent on gazing at the altar from which Our Lady looked down from among the plants and flowers arranged by Lucy and Sister Benedict. After the decade was finished, the procession formed again and proceeded, out of Andrea's sight, to the study. As strains of the Lourdes Hymn drifted up to her, Andrea experienced a strange emotion, which she supposed was the first religious feeling she had ever had, unless one counted the day in the chapel.

She went down the stairs and stood at the door of the study. The procession was just leaving, and she followed it, taking care not to be seen, into the gym, where the altar was on the stage, the plants arranged either side in descending order of size with the great arum lilies rising up in front from tall brass vases.

In the gym the processional gathered round the altar. Andrea stood well at the back, but everyone was so absorbed that they would not have noticed her. Even the junior girls, who usually fidgeted and turned their heads all the time, had been thoroughly drilled by Mother Christopher into an appreciation of the horrors that would befall them if they so much as fluttered an eyelid at the wrong time. The fear of the Lord was instilled at an early age in the convent. God was seen as rather a forbidding old man who did not like people to talk or laugh, except at specified times, and who seemed to prefer punishing people to rewarding them. This was in contrast to the Baby Jesus and his mother, who were very kind and loving, and were always trying to stop God the Father from being too harsh.

This image of the Holy Family was very confused and diffuse in the minds of the young girls, and sometimes it never really clarified itself even when they grew up, so that a proper understanding of theology was denied them, due to such a distorted and simplistic beginning.

In the gym the winter sunshine filtered on to the girls in their white veils. Andrea stood by the window and looked at the hard dry land and the skeletal trees and the cold water of the lake where the swans sheltered on the island in the middle. Beyond the walls were the slate roofs of the houses, which seemed to snuggle up against the convent like the cottages of fiefs around a medieval manor. The chimneys gave off spirals of whispy black smoke, and the contrast between the spacious grounds and the cluttered town was like the difference between youth and old age: one seemed to offer promise, the other to have realized, however reluctantly, that it was past.

Andrea thought how drawn she was to the convent, how half in love with its quaint predictable ways and the quirks and frailties of those within. She now accepted and welcomed this strange existence, as though the life of community surpassed that of independence, and love had taken the place of indifference.

As the procession began to re-form, Andrea went ahead of it and returned to the balcony. There it passed her on its way to the chapel. The fact of being a part of the procession made the individuals of which it was composed cohere, giving it a flowing, moving quality, rather like a liquid substance. Andrea attached herself to the end of this continuum and stood at the back of the chapel while it separated neatly into rows, like segments being chopped off a conveyor belt. Now they became recognizable and identifiable again as individuals. They started to fidget and move around, cough and have a giggle or two. As the opening hymn of the Benediction began, Father Vincent appeared in a golden cope attended by two little altar boys who had been borrowed from the council school for the occasion.

One carried a censer from which a thick cloud of incense mushroomed upwards, and the other held back one side of the priest's cope. Usually Mother Monica or one of the nuns would carry the censer, and kneel on the bottom step of the sanctuary. But on special occasions altar boys were drafted in, and caused a great stir among the girls, who, but for Father Vincent and the handyman Ben, hardly saw a man from one end of term to the other.

Andrea had never attended a religious service in her life. She watched it with the awe of one who is introduced to an enchanting spectacle for the first time; like going to a pantomime spectacular or a large continental circus. Father Vincent moved gracefully at the altar, placing the golden monstrance in the centre and bowing and genuflecting a lot. The little altar boy made great play with the censer, wafting it to and fro like a pendulum and assuring that the altar was almost obscured at times – and the front half of the congregation nearly asphyxiated – by the billowing white smoke. Its pungency, combined with the smell of hot candle grease, was delicious. Mother Mary Paul had done very well with the choir. Aided by her harmonium it gave a spirited yet reverend rendering of the Benediction hymns, and a motet to Our Lady by Palestrina as its central piece.

With this assault on her senses, Andrea experienced a gradual lifting of the spirit that had begun with the procession and now reached its apex in a positive flooding of the heart with feelings of warm emotion. In order really to belong, one must obviously be part of this. As the service ended and Father Vincent paced down the aisle towards the vestry at the end of the chapel she slipped out and went up to the classroom, where she pondered the interesting things she had seen and the intensity of feeling, warm and sensuous, that the experience had provoked.

In the afternoon after a lunch of chicken, trifle and lemonade the play group of the night before met again in the sixth form classroom. But this time it was in the nature of a council rather than a rehearsal. Reverend Mother had seen all the other participants of the seance before the procession. She had lectured them on the wickedness of the enterprise. Their behaviour, she informed them, had been worse than Andrea's because she was, alas, still a child of darkness, whereas they were the children of light. She quoted Luke 16, verse 8 to illustrate this point, and had another uplifting passage of Ecclesiastes backed by Ephesians 5, verse 8 to continue the light theme. At the end of the homily, she confided to them her hopes for Andrea's ultimate spiritual salvation, and urged them to set an example by their own piety, goodness and devotion. Then she wished them a happy feast day. One way and another it was quite an edifying experience, and they felt purged and cleansed of their sin.

'I still don't think it was wicked,' Andrea insisted, to their dismay, when they rejoined her. 'But I told Reverend Mother I did so that she would not send me to my aunt.'

'But I suppose you really were sorry?' Judith wondered if, after all, the Devil really did inhabit Andrea.

'Well, I was sorry about the fuss, and what happened to Anne and Lucy. That part was ghastly.'

'But was the seance fun or were you really serious?' Virginia wanted to know.

'A little of both, I think,' Andrea said carefully, realizing that somehow the girls had subtly changed sides and she must be guarded.

'I think the seance was silly, and so was the fuss,' Clare said. 'It was really the fault of Lucy, as usual . . .'

'Oh—' Andrea began; but Virginia came in quickly to forestall another argument.

'Did you enjoy the procession? I saw you in the chapel.'

'It was lovely. I've never seen a religious service before.'

'Never?'

'My father does not believe in God. I think my mother did, but she was rather scared of my father and would not do anything he didn't want.'

'How can someone not believe in God?' Judith wanted to know.

'Quite easily, obviously.'

'But He is with us, in the chapel.'

'Where exactly?' Andrea asked with interest.

'In the host in the tabernacle. We call it the Blessed Sacrament.'

'But how can that bit of bread be God?'

The girls were rather shocked at such treatment of sacred things.

'At the consecration of the Mass,' Virginia explained, being the most learned in religious doctrine, 'the priest turns the bread into the body of Christ. It is called transubstantiation. It is one of the central mysteries of our faith. How God shows himself in the form of bread, and is always with us.'

'Why bread?'

'Because it is food. It is a kind of analogy for the way Christ feeds our souls.'

'I find it rather hard to believe, ' Andrea said politely. 'I mean, that God is really there.'

'It is an article of faith,' Judith said. 'We believe it because we know it to be true. We have been told so by the Pope, who is God's representative on earth.'

Andrea sighed. 'It's very difficult isn't it? I mean to take in all this? But I liked the service with the singing, and what that man was doing at the altar.'

'That man,' Virginia said with emotion, 'is Father Vincent. He is a priest, not a man.'

Andrea giggled.

'I mean, that is to say,' Virginia corrected herself, 'he is a very special sort of man. He is consecrated to God.'

'Like the nuns?'

'In a different way. He is ordained to be God's priest, and is not like an ordinary human being.'

'He has no wife,' Clare explained. 'It is called being celibate.'

'You give up earthly joys for heavenly ones.' Judith added.

'But may he not want a wife?'

'No, he may not.'

'He doesn't feel the urge. He is above it.' Virginia thought they were doing rather well, and Andrea would soon be converted. 'He is actually higher than ordinary men.'

'I don't see why he should be just because he hasn't got a wife,' Andrea said. 'He is not above my father.'

'He is, I'm afraid,' Judith said gently. 'It's the same with our fathers too; he is above them. St Thomas said that priests were definitely higher.' She had just been doing St Thomas in doctrine class. 'And nuns; they are higher than ordinary women.'

'I don't see it at all. Just because they have no sex why are they better than anyone else?'

'Because sex is rather base, I'm afraid. St Augustine more or less said that; so did St Paul. Have it if you must, but better to do without.'

'But we talked about this yesterday. You said no sex makes you frustrated.'

'Ah, but that only applies to ordinary people. Not to priests and nuns. They do not want sex; they have put it away from them. Therefore they are not frustrated.'

'So the lay mistresses are frustrated, but not the nuns?'

'You have it exactly. They have taken a vow of celibacy, so they do not get frustrated. Once you take that vow it's all right. The urge leaves you.'

'It seems funny to me.'

'It's called grace,' Clare explained. 'Grace intervenes and stops you feeling like sex. That is why they are not like ordinary men and women. It is a very mysterious thing.'

'It *is* mysterious,' Andrea agreed.

'Perhaps you would like to know more about it?' Judith thought it was time to press home the advantage they undoubtedly had. 'We once had a non-Catholic girl who was under instruction. That meant she was learning to become a Catholic.'

'But I don't want to become a Catholic.'

'She didn't either, in the end. Mother Veronica instructed her. I think she was a bit severe, and put her off.'

'My father doesn't believe in religion. He would never let me.'

'What a pity. That's because he has no faith, you see. I'm afraid he won't go to heaven.'

'Won't I go to heaven?'

Virginia looked worried. They must not frighten Andrea if they were to save her.

'Well . . . You see there is a special place for people who are not Catholics. It's quite nice, but God is not there. If you want to see Him you must go to heaven. It's called the Beatific Vision, seeing God.'

'Oh dear. It's rather worrying isn't it?'

'It is, rather. But you won't die yet, so you have plenty of time to think about it.'

'How's Anne?' Andrea said, reminded of death. 'Has anyone seen her?'

'She's still in the infirmary. Sister Matilda won't let anyone see her. She says she must rest.'

'She must. She had a shock.'

'It was a nasty thing to do.' Clare looked severely at Andrea.

'It was a nasty thing to say,' Andrea riposted, looking defensively at Clare.

'*I* didn't push the glass.'

'Someone did. It didn't move itself. Reverend Mother says it is absolutely impossible.'

'Look, let's get on.' Virginia picked up her copy of the script. 'Let's do the bit where Bob Cratchit asks Scrooge for a rise. Scrooge, on stage.'

Everyone giggled because Virginia had impersonated Miss Clark's voice.

'Then we can do my part,' Judith said. 'We never seem to do it.'

'That's because you're so good. Come on, let's begin, or we'll miss tea and there are cakes today.'

Everyone scrambled for their scripts. Thoughts of religion and death, hell and heaven, celibacy and sex evaporated at the prospect of cakes for tea.

*1943*

The play was performed three times in the school: for the nuns and boarders, for the parents, and once more for anyone who hadn't seen it. It took place in mid-January, about two weeks after the end of the Christmas holidays. The reason it was not held before Christmas was that Advent is a semi-penitential season, not as solemn as Lent, of course, but certainly no time for girls to be junketing about on the stage in men's clothes and make-up.

The most important performance was the one for the parents. The Bishop always came too, and sat on a high chair in the middle of the first row so that those sitting immediately behind him could see nothing. The Bishop wore a large and very splendid ring, with a purple stone in an elaborate gold setting, on the fourth finger of his right hand. He displayed this ring by the way he placed his hand on the arm of his chair, letting it lie there gracefully. His fingers were soft and white, beautifully kept and a little plump, and they just very lightly clasped the arm of the chair so that the ring was shown off to perfection.

The Bishop was not an elegant man, he was too fat for that, but he was a very important one, and this was the thing that mattered, not his elegance. He took snuff, and always carried a large brown-stained handkerchief half in and half out of the pocket of his soutane. The top of his nose was a little brown tinged, too, and the hairs sprouted unbecomingly from his nostrils. Around the black soutane he wore a broad purple band, which, however, was useless in the control of his corpulent stomach, which had positively run wild. Round his neck was a gold chain, and from this hung a big gold cross, which was tucked into the purple band so that, because of the rotundity of that part of his anatomy, it stood straight up and left a great gap between it and the Bishop.

The Bishop had been in his see for nearly twenty years and he was a self-indulgent yet benign old man, authoritarian, orthodox and hating anything that deviated, however slightly, from the norm. He had little wings of grey hair on either side of his purple skull cap, which toned nicely with his complexion. He had a very friendly smile, and was particularly attached to Reverend Mother, with whom he would drink sherry in the parlour whenever he came to call. He enjoyed the annual school play because it was preceded by a particularly good dinner, which was also attended by the Canon of the local church, Father Vincent and one or two of the more distinguished parents.

Because of the intervention of the holidays, the two weeks before the play was a period of quite frenzied activity. Curtains were put up, scenery was made and painted, clothes began to arrive in hampers from London, lights were strung up by Ben and adjusted, and Mother St John had hysterics nearly every day.

Apart from the main actors were all those who played subsidiary roles, who did the lights, or acted as dressers, or moved furniture between the acts. And then, of course, there was Lucy, who came into her element with the display of flowers under the footlights, and the adornment of the altar to Our Lady, which was moved from the stage to the side of the gym. She spent days before the event in the greenhouse, bringing each flower to its supreme moment, watering, and loosening the soil. She gave little attention to her other role as curtain puller, but this was considered a mechanical thing, as Miss Clark would be in the wings to give directions.

Andrea had never known anything like the excitement leading up to the play. Lessons were hardly bothered with at all and homework was sketchy. Meals were gobbled up and the girls would rush away to polish their lines, rehearse the carols, help put up the curtains or make last-minute stitches in costumes that had split in some inconvenient place.

The performance for the nuns and the boarders was on a Saturday afternoon. It was really the dress rehearsal. Miss Clark had been there all day, contriving to appear calm with a fixed, determined smile on her face that was meant to emanate an atmosphere of unruffled serenity. Miss Greene, the art mistress, was working away at her scenery assisted by some of her more talented pupils, and Miss Larkin was taking the choir through the carols, which were sung offstage during the play.

At two o'clock Reverend Mother led her nuns into the

gym. She sat where the Bishop would sit for the main performance, only not on such a high chair. He also had a little dais, which Reverend Mother did not. The boarders followed in order of seniority, the small ones sitting on benches at the front, the older girls on chairs behind.

At two fifteen the curtains swung apart, and the prologue – especially written by Miss Clark, who liked to add her own accomplishments to those of the great masters whenever she could, and was not averse to interfering with Shakespeare, never mind Dickens – appeared and recited her piece. Off-stage everyone waited anxiously for their cues, and the more nervous huddled in corners with those who were assisting with the performance, urging them to hear their lines.

The play was in three acts, each with three scenes, quite short. The first act consisted of background, and also showed some episodes in the life of the young Scrooge transposed from the haunting scenes of the actual story. The last scene showed the death of Marley, and the ensuing years of mean-ness on the part of the ageing Scrooge. The three scenes of Act 2 were the haunting scenes with Marley's Ghost and the Ghosts of Christmas Past and Present. The final act had the last haunting scene and Scrooge's conversion. It was quite an ambitious work and had taken Miss Clark six months to write. Apart from her prologue and the transpositions, she had stuck very closely to the story and dialogue.

The prologue was clapped and retired, and the curtains parted to reveal the young Scrooge, alone in his schoolroom at Christmas time.

The rehearsal was a success. Only a few stumbled over their lines, and the haunting scenes were judged very effec-tive because of the special lighting tricks engineered by Miss Greene, as well as the skill of the players. Only Martha Oldwhistle was thought to be unsuitably cast, in the role of Christmas Past, because of the trouble she had controlling her nerves and the fact that her voice was so weak.

Scrooge and Marley's Ghost were considered outstanding, though Reverend Mother had her customary kind word for everyone when she received performers and helpers in the playroom afterwards. On this day she gave a party for everyone connected with the play, and there was fizzy lemonade or still orange juice instead of tea, exciting sandwiches in the usual feast-day style, and little cakes with hectically coloured icing where one of the cookery sisters had been incautious or overzealous with the cochineal.

After the party the girls went to tidy their things because there would be no more rehearsing until the great day the following Monday. Miss Clark was accompanied by her two star players from the party. Scrooge and Marley's Ghost walked on either side of her back to the gym, chatting about what a success the afternoon had been.

'You two were marvellous,' Miss Clark said, pink with excitement. 'You are a born actress, Andrea, I know you would be.'

'She was actually quite good,' Clare said carefully.

'But I thought *you* were terribly good,' Andrea said generously, 'and in such a long and difficult role. She didn't forget one line, Miss Clark.'

Clare's face turned a reddish-brown. The days of the play had been so busy that her preoccupation with the 'thing' she had about Andrea had dissipated in the general commotion. Now this generous praise made it stir again, and the emotion was such that she started to cough, and had to be thumped on the back by Miss Clark.

'It's very nice of you to say so,' Clare said at last to Andrea. Then they smiled at each other in the first friendly way for ages, and the beginnings of the rapport that was to last them for the rest of their schooldays took root.

Andrea put an arm round Clare's shoulder, and Miss Clark experienced a spasm of jealousy, having seen that smile, and said briskly, 'Now come along, girls. We must not linger. You were both excellent.'

Although their relationship was such a sophisticated one, Virginia and Andrea were generally considered best friends, despite the age difference. Their association was based on little more than mutual admiration, and the need on Andrea's part to have someone. Beyond that it went no deeper because

Virginia simply did not have the emotional equipment for anything more profound. Whereas she and Clare had a similar temperament in that they cultivated attitudes in order to conceal what lay underneath, Clare had a much greater potential for warmth, while Virginia, cold already, would find her emotions more frozen as she grew older. Andrea's development lay now somewhere between the other two; she could still act a part and was ready to take, but also she was more open and eager to give.

Virginia, however, was piqued when she saw Clare stroll into the gym with Andrea's arm round her neck:

'Hurry up, you two!' she called. 'There's plenty to do.'

Anne Wedgewood, recovered from her trauma, was sweeping the stage. If anything, the others who had taken part in the seance were just a trifle cool with her because, after all, the turmoil that night had resulted from her hysteria. But Anne was not as sensitive as Lucy, not so adept at sorting out or experiencing the nuances of likes and dislikes, so she behaved quite cheerfully. Lucy, on the other hand, had avoided all the girls who had been in the parlour, in case someone still blamed her for the catastrophe. She had been very busy with her plants, and had taken no real interest in the play at all.

'I think the rehearsal went off very well,' Virginia said as Clare and Andrea came up to her. 'You were marvellous, Andrea. I knew you would be.'

'So were you, and Clare was wonderful, I thought,' Andrea said smiling.

Virginia grimaced.

'Ye-s,' she paused, as though to register doubt. 'Ye-s. I suppose so.'

Clare glared at Virginia and went backstage.

'There's no need to be nasty!' Andrea whispered.

'I'm not!' Virginia hissed back. 'Why tell her she's good when it's so obvious she knows it?'

'That's mean.'

'Girls!' Miss Clark trilled. 'Will you give Miss Greene and me a hand with this set?'

Miss Greene was the youngest member of the staff, and had come straight from the Slade School of Art, followed by a year at the Institute of Education. It had been her great longing to be a real painter. But she found that a talent that had seemed exceptional at her convent school in Birmingham was not so remarkable at the Slade. Besides, her sheltered upbringing and her own personal modesty and reserve had made her uncomfortable with the idea of painting people in the nude. She knew painters were supposed to overcome this, like doctors. But her first sight of a male model in the life class had made her feel so odd that she had resolved to concentrate on still life rather than people. Moreover, she thought it was dreadful the way women were prepared to take all their clothes off to be painted, and then would just stand round chatting with the students afterwards, as though they had never displayed their bodies to the public view. Besides, the students made rude jokes afterwards about the models, and she thought the whole thing was very distasteful indeed. She loved nature, and sometimes in the summer would take her easel into the park, or her sketchbook, and sit among the trees. But now she had on her green overall and was laughing and happy as she, Miss Clark and the girls staggered under the weight of the set she had painted to go in the Cratchits' sitting room.

And now it is the night of the play. The Bishop has arrived, driven over in his aged limousine by his secretary, and is having sherry with the distinguished guests invited to meet him. One of them is Andrea's aunt, another Virginia's father. Clare's parents are not invited, because they came last year, but they will be among the audience.

Dinner is served in the parlour by two of the sisters, supervised by Reverend Mother, who flutters close to the Bishop to see that he has everything he wants, and that it is just right. It is, of course; just as with any other women, nuns like to excel themselves when they cook for men.

Virginia's father is a very sophisticated man, and his

daughter takes after him. They also resemble each other in appearance, tall and dark haired with very straight noses, and eyes deeply inset under brows that almost meet in the middle. He always comes to the school play, because his daughter is in it. It is the only time of the year he comes to the convent, although he makes an effort for prize day if Virginia is to receive a prize. Because he likes to eat well, Father is rather portly, but not so much as the Bishop, although he might be if he doesn't watch his diet. Anyway, he is much taller and his hair is still dark, though receding. He is in his late forties and Andrea's aunt, despite her devotion to dogs and horses, finds him an attractive man, and is glad she is sitting next to him. They do not know about the sophisticated relationship between Virginia and Andrea.

There are eight people altogether; they include a couple whose daughter has just joined the school, but they are very rich, and it is hoped they will hand over a lot of money for the upkeep of the convent, besides the school fees. The Canon is there, and Father Vincent; and, of course, the Bishop's secretary, a Monsignor, is dining too.

Andrea's aunt is next to the Bishop. She tells him with a gay, disarming cackle that she does not approve of his religion. The Bishop pretends to find this amusing. Secretly he is shocked; but he has already had so much sherry that his indignation is blurred, like his senses. Virginia's father pretends to be shocked too, though heaven knows why because he has not been inside a church for years. He feels that his vigorous sex life somehow excludes him. He is right.

It is a very good dinner party. The wine has been selected by the Canon, who keeps a good cellar despite the war and sells bottles to Reverend Mother at slightly more than the price he has paid for them. She buys her sherry from him too, at a likewise inflated price.

Virginia's father has not caught the name of Andrea's aunt. But when Reverend Mother mentions it again, he is impressed. It is a well-known family, and he rightly judges that she must be very rich. He immediately takes more interest in her than before because, although he is not poor, he makes good use of money and can always use more. He has mistresses in the north, as well as the exotic one in London, and they are as expensive to maintain as a string of racehorses. Besides, he is considering another mistress in London, because the exotic one is getting rather old; she has passed twenty-five and he is only really amused by young women, sexually speaking.

So he pays more attention to the aunt and she is flattered. She seems to blossom like a young girl, because the horsey men with whom she spends so much time seldom appear to notice she is a woman. She dresses and behaves as they do, so they can be forgiven for this. She is the first astride her large hunting mare, and the yells she utters on the chase are six times as loud as any man's. They frighten the foxes more than the baying of the hounds.

But this evening Aunt has on a very nice dinner dress she has bought with some black-market clothing coupons. She has had her short hair done in a softly waving style. Also a facial, at the hairdressers, that makes her look if not younger, then at least as old as she is. Usually she looks much older. She has also had her moustache removed with depilatory wax, and keeps stroking the unaccustomed smoothness of her upper lip. Aunt is forty-five, two years younger than Virginia's father. She does not like sex, and was relieved when her husband died. But if she knew how obsessed Virginia's father was with it, she might pretend.

There are cigars and cigarettes, and there is port. Before this there were delicious hors d'oeuvres, rare roast beef with vegetables grown under cover, and a trifle with a lot of sherry in it. But there is not as much as there might have been, because the nun who put the sherry in developed a liking for the taste herself, and finished the bottle.

From the extent of the feast, one would not have thought there was a war on, but nuns have a way of getting things that ordinary people do not have. They are pitied for their poverty and deprivation, and tradesmen are generous with them. They do not realise that the nuns could buy and sell them, and a lot of shops besides. The butcher is indulgent with large cuts of meat, and doesn't count the coupons. Anyway, he had a daughter at the school.

At just after eight o'clock Reverend Mother nods to the Bishop, who gets up and says grace, stumbling slightly over the words, because the extent of his eating and drinking has befuddled him. He hopes to have a good sleep during the play; he usually does, because he is not the least bit artistic. His secretary helps him to the door; Virginia's father smilingly gives his arm to Andrea's aunt – oh, she is charmed – and the procession moves out of the parlour, along the corridor, through the study and into the gym.

Inside the gym, the seats go right to the back. The curtains are drawn on the stage, but the footlights are on and everyone admires the gorgeous display of flowers underneath. There are even early daffodils and hyacinths, which glow in the light. There is a hum in the room, and every seat is packed. The atmosphere is charged with anticipation.

Sixth form girls show the party to their seats in the front row. Reverend Mother fusses, but pretends not to by smiling a lot. Mother St John, her nerves positively jangling a little tune of their own by now, keeps nervously out of the way. She hovers at the back of the hall, snapping at any girl who comes near her; but she is smarmy with the parents and they see a good number of her huge false teeth; some even see where the plate ends on either side at the back of her mouth.

As the Bishop enters, and at a sign from Mother Michael, the headmistress, to a girl who is peeping through the curtain, Miss Larkin starts up the backstage choir in a vigorous rendering of '*Ad multos annos*'. This is a hymn that is usually meant to wish the Pope a long life and reign; but it is always sung for the Bishop on this occasion and he is gratified.

Everyone rises. The Bishop bows and raises his hand in blessing as he goes down the middle aisle. Some people even kneel and cross themselves, because this is the custom. But others can't because they are so tightly packed. The Bishop manages to get to his throne on the dais without falling on his face. But his secretary helps him; and so does Reverend

Mother, who has the nerve to give the Episcopal bottom a little push from behind.

Then the Bishop sits down, with that graceful hand displaying his ring because it is spread on the arm of his chair, the fat white fingers gently clasping the sides. The audience now take their seats once more. A few latecomers are hurriedly shown in. They will get the wrong seats, but these will be laughingly rearranged with a lot of 'how do you do's?' during the interval. Talking breaks out again. There is a volume of shuffling and coughing. Then, suddenly, the curtains part, the prologue enters, the stage lights are dimmed, the audience is quiet, and the Bishop takes a loud pinch of snuff. The annual school play has begun.

> *A Christmas Carol, by Charles Dickens. Dramatization by Jennifer Clark.*
>
> *Act 1, Scene 1. A deserted schoolroom. Young Scrooge sits mournfully at a desk. Enter a bright, laughing little girl, his sister.*

> 'I have come to bring you home, dear brother!' she calls, running to him.
>
> He looks up; his expression registers hope.
>
> 'Home, little Fran?'
>
> 'Yes, home for good and all. Home for ever and ever. Father is so much kinder than he used to be that home's like heaven!'

The audience laugh at this, and begin to settle down. The school play is obviously going to go well.

And, at the beginning, everything did go well. The youthful scene was touching and lively, the Cratchits at their most poverty-stricken, and Marley died a lingering and painful death, leaving Scrooge sorrowful but meaner than ever. The act finished with his grudging permission that Bob Cratchit could have a whole day off for Christmas Day.

'Be here all the earlier next morning!' he said in threatening tones.

The curtain fell to applause. In between the scenes carols were sung by the off-stage choir, which, despite its efforts, had a rather sepulchral tone because of the heavy mass of curtains that intervened between it and the audience.

By the first interval everyone was thoroughly into the spirit of *A Christmas Carol*, and the Bishop, accepting a cup of coffee and a glass of port in his seat because he didn't feel like going all the way to the parlour, told Reverend Mother that he thought it was the best play the school had done. He had even remained awake most of the time, mainly because the carols woke him up during the scene changes. Anyway, it was certainly much better than a doubtful Restoration comedy that had been played the year before. Even though the double entendres in the original had been cut the Bishop had said it was shocking in its suggestiveness. Besides, he had not been able to sleep at all because he was so busy listening for the bawdy bits.

During the first interval parents either stayed in their seats or went to the science lab, where coffee was available. Virginia's father again escorted Andrea's aunt, and told her about his young daughter who played Bob Cratchit, and how badly she needed the loving firmness of a mother. Andrea's aunt listened with interest, and told him, in turn, that she acted in loco parentis for the daughter of her brother, and all about the loving care and attention she lavished upon her – more like a mother, she was, than an aunt.

After ten minutes or so Mother St John rang her little bell, more delicately this time, and the parents trickled back for what was, really, the climax of the play: the haunting scenes, which would result in the conversion of old Scrooge.

The stage that was constructed at the end of the gym was a real theatrical stage, except that the number of exits was limited to one, which led into the day girls' cloakroom. This meant that when the play was on the players had to be sure to be on the right side before the curtain went up. The wings were created by three sets of black curtains, and in front was the main curtain, in rich green satin, which was highered and lowered by two girls manipulating the ropes at either side.

The curtains were only put up for the play. The rest of the year the stage was bare, except for the altar to Our Lady in the middle, which had now been moved to the floor of the gym, and stood in the far left corner, with the end of the stage and the wall forming a right angle to it.

Above the altar hung the left front curtain, which was separated from it by a foot or two to allow for the drop. The stage lights ran in a box along the front, and beneath were Lucy's plants and flowers. Our Lady's altar was richly adorned, in honour of the occasion, with yellow and white chrysanthemums, arum lilies and tall fir trees on the floor at either side. There were two tall brass candlesticks on the altar, and an array of smaller lights in front, none of them lit, of course, during the performance.

The curtains were controlled by Lucy on the right of the stage, away from the altar, and a girl called Margaret Hollingsworth on the other side. The cue for raising and lowering was given by Miss Clark, who stood next to Lucy, acting as stage manager.

When the audience was settled, Miss Clark gave the signal and Lucy and Margaret heaved on the ropes. The curtains swung back and up, and the ropes were secured on hooks at either side. The stage was in darkness because Miss Greene had planned a very imaginative lighting effect for the apparition of Marley's Ghost. This had worked well at the rehearsal, but she intended to do even better this evening and introduce a special spot when Marley actually spoke.

Scrooge stood looking towards the wings, from which fearful sounds could be heard approaching. The light was pale and eerie, except for the glimmer of Scrooge's fire, made from orange paper over a light bulb to the right of the stage. Suddenly the clanking noise stopped and Marley's Ghost, head wrapped in a bandage, stomped heavily in, dragging the weight of the chain behind him. Cash boxes, padlocks, purses and a ledger or two trailed from this to the ground.

'How now!' breathed Scrooge. 'What do you want with me?'

'Much!' said Marley, his voice hollow because of the bandage.

'Who are you?'

'Ask me who I *was*!'

Lucy, because of her dislike for Andrea, deliberately let her eyes wander; she hated to see Andrea and Clare playing so well together. Consequently she was sitting on her stool in the corner while all this was happening, and her eyes strayed for a moment to the flower display she had created on Our Lady's altar, at the far side from where she was. She was particularly proud of the effect she had made. The flowers glowed like beautiful wax in the light from the stage, all very dim and subdued. Lucy sighed contentedly when, suddenly, she saw a red spark, which made the brass altar candles in their brass candlesticks seem to light up and burst into flame. In a vision of the most powerful intensity Lucy saw the whole of the altar catch fire and burn down the school.

'In life I was your partner Jacob Marley,' from the stage.

'Oooooo!' screamed Lucy from the wings. 'Fire! The place is on fire.'

Miss Clark tried to grab her, but Lucy freed herself and tore across the stage. It was one of those second-splitting occasions when those who watched were powerless to act, their minds completely unattuned to a new situation. But as Lucy ran, her eyes transfixed on the altar, the light disappeared and she saw it was not a fire at all. Instead, the whole stage was enveloped in a red light that came from the dramatic spot that Miss Greene had put on when the ghost announced who he was. But too late. Lucy, trying to halt herself, swung on the far curtain, caught her foot on the edge of the box containing the footlights and fell heavily off the stage. For a second the curtain swayed and sagged; then it fell with her. For a paralysing instance everything seemed suspended, and then the whole rail came down. The far curtain fell apart as the rope snapped and spread evenly over the whole of the front row, including His Lordship, the Bishop.

Marley's Ghost and Scrooge rushed to the front of the stage with Miss Clark, who, too, had been momentarily deceived by the unexpected light, and knew what had happened. The rest of the cast emerged from the wings and gaped at the awful scene before them. Ladies in the audience were screaming, and there were shouts of 'Fire! Fire!' until it was taken up as a great chorus by the whole of the room. 'FIRE!'

'Lights!' yelled Miss Clark.

Miss Greene put on all the stage lights and then rushed through the cloakroom to the outside door of the gym and switched on all the main lights there.

The scene, which was now flooded with light, would have been hilarious had it occurred in a Marx Brothers film and not in the gym of the Convent of the Blessed Apostles during the school play. The Bishop and a row of distinguished guests were writhing in grotesque positions under a mass of green curtaining. The central, elevated piece was undoubtedly His Lordship, and to his right and left curious manifestations were taking place, as people struggled to free themselves of the stifling folds. It was like a heaving green sea, ruffled and stirred to boiling point by a storm.

Some of the men in the audience had immediately dashed forward. One grabbed a fire extinguisher attached to the wall halfway up the room and started spraying foam on the heaving contortions of the Bishop. Another had taken the fire extinguisher on the other side of the hall and was aiming it at the mass on either side of the Bishop. Yet another ran outside to the corridor, asked a passing nun where the phone was, and summoned the police, ambulance and fire brigade by dialling 999.

Meanwhile, the most sensible parents saw there was no fire, but the two men had almost exhausted their extinguishers by this time and the curtains had a little belt of foam on the top, like the white crest on a wave. People nearest to the front tugged and tugged at the curtains; but in the confusion some pulled this way and some that so that nothing constructive happened.

The first to emerge from under the curtain was Reverend Mother, because she was so small and had managed to crawl out. She had decided that her hour to die was not yet come, and had just slithered along on the floor. Because the curtain was in two parts, very soon others started to appear. Virginia's father helped out Andrea's aunt and then, with the aid of the helpers, pulled the curtain from his side of the row. The Bishop's secretary, when he was freed, became hysterical at the sight of his master enmeshed, and tore at the curtain, helping to entangle it even more.

The authoritative voice of another parent barked 'Stop!' and, helped by Virginia's father and three others, wrenched the fire extinguisher out of the hands of the diligent parents, directed the helpers to the side of the curtain and called 'Lift!'

They lifted, and the purple slipper of the Bishop appeared, then very gradually the rest of him. His hands were clawing wildly above his head, and his skull cap had fallen over his face. The patches of sparse hair clung wetly to his head where the foam had penetrated. His face was dappled with frantic purple patches, and he kept opening and shutting his mouth like a huge fish coming up for air.

Hands, many hands, went to the rescue of the Bishop and helped him off his chair. Dr Bingley was holding on to his wrist in an attempt to take his pulse. The secretary produced a large white handkerchief and tenderly wiped His Lordship's gleaming face. He gently placed the skull cap on top of the reverend skull, tucked the cross, which had been swinging like an overworked pendulum, back into the purple sash, and brushed the shoulders of the black soutane.

Chairs had been put back in place and the audience gathered in chattering groups. The entire cast of the play was still assembled on the stage, as though for the final curtain. But there was no self-conscious pleasure on their faces, just bewilderment as they gazed on the scene of utter discord. Miss Clark wrung and unwrung her hands, contemplating dark thoughts of suicide. Her first literary effort, ruined. She sank her head upon Clare's shoulder, uttering little moans.

Inside herself, however, though shocked, Clare was laughing. She had never in her life seen anything so funny as the fat old Bishop emerging like a teetering drunk from the curtain. Next to her Andrea caught her eyes, and for a moment their shoulders shook in unison.

It was then, in that instant, that fractional pinpoint of time, that their rapport was cemented. Out of the whole cast only they appreciated the farcical quality of the situation; only they could rise above a tragedy and turn it into a comic human situation.

There was, of course, no thought of proceeding with the play. The senior nuns had come scurrying into the gym, and, as the last arrived, there was a clang of bells outside as three fire engines, two ambulances and a police car came to a screaming halt by the main door. Reverend Mother had a quick word with Mother Michael and Mr Clearwater, and the three of them hurried out of the gym to stay the avalanche of uniformed men about to descend on the convent.

Outside there was the noise of voices, heavy steps and car doors shutting. All those in the gym not otherwise engaged ran to the windows and looked into the drive, which was as bright as day because of the lights from the vehicles. Heads peered from dormitory windows and lights went on in the quarters of those nuns who had been safely tucked up in their beds.

On stage the cast had split into groups. Miss Clark was being comforted by Mavis Myers and Judith Lynch, and Andrea and Clare were getting a scolding from Virginia Clearwater for their behaviour, for finally they had had to retreat behind one of the black wing curtains to have a really good laugh, and there she had found them clutching each other in a gale of paroxysmal mirth.

When order was more or less restored with everyone looking out of the windows and the Bishop drinking a glass of brandy that had been provided by a thoughtful Sister Angela, someone thought of the cause of it all. The curtains were still lying where they had been pushed back against the stage.

'Where is Lucy?' Miss Clark gave a shrill little scream and peered downwards from the stage.

'Lucy, Lucy . . .' A hubbub broke out, with everyone

looking at everyone else, and there was an exodus away from the windows and towards the stage. No movement came from the mass of curtains.

'Lucy!' Miss Clark gave a very spectacular and unlady-like leap from the stage and began to pluck frantically at the curtains. The Bishop was left all by himself holding the brandy; even his secretary deserted him. All peered at the curtains. Anxious hands tried to move them, but nothing happened until Dr Bingley mobilized half a dozen males and got the operation properly organized. Everyone dreaded what they might see.

What they saw was a very still form, flat on its back by the altar, lying beside the crushed statue of Our Lady and the debris of the flowers and shrubs. It stared up at them, and someone whispered, 'She's dead.'

'She's dead, she's dead.' The awful words circulated round the hall and there was a furtive movement to the front.

'Lucy!' Miss Clark, Mother David and Dr Bingley knelt beside the still form, which raised its head in a feeble way and said:

'I'm all right, miss.'

Lucy had been saved from asphyxiation by the fact that the weight of the curtain had been borne by the front row, so that it formed a kind of tent and hardly touched her. All the time she had been able to see the bright lights above her, and her ears had been attuned, oh so much attuned, to the furore her impulsiveness had caused. The fact that the statue had been smashed weighed far more in her remorse than the possible death by smothering of the Bishop and distinguished guests. She had prayed to Our Lady for forgiveness, and had lain perfectly still in the hope that everyone would forget her and she would be able to creep away, or, better still, that it would turn out to be a bad dream.

'Oh, Lucy, what a silly girl you are!' wept Miss Clark, tears released at last, and clasped Lucy's head to her bosom.

Lucy gently withdrew from the strangulating embrace and propped herself on one elbow.

'I thought it was on fire. I thought the statue was burning.'

111

Dr Bingley felt his patient's pulse, pronounced it alive and stood up.

'Now can someone explain just what happened?'

They drew Lucy up and sat her on a chair, from which she avoided looking at the Bishop, who was still groping for air.

'I know how it happened,' Miss Clark said. 'It was just at the beginning of the scene with Marley's Ghost. The stage was lit by a solitary white light. When the ghost said who he was, Miss Greene introduced a sudden bright red spot. Lucy can't have been looking at the stage, because she suddenly said "Fire!". I looked in her direction and saw that the light had been caught by the brass candlesticks on Our Lady's altar at the side. It did look for a moment as though it was on fire. I grabbed Lucy, but too late.'

'When I ran, miss, I saw that the light was not from the altar, but the stage. I tried to stop myself . . .'

Lucy began to weep now.

'Silly child,' Miss Greene said gently. 'It was really my fault for not rehearsing the lighting properly.'

'Lucy should have been looking at the stage,' Mother St John said, having joined the group after having her private burst of hysterics in the day girls' cloakroom. 'Naughty girl.'

Lucy wept the more. Dr Bingley said she had better go to bed. She was taken by Sister Benedict straight to the infirmary, where Sister Matilda, woken from a righteous sleep, gave her two aspirin tablets and a large spoonful of castor oil.

By this time Reverend Mother had returned with a man in a peaked cap, braided, with three pips on his shoulder. This was the police inspector, who gazed wonderingly at the confusion in the gym. Because the altar was in ruins it was some time before the cause of the disaster could be explained to him. Then everyone looked up accusingly at the giant red spot, which was still on in the middle of the stage. Miss Greene took this to be her cue, and silently disappeared. But the inspector was a jolly man, and Reverend Mother had been charm itself, so everyone was laughing by now, except the Bishop. He was not laughing at all.

Two of the senior girls were folding the fallen curtains, and Sister Angela was sweeping up the remains of Our Lady. Sister Benedict was trying to re-pot the fallen plants. Clare and Andrea had controlled themselves by now, and were talking to Clare's parents and Aunt. Mr Clearwater had nobbled Virginia, and was telling her what a bad show the whole thing was.

The inspector was smiling and nodding, and then he left to give his men instructions to go home. The junior players were taken to bed by Mother Christopher after they had been given hot milk in the refectory by Sister Francis, who also had been woken from her bed. She grumbled a good deal about *that*.

Mother Michael made an address from the stage to those who remained. She explained the cause of the accident, apologized and said there would be two more performances of the play when order had been sufficiently restored. The parents gave her a polite little clap, and left in orderly fashion, having a word with their young if there was the chance. What a night it had been.

The inspector returned and helped to escort the Bishop into the parlour. There they were joined by any people of importance and partook of brandy provided by Reverend Mother, coffee and the stale, highly coloured cakes left over from the party two days before, which Sisters Angela and Francis produced. They were all laughing quite heartily by now, except for the Bishop, who was inclined to think the whole thing was a non-Catholic plot against his sacred person. All he wanted to do was to go back to his palace, have a good sleep, and a check-up from his doctor the following morning.

The Bishop was the first to leave. All the others seemed set for a merry party in the parlour, and the Canon sent Father Vincent over to the presbytery to fetch some more brandy – for which he would charge Reverend Mother, allowing for his usual margin of profit.

The girls went to bed, and Miss Clark got tipsy at the party in the parlour. The lights in the gym were finally extinguished, and gradually they went out in the rest of the house as people prepared for sleep. But they stayed on in the parlour until after midnight, and Mr Clearwater had to drive Miss Clark home, even to put her key in the door. But he didn't want to go any further, because she was not of the age that appealed to him – nor of the appearance either.

Reverend Mother thought the convent would never recover from the shame of the evening. She had hovered hopefully over the Bishop when she had seen him to his car, but there was no word of understanding, or even a blessing. Trust a bishop not to understand. Still, those in the parlour had had a good time, and no one had been seriously hurt.

"There is a time to weep, and a time to laugh; a time to mourn and a time to dance," she told herself, comfortingly, on her way up to bed.

The following day Mother Michael called a meeting for the staff, to explain what had happened and to decide on new dates for the play. At the morning assembly of the school she had made a very dry statement to the effect that the curtain had simply fallen down and the play had had to be cancelled. However, it did not take the school long to learn that the situation had been rather more complex, because so many parents had been there the previous night. The news became known in a mixture of fact and sensation; one of the wilder rumours being that either Lucy, Andrea or Clare had deliberately hurled themselves off the stage taking the curtains with them. A few said the Bishop was dead, and some believed there had been carnage in the whole of the front row. Little serious work was done in the classrooms that day.

Lucy was still in the infirmary, suffering from self-induced shock. She had decided to induce it, even though she felt quite well, every time she awoke and relived the terrible moment the night before when she had started to fall. Because of what she had done she kept on saying she wanted to go to confession. But Sister Matilda sensibly called not Father Vincent, but the doctor and he prescribed a mild sedative and two days' rest.

The meeting was held after school, as it was impossible to arrange it at any other time. The staff were mostly exhausted because of having to cope with questions to which they did not really know the answers themselves. The most fanciful stories were firmly squashed, which only made them gain wider currency. The staff gathered at four o'clock, with cups of tea in their hands, grateful that the day was almost over.

Mother Mary Michael was one of the most normal as well as the most gifted and accomplished nuns in the school. She belonged to that generation of women who entered religion because they really felt they had something to give, instead of merely wanting to escape from the world.

Those nuns who entered for the wrong reason were as inadequate as religious citizens as they would have been as ordinary ones. A discontented and unhappy woman did not make a good nun.

Mother Michael had become a convert to Catholicism when she was in her second year studying modern languages at Cambridge, just after the Great War. She was a clever, attractive and popular girl. After getting first-class honours, she stayed on for further study and became engaged to a young don who had just taken up a fellowship at Trinity. They were both terribly happy, their parents were pleased; nothing could go wrong.

And nothing did actually go wrong, except that the then youthful Mother Michael had a Call. It had been quite clear and there was no mistaking it. She believed ever afterwards in the idea of vocation, because God had called, and she had responded. It was not that she loved her fiancé any less, or ceased to love him at all. She only knew, through this mysterious calling, that she must enter a teaching order and devote her whole life to God and not to him. The fiancé, who was not a Catholic, never understood. They had been within a few weeks of their marriage, and he just could not see it. A few years after this, when he was thirty, he killed himself; but it had probably nothing to do with Mother Michael.

She entered the teaching order as soon as she left Cambridge, after taking guidance from a Jesuit as to which one she should choose. Despite the few absurd people who did join for the wrong reasons, there were also some very clever women in the Order, and Mother Michael immediately felt she had come home.

Since that time she had never doubted the reality of her calling; and she had enjoyed every moment of her religious life. She didn't even mind when she was sent from the beautiful and exclusive girls' school of the Order in the south to this cold northern town to be headmistress.

Mother Michael had changed over the years, and she was no longer pretty. This may have been because she wore very large horn-rimmed spectacles, and because the years of discipline and frugality had made her face thin and chalk-white. She was always busy, never gossiped, and her disposition was mild and tranquil. She did her job very well, believed in strict discipline for the girls and the virtues of early to bed and early to rise, with a mixture of work, play and prayer in proportion. She thought this turned out girls who were healthy and happy in body and mind.

No one liked Mother Michael very much, because, despite her obvious gifts and her sense of justice and fairness, there was so little that was really human about her. She was like a very well-maintained machine that never broke down. Many of the less stable nuns were loved, just because of their weakness and fragility, qualities that evoked response because they were natural. No one actively disliked Mother Michael, because there was no earthly reason to do so, and almost everyone respected her. She was the only nun whom Reverend Mother considered at all as an equal, because she was firm and held her ground, though always in a respectful way.

One would have thought that the trivialities of convent life would bother someone like Mother Michael, but not at all. She saw it all as a part of God's plan for her, and she accepted it with equanimity.

Mother Michael entered the staff room with the nuns who actually taught in the school: Mother David, Mother Mary Paul, Mother Christopher, Mother Euphrasia, Mother

Veronica and Mother St John. Although it was a teaching order there were not all that many clever nuns about, and they had to be dispersed among the other houses in the country. Some of the nuns who lived in the convent were retired, and others taught in the Catholic elementary schools in the town.

Mother St John taught scripture, very badly, to the lower forms, and Mother Christopher was in charge of the junior school. Mother St John was still in a bad mood because the events of the night before coming so soon after the seance had brought on an acute attack of nervous dyspepsia, and she sat there quietly, scowling and belching all the way through the meeting. The lay staff rose as the nuns came in, clutching their cups and biscuits in their hands. Nuns and lay staff were always terribly polite to one another.

Mother Michael sat in one of the chairs that had been casually arranged round the room and folded her hands in her lap.

'This meeting has been called, members of staff, to tell you exactly what occurred last night, so that you will be able to quell all the wild rumours that are circulating. I also want to arrange new dates for the play.'

Mother Michael spoke precisely and never uttered one word more than was necessary to convey meaning. She told them very clearly what had taken place, and how Lucy Potts had contrived to have the optical illusion whose results had been so spectacular. She made it seem all very ordinary, almost normal.

She was watched by Miss Clark, who was dressed in sombre brown for the occasion, unrelieved by any of the bright spots of colour she usually favoured. The awful day had been made worse by a subsequent hangover, and she had made most of the forms she taught read quietly during her classes, while she held her throbbing head in her hands and stared at her desk.

Miss Greene blushed when Mother Michael came to the light effects that had caused the trouble.

'Why was it not rehearsed? Surely it was rehearsed?' asked Miss Goldie the Latin mistress.

'Even if it had been,' Mother Michael neatly circumvented the question, 'Lucy Potts would still have been gazing at the altar. She is such a dreamer.'

'She has an obsession about those plants of hers,' Mother David said mildly.

'Oh, not an obsession, surely. Affection perhaps,' Mother Michael corrected her.

'*Obsession!*' Mother St John insisted, getting it in quickly between burps. 'That is just what it is. An obsession.'

'Most unhealthy,' said Mrs Battley, who taught modern languages.

'*If* I may conclude?' Mother Michael said firmly. She finished the talk with a note of deprecation in her voice for the insult that had been done to the front row, and, above all, to His Lordship, the Bishop.

'His Lordship, the Bishop,' Miss Goldie echoed in awed tones. 'How frightful.'

Miss Goldie had taught Latin in the school for as long as anyone could remember – as far back as the Roman occupation of Britain, for all they knew. In fact, no one could remember further back than Miss Goldie, and although she had not been present when the foundations of the school were laid she had appeared pretty soon after. In her time she had seen nuns and teachers come and go, die and retire. Now she was nearing retirement herself, and deeply resented the prospect. She should have retired before the war, but a shortage of classics teachers had made the school glad of her services.

Miss Goldie's idea of the Latin language was hardly romantic. She concentrated on syntax, favoured soft clerical pronounciation and abhorred writers like Ovid and Catullus. The girls were brought up on Caesar and Cicero, with a touch of Horace for light relief. She had a whiskery chin, a mandarin moustache and always wore purple or black. Her still-dark hair was secured in a firm bun two inches from the nape of her neck. She kept her handkerchief secured somewhere in the nether reaches of her drooping bosom, and groped for it from time to time, quite unself-consciously. She was the senior teacher in the school, and much feared by the girls. She was deeply and austerely religious.

In her youth Miss Goldie had wanted to be a nun. But her attempts to enter religion had always been frustrated by her mother, who had announced that she was dying in her early twenties and had been, figuratively, on her death bed ever since. She had just celebrated her ninety-fifth birthday – from the bed in which she had passed most of her life. Miss Goldie was now seventy, though she could pass in appearance for fifty or so, and was convinced her mother would outlive her. There is nothing quite like hypochondria for a long, if fruitless, life.

Miss Goldie was great friends with Miss Moppatt, who had been teaching history in the school for a likewise record number of years. Miss Moppatt had never taught anywhere else, and her grasp of history was still as vague as it had been when she had obtained her lower second-class degree. She relied on the works of Hilaire Belloc, because he was a 'safe' Catholic, and otherwise made do on a hazy and ineffectual memory. No one ever did very well in history in the school, and Miss Moppatt's methods caused Mother Michael, that enlightened nun, much suffering.

Their friendship was the only thing that made life tolerable for Miss Moppatt and Miss Goldie, for Miss Moppatt had very old parents too, and had lived with them all her life. They were over eighty, and she was sixty.

Miss Moppatt, small and thin, favoured brightly coloured materials for her otherwise drab dresses, whose style, high at the neck with long sleeves and a hem halfway down her calves, never varied. She had listened carefully to Mother Michael's narrative, saying 'terrible' at intervals, and she nearly swooned at the idea of the Bishop drowning beneath waves of thick curtain material. She was very religious too, but secretly believed in God as one person rather than a Trinity. She thought He manifested Himself as the Sacred Heart of Jesus, and prayed to Him only under this guise.

119

The staff sat thoughtfully for a while when Mother Michael had finished. They all avoided looking at Miss Clark and Miss Greene.

'Of course it was really nobody's fault.' Mother David was trying to be fair.

'W-e-ll,' Miss Goldie was doubtful about *that,* 'nothing happens by itself. It was clearly *somebody*'s fault.'

'*My* fault,' Miss Clark said with a tragic expression on her face. 'It should have been rehearsed.'

'*My* fault,' Miss Greene insisted. 'I should have told you about the new spot.'

'This is complete nonsense,' Mrs Battley said firmly. 'It was clearly the fault of that ridiculous girl Lucy. I have never known a child with such an innocent, even foolish, expression on her face cause so much trouble.'

'Exactly,' Mother St John said. 'There was the seance. And before that—'

Mother Michael lifted her hand.

'Please. This is not an inquiry into the behaviour of Lucy Potts. She obviously had an illusion of fire. She is perhaps not *quite* as responsible or thoughtful as she might be, so—'

'Lucy is a silly child,' Mrs Battley said. 'She should never have been given the job of pulling curtains in the first place.'

Miss Clark coloured and looked fiercely at Mrs Battley, who was the only married member of staff, and had two young boys at Downside. Mrs Battley shared the teaching of modern languages with Mother Michael, and was a practical, pragmatic woman who felt very much the superiority of her married status, and remained rather aloof from the staff, whom she pitied.

Not that she was very happy with her husband, who was a civil servant, but at least she felt she was fulfilled, whereas the others were not. She had her boys to remind her of those rather far off distant days before she and her husband had grown tired of each other and begun to live a celibate life of mutual, if rather contemptuous, toleration.

'Surely curtain pulling could be done by the simplest

mentality,' Miss Greene said. 'You can hardly call it a responsible job.'

'I do call it responsible,' Mrs Battley said. 'I do.'

'Lucy is not quite herself, these days,' Mother David said delicately. 'If you remember she used to be very friendly with Clare Bingley. But ever since Andrea came that seems to have finished.'

'They were never suited anyway,' Miss Larkin, the singing mistress said. 'It was not a friendship at all. Clare merely used Lucy.'

'But Lucy was very attached to Clare,' whispered Miss Parker, the science mistress, who had a nervous disposition due to a childhood illness, and stammered a little when she spoke. 'S-she was v-v-very attached.' She was all right in class when she had to repeat mechanical instructions and formulae, but she was hopeless at making any original contributions to a conversation.

'One can hardly blame Andrea,' Mrs Battley said. 'She is always very sweet with Lucy.'

'It is more accurately Clare's fault,' Mother St John intervened. 'Clare is behind everything that goes wrong in this school.'

'But *this* time, Mother—'

'This time too. By being so nasty to Lucy she has upset her. I see it now.'

'Until Andrea came, I do not recall so many incidents of this kind occurring,' Mother Veronica observed in a detached, chilly voice. She was one of the few people in the school who was neutral in her attitude towards Andrea because she never showed any desire to court her, or invited her to sleep in her dormitory. She also had little aptitude for mathematics.

'Odd, too, that Andrea was on the stage last night when this thing happened.'

'You cannot blame Andrea for that! What a horrid thing to say. Her main scene was ruined,' Miss Clark spluttered in defence of her favourite.

'But the seance *was* her fault,' Mother Veronica said. 'I often think she was not punished enough for that. In fact,'

121

she looked across at Mother St John, 'she was not punished at all. Anyone else would have been expelled.'

'Mother, please,' Mother Michael chided. 'That was not for us to decide. That incident came under the personal control of Reverend Mother. You do not criticize that, do you Mother?'

'Of course not, Mother. It is only that I have had other disturbing news about Andrea, and her influence really seems to be quite pernicious. Last night in the middle of the disturbance Andrea and Clare were found behind a curtain engaging in hysterical laughter.'

A complete silence, profound and shocked, followed, broken by Mother Michael.

'May I ask how you know this, Mother?'

'Of course. Virginia Clearwater told me in the dormitory last night. She was very distressed, because His Lordship could have been killed. She said that while everyone was trying to help, Clare and Andrea were giggling helplessly behind the curtain. Then she asked them what was the matter, and they said something uncomplimentary about the Bishop and asked her if she did not see the funny side. She replied that she certainly did not, and reprimanded them quite severely.'

Mother St John's face was even more chalky than usual. 'It must have been Clare's fault.'

'Certainly not,' Mother Veronica countered. 'I am sure it was Andrea. I know she is favoured by many people here, but sometimes I have my doubts about her.'

'Whatever can you mean, Mother?' exclaimed Miss Clark.

'What I say. She is a trouble-maker, but tries to disguise it by pretending to be so nice to everyone'

A little chorus of protests and disclaimers broke out in the common room. Most of the staff agreed that, except for the unfortunate fact that she was a Protestant, Andrea was a model child and pupil. Miss Clark got up and walked over to Mother Veronica, shaking her finger at her.

'You have no right to say that! It is most unfair!'

Mother Veronica's composure evaporated, and she stared

uncomprehendingly at the waggling finger of the English mistress. She could not even voice a reply, and just gazed at the finger as if it put her in a state of trance.

'Miss Clark!' Mother Michael said. 'Please control yourself. That is no way to talk to a colleague, and . . . a nun.' She dropped her voice a tone or two in respect. 'Moreover, you know the children are told never to point. Kindly take your finger away from Mother Veronica's face.'

The silence in the room came to Miss Clark, but remotely, because inside her own skull there was a noise of pounding. She didn't even remember crossing the room, and stared at Mother Veronica almost in wonderment as to how she got there.

'I-I'm sorry. I don't know what's the matter with me. I am overwrought.'

She sat abruptly down in a chair, and stared at the ceiling. Then her shoulders shook violently, and the tears rushed out. Cynthia Greene and Mrs Battley immediately went over to her.

'Really!' Miss Moppatt exclaimed. 'I have never seen such a scene in all my years at the school. Have *you*, Miss Goldie?'

Miss Goldie shook her head vigorously.

'Never.'

'Please, members of staff. Please.' The normally imperturbable Mother Michael was quite agitated. 'This must cease. Miss Clark, you may leave the room if you wish.'

Miss Clark shook her head; she didn't wish to be seen in the corridor by the girls. Mother Veronica was looking terribly distant and dignified. The whole incident had been a shock and an affront.

'I'm sorry, Mother.' Miss Clark blew her nose on Mrs Battley's handkerchief, and rubbed her eyes on her sleeve. 'Mother Veronica, I am *so* sorry. But I do think it was an unfair thing to say about Andrea. Terribly, terribly unfair.'

Mother Michael again lifted a hand.

'Please, no more about Andrea. It is true she has been involved in one or two disturbances since she came to the school. But the poor girl has never had the benefit of a happy and stable family life. I am sure she does her best.'

'Perhaps she was only giggling last night through nerves,' Miss Greene suggested. 'Like the Chinese.'

Mother Michael raised her eyebrows.

'The Chinese?'

'They laugh when they are upset, Mother.'

'Ah.' Mother Michael clearly thought this was an inspirational idea to explain Andrea's conduct. 'She may have travelled in the Far East with her father, and picked it up there.'

'Well, where did Clare pick it up then?' asked Miss Goldie in a sceptical voice. 'She has not travelled in the Far East, as far as I know.'

'She got it from Andrea.' Miss Greene warmed to her theory. 'It is catching. Laughter is very catching.'

Some looked with astonishment at Miss Greene, others smiled. One even lit a cigarette, and the tension in the room relaxed.

'Members of staff,' Mother Michael said, 'it is time we closed this meeting. I do not propose to take punitive action over last night against anyone. I am sure the girls were giggling due to nerves, if not,' she gave a dry little smile, 'to Far Eastern influence. It is true that Lucy may be a little unhappy because of Clare, but there are plenty of other nice friends for her. She is very interested in her plants, and I will ask Sister Benedict, who is fond of Lucy and understands her, to have a talk with her. Now, I think we shall have another performance of the play on Friday, and the last one on Saturday as planned. I am getting some men in to see to the curtain. Reverend Mother has written to the Canon and His Lordship. There, I am sure, we can let the matter rest. After all, my dear members of staff, girls will be girls.'

With this comforting platitude the meeting ended. Mother Michael led her cluster of nuns from the staff room like a duck shepherding its young. Those who remained poured themselves more tea and lit cigarettes. Miss Clark had recovered from her outburst, but was still sniffing into Mrs Battley's handkerchief.

In ones in twos the staff gathered up their books and put them in briefcases or on to their shelves. Then they left to return to that other part of their lives, less important and sometimes dull, but also significant, which was lived away from the convent, the nuns, and those disturbing, awkward pupils.

# Six

After 1945 one could travel round Europe and see the scars left by the war. Cities, towns, villages and country-side – nothing escaped. People were killed in blitzes or bombardments, or they were executed up against walls for their patriotism. In the concentration camps during those awful years over six million Jews were quite deliberately gassed. A terrible shadow of destruction dwelt over all humanity.

Yet the war scarcely touched the town lying in the peaceful northern valley, above the river that flowed sluggishly into the Atlantic. At the beginning there were a few alarms as the enemy bombers passed over on their way to the industrial towns on the estuary. Then the sirens would wail, and in the convent the girls would gleefully scuttle down, dragging blankets and pillows with them, to the cellars, which Reverend Mother at the outbreak of war had, at great expense, converted into shelters. After 1942 the shelter was never used again and, as far as the girls in the school were concerned, a rather exciting chapter, full of opportunities for heroism and romance, was over. Apart from this the war might not have existed, except for the food. But institutional food is invariably bad, so this was not really any deprivation to measure against that which other girls were suffering in occupied Europe.

Some of the girls' fathers went to the war. Others were in reserved occupations, or were too old. Hardly any of them died, except from natural causes. The impact of the war, then, hardly touched the girls at all. Occasionally they would see nuns and mistresses talking in a grave little huddle, looking solemn, and special prayers would be asked for in chapel that night or during the school assembly.

And so in Europe offensives and counter offensives went on, cities fell and were recaptured, demarcation lines expanded or shrank. Millions had their lives completely changed by the war; they lost their homes, or became refugees and had to flee to foreign countries and try and resettle there. Mothers lost husbands and sons, children lost fathers and brothers.

But in the northern town few had their lives changed. No one had to go to another country to live, and no one was put into a concentration camp because of their race or the views they held. The war passed the northern town by. But whether it was truly thankful for this is an open question. It simply did not know what it was missing; and when later the opportunity came to find out, the memory was forgotten, and gratitude was only half hearted for something that had happened so long ago.

'We had a simply super time,' Clare told Andrea one day when they were talking about the time they used to have airraid alarms. 'We would come down in pyjamas and dressing gowns. We had chocolate to drink, and cakes. Occasionally we slept in the cellar all night. It was terrific. I was sorry when it finished.'

But Andrea knew more about the war than that it was fun. Her father often spoke about it, and they had lived in Kensington when the City of London was nearly destroyed. Andrea had been very frightened by the noise; she could hear the aircraft overhead and the muffled thuds in the distance. Her father would talk about what Europe was suffering, and about the places he had been posted to in the thirties: Bucharest, Budapest, Rome and Warsaw. Andrea used to marvel that she had visited all these places, and she would cling to those memories because her father told her that nothing would ever be the same again.

She worried about her father now, all alone in that place

in the Middle East, Damascus. But Reverend Mother told her Damascus was a very safe place to be, because the Nazis would never get that far. Churchill would stop them long before that. Reverend Mother thought that Churchill was like God, and she carried a picture of him in her missal. Sometimes she almost prayed to him, instead of for him. She was sure everyone's destinies were in his hands, and that he would deliver them all. Andrea listened gravely to Clare; but when she had finished she said:

'I don't think it is super at all. Think of all the people being killed in Liverpool by the bombs.'

'Oh, you know what I mean. I don't mean *that*! It was horrible about the people being killed. All the same, it was exciting for us, at the time. You know.' Clare flushed a little.

The girls were sitting in the early spring sunshine on a bench outside the cloakroom, during the half-hour recreation period before tea. In the playground below the more vigorous were having a quick game of netball. A gaggle of squawking juniors was playing rounders on another pitch. Others were strolling round the lake, hands in the pockets of their coats, because it was still chilly. But this patch outside the cloak-room was always warm, because it was protected by the wall of the building. The two sat coatless, with their lisle-stockinged legs stretched out before them and their arms folded.

Since the play Andrea and Clare had become inseparable; they were established 'best friends'. The fact that they had been the only two to see any humour in the sight of the Bishop enveloped in a large stage curtain had made a certainty of something that only Clare had known existed before: their essential compatibility. It seemed astonishing to Clare that Andrea had taken so long to recognize it. But now that she had, they were as one. It was the end of a wooing; the beginning of a partnership.

Clare had been helped by the attitude of Virginia Clearwater, who had reported their giggling to Mother Veronica. This treachery had shocked Andrea, and the two united against her. Andrea and Virginia now scarcely acknowledged each other. Their sophisticated relationship was clearly at an end.

Compared to what Clare had to offer, Andrea saw that her association with Virginia had been so superficial. Clare and she thought exactly on the same level, if they did not agree about everything. It was the way they appraised things that was so important; the processes of minds whose mechanisms were so similar. However it was more of a marriage than a love affair; it was an essentially suitable liaison.

Clare found in Andrea the first best friend who was worthy of her. All the others, like Lucy, had merely been foils to a brighter talent. Clare's discontent, her rudeness and bullying had come from an uncertainty about herself. But now Andrea seemed to complement that part of her which had been detached and insecure. Clare began to mellow, because the necessity for hostility had been removed from her life.

In the close confines of the convent, and in the warmth of Clare's affection, Andrea's real nature emerged as the depth of her feelings, hitherto partly hidden, swept to the surface. She felt herself surrounded by love. The warmth and approval of those about her gave her an almost sensual satisfaction. It was the security that she, too, had badly needed; now the environment made its contribution and she did not need to rely solely on those instances of devotion which, because they were isolated, could not cohere and provide a safe web for her to rest on.

Later in life Andrea was to have many lovers, and people who were shocked by the way she flitted restlessly from one to the other would not know that she was looking desperately for the love that she had known from her fifteenth year in the convent, and that was to cease so abruptly when she left it for the uneasy world of later adolescence and adult life.

In religion Andrea found another vehicle for her emotional temperament. The wishes of her father and aunt became gradually eroded, rather than openly defied, and she went to the services as she wished. She used simply to sit, listen and absorb, conjuring up for herself images of a very rarified and beautiful place that had the mystical quality of the pictures she loved by Giotto, Cimebue and Simone Martini.

Although Reverend Mother was anxious to pluck as many souls as she could from life's garden (another felicitous phrase of hers from her homily about the conversion of souls), she did not care to grab them before the roots had time to implant themselves in the soil of the Faith. While she would do all she could to encourage Andrea, she would do nothing to stampede her into the fold. She thought it best that Andrea should do just as she liked, without feeling either compelled or deprived. She was exactly right. Aunt, though not deliberately deceived, knew nothing; Andrea was happy, and the nuns waited in hopeful anticipation of things to come.

In the Easter holidays Andrea went home with Clare to her parents. The Bingleys were warm, responsive people and they liked Andrea, whom they had already met at the school. They came to visit a good deal more often than Andrea's aunt. It upset Reverend Mother to see the girl neglected in this way by her family, and she was so pleased when Clare asked permission to take her home. In this normal, happy family Andrea was comfortable; it seemed like a natural extension of the convent.

Aunt was relieved not to have her niece for the holidays. She was very involved with the business of her estate, and also with the interesting new relationship that had grown up between herself and Virginia's father. He had taken her several times to dinner in Manchester, and had been twice to Sunday lunch with her. For the first time since her husband had started to court her, over twenty years before, she had felt the stirrings of something that was quite unconnected with horses or the killing of small animals. One could not actually have called it physical desire, but it was the only kind of approximation to this pleasant feeling that someone like Aunt could have.

Mr Clearwater appealed to her, in a way that other men of her acquaintance did not. She started to take care of her appearance, and became coy and kitten-like in his presence.

She was, of course, hoping to encourage some interesting initiative on the part of Mr Clearwater.

But although he paid her the most gracious compliments, and was as attentive as any man could be, he did not make love to her. Nothing remotely physical happened. Mr Clearwater was after Aunt's money, not her body. If possible, he didn't want to marry it; he wanted to invest it in the numerous companies in which he had a financial interest. He had plenty of bodies that were far younger and more attractive than he imagined Aunt's to be; only their upkeep was costing him more and more.

His tactics – which, as it happens, were very skilful and correct – were to keep Aunt's interest just on the boil by the charm of his manner and his air of extravagant elegance. He thought he could play along like this for quite some time; and then he might have to take stock of the situation and, perhaps, redeploy his forces.

Both Aunt and Virginia's father were scheming in their way, but for different things. They deserved each other, and no one need feel sorry for them.

In the spring and early summer the grounds of the convent gradually lost the barren aspect of winter. The formal flower beds showed patches of vibrant colour; daffodils, bluebells and primroses proliferated in the woods, and the sticky brown buds opened on the chestnut trees. The swans on the lake shook off their inertia and started to breed, much to the interest of the junior girls, who would spy on them from the dormitory windows in the lengthening evenings. Mother Christopher would haul them back with sharp little exclamations of reproof. She had often told Reverend Mother that the activities of the swans in the spring were an unhealthy sight for the girls to observe. But Reverend Mother told her not to be ridiculous. All nature was alive at this time. Besides, she had been given the swans by the Bishop and was sure their behaviour could do nothing wrong or damaging to their young.

The beginning of the summer term was a period of change

131

and activity in the convent. The girls put on their summer uniform of light blue dresses, soft white collars and dark blue ties, which were fixed to the neck with press-studs. The thick blue overdrawers were exchanged for cotton ones, and the junior girls wore white socks. The seniors wore thick lisle stockings all the year round; in the summer they became rather hot and smelly, because they were not changed often enough, and they stuck together when they came back from the laundry.

The games changed from netball to rounders and tennis. This was a time of tension, too, because summer exams were approaching, and those in the Upper Fifth sat for their School Certificate. But for those in the Lower Fifth exams were not so important, and they threw themselves into sporting activities, or prepared for the needlework and art exhibitions and the concert, which were a feature of prize day at the end of the term.

Early in the summer term an event took place which was one of importance to the Church, if of no direct interest for the convent. Boys of the diocese between the ages of about twelve and fourteen were summoned to be interviewed by the Bishop to decide whether or not they should go to the seminary and train to be priests. The Catholic Church had an idea that if you caught them young enough you kept them. Usually it was right.

The ones selected had already shown proficiency in examination, and an inclination to piety that had set them apart from the rest of their schoolmates. Most prolific Catholic families considered it an honour to have a priest in the family, so that the tender age at which this important decision was made did not trouble them at all. Besides, it took care of their education and they could always change their minds later on.

About fifty young boys came to the convent, and the gym and playroom were put aside for them as they waited for their interviews with the Bishop and priests in the parlour. The rooms where the boys waited were strictly out of bounds to the girls, who were kept in rigid seclusion in the study or their classrooms, or sent straight down to the playground under strict supervision.

However, as Mother Michael had said in her unimaginative way, girls will be girls; and the Bishop would probably have added that boys will be boys – because he was also an unimaginative kind of man. Neither of them would have intended by this to make any kind of allowances for what the young will actually do.

But the occasion that put paid to the priestly aspirations of six of the would-be seminarians occurred on the second day of the interviews of this particular summer term; and involved Lucy, who, needless to say, had escaped the vigilance of Mother St John, and was busy tending her flowers in the greenhouse.

The last lesson of the morning in the Lower Fifth was Latin, taken by only the cleverest girls in the form. Miss Goldie carefully weeded out the scholars from the dullards at the end of the Upper Fourth, and those she retained would take Latin for School Certificate. The alternative to Latin was Scripture, which was usually taken by Mother Veronica. But on this particular day – a day that was to rank with the seance and the fall of the curtain in the darkest annals of the convent – Mother Veronica was in bed with a severe attack of summer flu. Mother St John, who also taught Scripture, had a class with the third form. Accordingly the Scripture pupils in the Lower Fifth were given a free period, and were supposed to be in the study doing their prep 'on their honour'.

Now Lucy had as little aptitude for Scripture as she had for anything else; and instead of going to the study she slipped out to the greenhouse to inspect the progress of the summer hibiscus and lilies, which she was nurturing for the Feast of Corpus Christi, two weeks away.

Since the episode of the play, Lucy had become more withdrawn than ever. She had no best or even close friend among the girls, and divided her free time equally between the chapel and the greenhouse. Lucy had thoughts of becoming a nun; a solution that had suddenly presented itself to her

133

predicament of how to get on with people. Lucy thought of all the funny nuns in the convent whom one never saw, who were tucked away in the secret confines beyond the nuns' passage or who seldom spoke to anyone, and thought all she would have to do would be to look after the greenhouse and never say a word to a soul.

However, she kept this plan to herself, and made her piety very unostentatious and personal. No one knew how bound up she was with her soul, that she said more rosaries than ever, and kept all her money to buy medals, holy pictures and devotional books from the school repository.

This was run by a half-blind nun called Mother Emanuel who never noticed anything, not even the fact that some of the girls didn't pay enough for their goods, or that she gave short change to others, who didn't like to mention it. The repository, or Holy Shop, as the girls called it, was in a little room off the hall, which was also used to entertain people who were not distinguished enough for the parlours. It was open once a week and on the nights before the major feasts.

The girls used to love to root among all the trivia of piety, which, if worn or used properly, would give them indulgences to ease their path to heaven. The odd thing about Mother Emanuel's activities was that they showed a profit. She had once been a teaching nun in another convent, and had come to this school in her retirement to do helpful little things. She was completely blind in one eye and wore a piece of gauze over the lens of her gold-rimmed glasses. She was bent with age and shuffled along the corridors, peering at the floor, one hand keeping in touch with the wall.

Apart from regularly giving short change, Mother Emanuel used to collect used Christmas cards, and holy pictures left lying carelessly around in the chapel. Then she would apply ink eraser to them, carefully and skilfully with her one good eye. She had become quite expert at this, and she would sell the newly restored pictures for a nice profit in her shop. Girls sometimes found pictures missing from their missals in the drawers of her shop, and would attempt to reclaim them.

Mother Emanuel was shocked at their inference, and swore that the pictures had only been bought from the supplier the day before. The girls would buy these second-hand pictures, carefully write over them and give them to their friends on feast days and birthdays.

It was a custom in the convent that on a girl's birthday her friends would put cards and presents in her place at breakfast time, as they came from Mass. The girls would drop them casually at the place, while the recipient stood there blushing hopefully. By this method it was easy to gauge who was popular and who was not. Everyone else just stood and watched, and they would snigger to themselves if the pile was a small one, or be eaten up with jealousy if it was large. Present giving was a useful means of either bestowing or currying favour, and the most popular girls always got the most.

So, here was Lucy, in her greenhouse when she should have been in the study doing the parables in St Matthew's gospel. She heard the door open, and, thinking it was Sister Benedict, did not turn until she was aware of a strange presence, hovering. To her surprise, she saw it was a boy of about her own age, with shiny slicked back hair and a new grey utility suit with long trousers.

Lucy was unnerved at the sight of the boy and dropped her watering can.

'What are you doing here?' she said.

'What are you doing here?' the boy replied cheekily, with the strong accent from the town.

'I am watering my flowers,' Lucy said with dignity. 'I am growing them for the Feast of Corpus Christi. You have no right to be here at all.'

'I'm waiting for my interview,' the boy said. 'We were told we could go for a walk by the lake because the girls were in school.'

'Then you should be walking by the lake.' Lucy picked up her watering can, took it to the tap and began to fill it. The boy stood by the plants and watched her as she started to water them again.

'That one's dying,' he said, pointing with a well-scrubbed finger. The parents of the boys, hopeful that their sons would aspire to God's altar, always gave them a good clean before they came to see the Bishop.

'It is not,' Lucy said. 'It is rather sickly, but it is not going to die.'

The boy chuckled.

'What's your name?'

'My name is Lucy,' she said primly. 'Lucy Potts.'

'Mine is George. I live quite near here. I sometimes come and serve Father Vincent on feast days. I come on the Feast of Corpus Christi.'

Lucy thought he must be all right with this pedigree, so she unbent a little.

'How interesting. Are you going to be a priest?'

The boy was silent.

'Well?'

'That's my parents' idea, not mine. My ma is very pi. I have got eight brothers and sisters and she wants one of us to be a priest. I'm the eldest.'

'Oh, but I don't think that is a right attitude.' Lucy's tone was disapproving. 'You should have a vocation.'

'Well, that's what this is for, to see, isn't it? I might have a vocation.'

'How old are you?'

'Fourteen.'

'I'm fifteen.' She felt more confident now that she knew she was older than the boy. Then the door opened again, and a young voice called:

'George! What yer doing there?'

George beckoned without turning.

'Come in, Mike, I'm having a chat with this girl.'

Behind Mike were four other boys, who trooped into the greenhouse, casting curious glances around.

'These are me friends,' George explained.

They were of various sizes, but all with neat hair, well-brushed suits and those very clean faces. Lucy was rather confused by the number of them.

'You should not be here,' she said. 'It is forbidden. You should be walking round the lake.'

'We should be walking round the lake,' one of them mimicked in Lucy's soft, precise, girlish tones.

'Well, you should.'

'Aren't you a good little girl?' the one who was called Mike said mockingly. 'Do you always do what you should?'

'I try,' Lucy said, attempting to still a little panicky feeling inside her. She didn't like the way the boys were gathering around. 'And if you are going to be priests you should do what you are told.'

She turned from them and went along the line of her plants with the watering can.

'Come on, let's go,' said one.

'I like it here,' said another. ''Sides, I think it is going to rain.'

'Isn't she a good girl?' Mike said mockingly. 'Look at her, doing what she is told.'

Mike was the tallest of the group. He had rather a dark unpleasant face, and his hair, shiny with Brylcreem, stuck up in places.

'Oh, please go,' Lucy said, turning towards them. 'It will be very unpleasant if you are found here.'

'It will be very unpleasant if we are found here,' came the mimic again.

'We should be walking round the lake,' said another, attempting the same imitation.

'Come one, let's go,' said a third, more nervously.

'Aren't you a good little girl?' Mike said again, looking at Lucy with a sinister expression. 'What's your name?'

'Lucy,' George said.

'Lucy, Lucy, sweet and juicy,' Mike trilled. 'Give us a kiss, Lucy.'

'How dare you!' Lucy began to back away. 'That is an awful thing to say.'

'Don't you like it, Lucy? Haven't you ever been kissed, Lucy? Isn't Lucy a pretty name, chaps?'

The others were just looking at Lucy, with no very real

interest. But they had gathered round her in a way that suggested menace. She backed to the shelf and leaned against it. Her fear started a reaction among them; a desire to tease and make suffer someone who was without defences. They were just quite nice, ordinary boys; but this frightened girl awakened their primitive male instincts, and they wanted to hurt her. She was afraid and she wasn't pretty. Had she been, they would have wanted to show off instead.

They closed in on her, and Mike reached out and pulled the string of her apron, which fell to the floor. Lucy's expression was horrified.

'Stop that! You must go. I'll . . .'

'What will you do, Lucy?' another said. 'You can't get out, can you? You're our prisoner.'

They all laughed at this. It was going to be very good sport. It even made the more nervous among them feel braver.

'Please go,' she appealed.

'Please go,' the mimic echoed.

The boys laughed again, and moved nearer. Lucy clutched the edge of the shelf with her hands.

'You shouldn't be afraid of us,' George said, again with an air of menace. 'What are you afraid of?'

'I'm not afraid at all,' Lucy said, making a pathetic attempt at boldness, 'I just think you should go.'

'She is afraid, she is afraid.' Another reached out and pinched her arm.

'Oh!' Lucy clutched herself. 'Don't! I hate being touched.'

'She hates being touched!' Mike flipped her hair with his hand.

Now they were all trying to touch Lucy. Another pulled her hair, one pinched her leg, and Mike tried to cover her face with his hand. One lifted the edge of her dress and tried to peer underneath.

'What colour are your drawers, Lucy? Show us your drawers.'

Lucy was terrified, but her fear was modified by her rage. She kept on kicking out at them, or trying to hit them back.

Mike attempted to lift her dress right up. Another stopped him.

'Now don't go too far. Or she'll tell on us. Will you tell, Lucy?'

'I will. I'll tell what you've done already.'

'Would you mention to Reverend Mother, to the Bishop about your drawers? Would you say that?'

'Yes I would. And I tell you another thing; when they hear about this none of you are going to be priests. I am going to be a nun, and it is sacrilege to touch me.'

George was a little frightened by this news, and stepped back, one or two of the others with him.

'Let's go. This is daft. She isn't worth it.'

But Mike took George's place in front and leered at Lucy.

'So you're going to be a nun? Fancy that.' Then suddenly he grabbed the hem of her dress and tugged it right up over her head.

'Blue drawers,' he said. 'Aren't they flimsy? I don't think.'

The boys sniggered, but without enthusiasm. They thought Mike had gone too far. One of them attempted vainly to pull the dress down again.

Lucy stood there displaying blue knickers, a woolly vest and lisle stockings secured at the top of her legs by garters. Apart from this display of underclothes there was nothing at all to see, but the situation was shocking. She clung on to the dress over her head, because she did not want to look at her persecutors. She felt like a Virgin Martyr waiting for the end. Yet to her surprise her feelings were not so much outraged as detached. She simply could not believe that this was happening to her.

George, as if suddenly aware of the possibly serious consequences of their behaviour, tried to pull the dress down; but Lucy held on to it.

'Only fun, Lucy,' George said placatingly. 'Look, we'll go now. Take the dress down. We haven't even looked.'

Lucy said nothing.

'No tits!' Mike said. 'She's not well developed, is she?'

'Shut up, Mike.' George went on tugging at the dress; but Lucy just as firmly held on to it.

And this was how Sister Benedict found them. She grabbed the garden rake as soon as the astonishing scene confronted her eyes, and laid about her as she advanced on the boys, who scattered like the money lenders in the Temple.

'Get away, get away.' She cried. 'Lucy!' Lucy had lowered the dress a fraction on hearing that familiar, well-loved voice, and now peeked over the hem. Sister Benedict caught it and sharply pulled it down. Then she swept Lucy into her arms, making soothing noises as she cuddled her. Lucy said nothing. She just gazed through Sister Benedict, through the boys, beyond the garden. It was very unnerving for her audience.

'Lucy, are you all right?' Sister Benedict said. 'Say something, Lucy.'

One of the boys tried to sneak to the door. Sister Benedict left Lucy propped against the shelf and ran after him, seizing him by the back of his carefully laundered shirt collar and grabbing the arms of two others on the way. When she got the three of them she banged their heads together. Sister Benedict was a very forceful nun, as well as strong. She also knew now that the situation was too serious to waste time on an enquiry. She took Lucy by the arm and made a sweeping motion in front of her with her hands.

'Get along before me. Straight to the Bishop. And if anyone tries to run, don't think I ever forget a face.'

The shock seemed much worse, now that it was over. Lucy started to shake, as though it was terribly cold, and then she began to weep. But Sister Benedict gently pulled Lucy by the arm and swept the six boys before her. It was quite a sight, emerging from the greenhouse.

The inquest on the incident in the greenhouse took two days. Lucy had once more been taken to the infirmary, and it was decided she was not well enough to see the Bishop on the first day. In her absence all the boys gave a very imaginative, and untrue, account of what had happened, one that made Lucy appear to have blended in her exotic personality qualities both of Mata Hari and the Rose of Tralee.

Then the Bishop had them all in one by one, and he heard six different versions of the truth. Reverend Mother, knowing quite well that Lucy was no siren, supported her charge. She was backed by Sister Benedict, who believed in Lucy. However, she had seen, and her conscience had made her tell the truth, that Lucy *was* holding on to her skirt over her head. She was clinging to it for protection, not lifting it for the boys to see underneath.

In a court of law the dispute would have revolved around intention; and so it did now. Was Lucy deliberately exposing herself or, as the nuns believed and as she had told them in the infirmary, was she too ashamed to look?

The good Bishop was most reluctant to believe that six of the selected candidates for the priesthood could have behaved in such a way without being gravely provoked. Surely they were trying to pull the skirt down, and the siren had pulled it up? But at the end of the afternoon and the six conflicting versions, quite apart from Lucy's own, he clearly did not know what to believe; and concluded that it was the work of the Devil.

This was an inadequate explanation for Reverend Mother, who asked the Bishop to return the following day with the parents of the boys concerned. Lucy was seen by a doctor and sedated. At first he attempted to examine her to see if she had been interfered with in any way, but she screamed so much that Sister Matilda refused to allow it. This could be taken either way: that she had, or that she had not. Lucy had found her own memory of the details receding as the effects of delayed shock took hold.

The stories that had swept the convent were by this time so magnified that Lucy was believed to have been assaulted six times by six boys under the age of sixteen. All that was really known was that something nasty had happened to Lucy in the greenhouse and she was now in the infirmary. The stories were all made up, and gathered colour as they were repeated by the girls with mingled horror and envy.

It should be said that the Bishop, scarcely recovered from his terrible ordeal with the curtain in January, was not best pleased at discovering that the centrepiece of the latest fracas was the same as the previous one. His immediate reaction until he saw her spotty face, her lank hair and her poor short-sighted eyes peering timidly at him through her thick lenses, had been to regard her as a harlot, bent on ensnaring his boys. He amended this, upon inspection in the infirmary, to dismissing her as an over-sexed simpleton who did not know what she was doing when she pulled her skirt over her head to reveal herself to the astonished and petrified gaze of his pure-minded and nobly motivated aspirants to the sacred ministry.

After the preliminary enquiries on the first day Reverend Mother and the Bishop discussed the matter over sherry in her room. Reverend Mother only drank sherry with the Bishop and the Canon, and it was a great honour to partake with her. As she liked sherry, and this was the only time she indulged, she invariably drank more than was good for her and sometimes had to lie down afterwards.

Not this time, however. No indeed. This time she wanted to keep her wits sharp about her for the encounter with her spiritual overlord; so she merely sipped, gazing at him reproachfully over the rim of her glass.

'You must know, my lord, that this plain girl is incapable of lifting her dress over her head. She is very pious. A restrained and retiring girl, caring only for plants and flowers.'

The Bishop also looked over the rim of his glass as a counter offensive, his gaze reinforced by a pair of gold half-lensed spectacles well down on his nose.

'Ah. Ah, Reverend Mother. Who knows what a young girl will do in the presence of personable males? It is the reaction of the species female to the species male.'

'To lift up their skirts at first sight! My lord!' Reverend Mother fortified herself with a hefty swig of sherry at the very idea.

The Bishop smiled in a worldly wise manner.

'Is that not, after all, why we keep young people apart? We know how they react.'

'I know how *my* girls react. They do not react to young boys, who have not even reached manhood, by lifting up their skirts.'

'Indeed, Reverend Mother?' said the Bishop, taking a delicate sip. 'Indeed?'

'Look, my lord,' Reverend Mother edged forward in her chair in her agitation then, seeing that her knee was in dangerous proximity to the black clad knees of the Bishop, hastily slid back again. 'I know and you know that Lucy did *not* draw her own skirt over her head. It was done by your boys. She was in a state of profound shock when Sister Benedict found her.'

'Perhaps because of what she had done. She had been the victim of an uncontrollable urge.'

'My lord!'

'It is possible.'

'It is not remotely possible, with respect to your lordship. Your boys came in seeking a diversion when they should have been walking round the lake. They teased the young girl, quite innocently at first. She responded by showing fright. They went too far. It is this nasty herd instinct that young people can have when they are confronted by a single victim. It is like a pack of wolves with a poor defenceless sheep.'

'Ah.' The Bishop felt he was losing ground. A point had been scored. He curled his hand round the stem of his glass. This was exactly his own suspicion, but he declined to voice it; even to believe it. After all, they were short of candidates for the priesthood in his diocese. He tried a new tactic. 'But this very child has already caused trouble. She brought the curtain down on my head.'

Reverend Mother sipped sherry incautiously; her mind racing ahead of the Bishop's. The honour of the convent was very definitely at stake.

'It is not at all the same thing. Causing a curtain to fall on a bishop, though lamentable, my lord, is not at all the same thing as voluntarily drawing up one's skirts over one's head, with the object of exposing oneself.'

The Bishop winced at the word 'exposing'. It was so very descriptive.

'But it does show she was unbalanced.'

'She is not unbalanced. She thought she saw a fire.'

'There was no fire.'

'It was merely . . . My lord,' Reverend Mother leaned forward again, appealing to his sense of fairness, his experience as a spiritual father, 'there is no question. Lucy did not do it; it was done to her. She is a sensitive little girl, very shy and given to daydreaming. When the boys came in she was watering her plants for the Feast of Corpus Christi. She is completely ignorant of matters concerning, er, the world, and such an action, even had she become, for some reason, deranged on the spot, would never have occurred to her. She simply would not have done it.'

The Bishop put down the sherry glass as a sign of disfavour.

'But she was holding up her skirt.'

'Because *after* it had been pulled over her head she was ashamed. One can understand it.'

'I would have thought that she would have drawn it down immediately.'

'Shock, my lord, shock. She could not bear to face her tormentors.'

The Bishop sat back, his plump white hand with the purple ring tapping the table.

'Well, Reverend Mother, it is very disturbing. If what you say is true, I lose six candidates for the priesthood.'

'But, my lord, we keep the honour of the convent. That is important too.'

'It is honour versus honour, Reverend Mother. Well, tomorrow we shall confront the young girl with the boys.'

'And Sister Benedict.' Reverend Mother got up. No doubt but that she had won. There was a defeated sag about the Bishop's shoulders. 'Besides, my lord, would you want unworthy priests?'

144

'But they are boys, Reverend Mother.'

'Ah, but soon to be men. What then, my lord, if this is how they behave at fourteen? What *then* I ask you?'

'Well . . .'

The shoulders sagged a little more, and Reverend Mother advanced on him with the sweetest smile imaginable; not in the swaggering manner of the victor, but as one who wins through virtue, and forgives in the gentle spirit of Christian charity. She took up his empty glass.

'Might I give your lordship sherry?'

Needless to say, what was undoubtedly obvious the next day when the little concourse met in the main parlour was that Lucy was innocent and the boys guilty. The versions were still divergent, but about Lucy there was the stern ring of truth. She gazed resentfully at her persecutors, and had not the manner of one who had deliberately raised her skirts over her head the day before. Also, the boys argued with one another, each trying to apportion blame, to claim innocence. When Lucy positively identified Mike as the chief malefactor he hung his head and convicted himself. The upshot was that the parents of the boys were asked to withdraw their sons' names as candidates for the priest-hood. The Bishop returned home in a fury and to have treatment for his seriously disturbed digestion, the result of overeating at a large convent lunch aggravated by sub-sequent tension.

Lucy was vindicated. She recovered rapidly from her ordeal and when, a day later, she emerged from the infir-mary she was the subject of speculation, at times admiration, among the boarders.

'Were you scared?'

'What did it feel like?'

'Did it hurt?'

'Were you completely naked?'

'Did they take *their* clothes off?'

'Did you stand up, or lie down?'

Lucy said nothing, she just shook her head and looked

145

about her in the proud and noble manner of one who had suffered, a mysterious smile on her face. Let them think what they liked. But no one really knew the truth, and this air of mystery, this reluctance on her part to talk or explain, helped to establish Lucy as a personality, a cross between the Scarlet Woman and the Blessed Maria Goretti, who had chosen death rather than rape. It was perhaps no coincidence that her patron, Saint Lucy, had died for a similar cause. As it states in the preamble to the Feast of St Lucy on December 13th in the Roman Missal: 'St Lucy gave herself to Jesus, and chose death rather than lose the incorruptible treasure of her virginity. AD 303.'

Despite its overtones of impropriety, Lucy was not slow to take advantage of the fame and notoriety she achieved as a result of the incident in the greenhouse. In time she became less reluctant to talk about it, even to put a little flesh on the bare bones of the story. The emergence of Lucy was a very gradual thing. What affected her was her importance in the eyes of others. She began to minimize, to herself, the negative and dubious aspect of her achievements, and to take advantage of them.

The first to take an interest in her were Andrea and Clare. Of late they had taken to discussing what would happen when they grew up, and the relationship between men and women. They yearned to know more; not only about the physical side, but about emotions too. How did one *feel*?

'I want you to tell us *exactly* what happened,' Clare demanded of Lucy when one day, not long after the episode, they had managed to lure her to their bench by the cloak-room, which was on the way to the greenhouse. Lucy, placed firmly between the two girls, pushed her steamy glasses up her greasy nose and stuttered nervously.

'Well . . .' she began.

'Yes?'

'Well, it was terrible really.'

She gave a furtive little smile as she said this, as though to indicate that it hadn't been half so bad at all. Andrea and

Clare had been very careful to detach themselves from the throngs that had surrounded Lucy upon her exit from the infirmary; they did not want to form part of the mob. But they had discussed it between themselves, and thought Lucy might add to their tentative explorations of the intriguing subject of adult life.

'Now come on, Lucy. We want the truth,' Clare said sternly. 'Were you stripped naked, or weren't you?'

Lucy went scarlet at the very idea – she'd had no notion that the story had got so wild. She hung her head. The two took it as an admission of the truth. They were equally excited and repelled by the idea.

'And then what happened?'

'They pulled my dress over my head.'

'Really? You were on the floor stark naked, yet with your dress over your head? Did they take it right off, or just pull it up?'

'Pulled it up.'

'How did they take your vest off?'

Lucy was not a good liar and should have stopped at this point. But the glory at being with Clare again was too much. She longed to impress her.

'Oh, they got it off all right.'

'But how? I mean, how, if your dress was still on?'

'They put that back on again.'

There followed the profound silence of disbelief.

'I don't think anything came off,' Andrea said after a while. 'I don't think anything happened at all.'

'Oh it did, everything came off,' Lucy insisted.

'But the dress was still on?'

'And shoes and stockings?'

'And knickers?'

'I was stark naked.'

Pause. Sceptical as they were, they did not think that Lucy – pure, virtuous Lucy – would make such a gross story up.

'And what did they do?'

'They just looked at me.'

'Just looked? Whatever did they want to look at you for?'

Lucy could not think why the boys should want to look at her naked flesh. She appeared as puzzled as her two inquisitors.

'I don't know.'

'Did they take their clothes off?'

'Oh no.'

'Did they undo their trousers?'

Lucy looked incredulous.

'Whatever should they want to do that for?'

'Because,' Andrea said wisely, 'that is how you have sex.'

Lucy had never been part of the Lower Fifth discussions on this awesome topic. At the notion that she had narrowly escaped having sex, she shook with relief. Then she remembered that she hadn't taken her clothes off at all; although the idea that she had had almost taken root in her mind. She had a vision of herself stark naked, holding her watering can and all the youths staring at her, wanting sex. But that was not what had happened, though she thought, by now, it would be wiser if nobody other than Reverend Mother and the Bishop knew it. They were unlikely to tell the truth about the episode to anyone other than one or two of the nuns, who would never mention it to the girls because of its indelicate nature.

If the truth were known she would look rather silly. Everyone would laugh at the thought of her standing there showing off her woollen vest and darned stockings, clutching her dress over her head. It was much grander and more important, obviously, to have had one's clothes actually *off*.

'No one undid their trousers,' she said. 'Sister Benedict came in.'

'It must have been a shock for her.'

'It was. She covered me up, and sent the boys away.'

'Did they feel you while you had your clothes off?'

'*Feel me?*' Lucy weighed this up in the moment she had. From the look on Clare's face, this was quite crucial.

'Oh yes, they felt me.'

'Where?'

'On my arm.'

'Your *arm*?'

'And my legs.'

She remembered the pinchings; that was being felt. She didn't see how she was telling much of a lie.

'Anywhere else?'

Andrea and Clare were firing these rapid questions, as if it were a court of law.

'Yes, all over.'

'Between your legs?'

'Yes, there too.'

By now Lucy was quite convinced of the importance of putting up a really good show. Clare was obviously very impressed. And seeing that it had not happened the notion did not disturb her at all, because she, quite literally, couldn't imagine such a thing.

'Goodness.' Clare was seeing Lucy with new eyes as one to whom interesting things happened.

'You were jolly brave, I think,' Andrea said. 'I would have gone mad. I would never have recovered. I mean, it's not as though those boys were anything to look at. Little monsters.'

'Oh, I don't know,' Lucy said with a suggestive wriggle. 'One or two of them were all right.'

'I prefer older men myself,' Andrea said. 'About eighteen or nineteen.'

'Yes, but the idea of being stripped in the greenhouse . . . Are you *sure* it happened, Lucy?'

'Sure.'

'She was in the infirmary for two days,' Andrea said reasonably.

'Three,' Lucy said, 'if you count the day it happened.'

'Poor Lucy,' Andrea said kindly. 'You must just forget about it all. Pretend it never happened.'

Lucy rolled her eyes. 'Oh, I could never do that. I shall remember it all my life.'

Clare giggled. 'I think she enjoyed it.'

'Clare, how could you? It was a terrible shock for poor Lucy, wasn't it?'

149

The irony in Andrea's voice escaped Lucy, who put a hand to her brow.

'A terrible, terrible shock.' She got up. 'I think I should go and water my plants now.'

'Be careful,' Clare warned. 'Lock the doors behind you.'

Lucy trotted off quite perkily, and the two gazed after her.

'I think she made it up. I don't believe her at all,' Clare said. 'I think if it had really happened it would have affected her far more. Timid little Lucy? She would never have got over it.'

'I think you're right,' Andrea said. 'But why should she make it up?'

Clare shrugged. 'To get attention.'

'She got that all right. I think something did happen, because the boys were punished. Even Mother St John hasn't mentioned it, and you know what a gossip she is. It was something serious, that's for sure.'

'But not like she said.'

'Not quite. I don't think her clothes ever did come off; that bit she made up, because when she was telling it it seemed to mean nothing to her at all. I ask you, if you're Lucy, does a thing like that mean so little?'

'Quite. It would be something, even for us.'

'Even for us.'

The two looked at each other with the understanding of a shared point of view. Then the tea bell rang, and they linked arms and went into the refectory. Linking arms was forbidden, though the two disobeyed this rule in common with many others.

Their friendship had gradually presented a challenge to Mother St John, and Andrea had slid down her scale of favourites until she joined Clare at the bottom. They never did anything actually wrong, but they never did anything right, either. They managed to evade, to circumvent rules and restrictions, rather than openly to flout them. So that although they were never in the places they should be, they always had a very good reason for not being there. They were determined to be as different from anyone else as they could, yet without giving offence. Consequently they were envied by the girls, looked up to and enormously admired.

They sailed through the summer term, as they had the one before, doing exactly as they liked. The girls lied for them, covered up for them and tried to be like them. Only they would get into trouble, and Andrea and Clare never did. They were more than a match for Mother St John. Clare benefited from Andrea's example, and Andrea learned much from Clare. They were a formidable pair.

At the prize-giving at the end of the summer Clare got the form prize for scholarship, as she had for the two previous years, and Andrea got a prize for general excellence. All the staff and most of the nuns clapped enthusiastically as they went up to receive their awards from the Bishop, who sat safely on his throne at the end of the hall. He had made sure there were no curtains above him on the stage as he sat down. He was also relieved to see that Lucy was not among those receiving prizes.

But Lucy was content. She had had the best term ever because of the fame of her ordeal. She had improved in temperament, in stature, even in looks – because a girl who has been stripped stark naked in front of six maniacal boys had a reputation to maintain; she must not let herself down. Besides, she had done the flower display for prize day – a display carefully circumvented by the Bishop as he stepped on to the rostrum – and everyone agreed it was a wonderful show. She was also not bottom of the form this year; there was one person below her.

There was a concert at the end of prize-giving in which the choir sang prettily, and Miss Larkin gave her solo rendering of 'Cherry Ripe', as she did every year, though sometimes she varied it with 'Where E'er Ye Walk'. This was acclaimed as enthusiastically as ever. Clare recited 'The Fighting Temeraire', with the help of a chorus, who did the 'It was eight bells ringing' part. To the pleasure of the Bishop there was a tableau in honour of Our Lady of Fatima, which was staged by Miss Clark and costumed by Miss Greene,

151

who wisely attempted nothing daring in the way of lighting effects.

Miss Goldie had written a very moving one-act drama in Latin about the siege of Troy, played by the sixth form, and Virginia Clearwater tore her hair very realistically as Cassandra, shrieking 'vae, vae victis' at the top of her lungs. The Upper Fourth did a dramatization of a story by Maupassant organized by Mrs Battley; though its effect was spoiled by loud snores from the Bishop in the front row.

Then there were the needlework and art exhibitions, and rounders and tennis in the grounds. There was a very gay end of term feeling, and the air was warm and smelled delicious with the fragrance of the trees and the flowers.

And so the summer term came to an end, and so did Andrea's first year in the convent. She felt as much a part of the school as anyone else, even though she was a Protestant. It was more of a home to her than her own home had been, a refuge as well as an inspiration. In retrospect she was to regard it as one of the nicest years of her life, though the ones that followed were just as good. It was only when she left and went into the world that Andrea was to find again the insecurity and uncertainty she had known as a child, and to weave once again that web of detachment and remoteness about her – and pretence.

Andrea was to spend part of the holiday with Clare, and part with her aunt. The girls packed their trunks, squashed their white panamas on their heads and went off for the holidays. But this was 1943 and in Europe it was one of the blackest years of the war. Other little girls were being trundled in cattle trucks to concentration camps, torn from their parents and herded into ovens to die. Men would die on battlefields, in the sea, or be shot to pieces in the air. Civilians were being bombarded, and would perish under the rubble of their homes. Columns of refugees trailed wearily all over Europe; animals would disappear from streets as starving populations tried to keep alive by eating them.

But in the north of England nothing like this happened;

and the children of the convent played safely in the holidays, knowing and caring very little about the rest of the world in wartime.

# PART TWO

The Way of Perfection
*1944–1946*

# Seven

'"Sexual" is a word I do not care for,' Miss Clark said with a tight little smile, '"Physical" will do very well, Andrea. I give you A-minus nevertheless.' She handed the exercise book over, and nodded her head, looking rather prim.

The girls were doing *Antony and Cleopatra* as one of the set books for their School Certificate, an examination only a term away, for this was spring in the following year. Andrea had found in the play a perfect expression for the developing intensity of her nature, a growing awareness of passion. She had brought tears to Miss Clark's eyes as the dying Cleopatra in the form reading of the play. She had put her all into the essay on 'The relationship of Antony and Cleopatra in the context of the Elizabethan ideal of love', although she had dismissed the Elizabethan ideal as flowery, and had insisted that the two characters were bound by a passion of a 'savagely sexual nature'. Miss Clark had underlined this in red with an exclamation mark, had scored out the word 'sexual' and substituted 'physical'.

'Their love is of an almost metaphysical nature,' Miss Clark went on, 'and Shakespeare was undoubtedly affected by the romantic ideas of his time. The notion of love in the sonnets has a transcendental quality. You certainly can't say this relationship was purely physical.'

'Sexual,' Andrea said firmly. 'I meant sexual. Don't you think physical would just have a bodily meaning, Miss Clark? "Sexual" expresses the unique relationship between men and women.'

The form were enjoying the argument taking place at Miss Clark's desk, to which the girls had gone up one by one to receive their essays back. Miss Clark gave a small tinkling laugh, as though to minimize the implications of Andrea's remarks.

'"Sexual",' she said, colouring slightly, 'is a process. It can refer to animals as well as humans. It is not confined to the unique relationship, as you call it, between men and women. What make this relationship unique are the spiritual overtones, an emotional involvement which animals do not have. In fact,' she took the essay book from Andrea's hand, 'now that we have discussed it – and, after all, this is the purpose of literary exercise – I don't think that phrase is well chosen at all. I would say,' she lifted her pen and held it poised thoughtfully in the air for a moment, 'I would say "they were bound by a passion whose overtones were of the purest poetry and lifted them up above their merely physical natures!"'

She wrote the sentence in the margin, while Andrea glared at her. Andrea had changed in the past year, and wore her hair fastened at the back by a ribbon. Her expression had not altered much, except that perhaps it was more assured, but her whole manner had changed from that of one who is merely receptive to one who imposes her will on people and events. She scowled at Miss Clark as she retrieved her exercise book without another word. If the same subject came up in the exam she would definitely use her original phrase, which included the word sexual.

'It's because she is repressed,' she informed Lucy and Clare afterwards. 'She is so old now and knows she will never marry, so she doesn't want to think about sex at all. What rubbish she talks about the "Elizabethan ideal". All those hey-nonny-nonnies, I ask you. That is the trouble with being taught by women who are unmarried. They are unfulfilled.'

'Mrs Battley is married,' Clare said. 'It doesn't seem to make any difference to her. She is always very funny about the French Romantic poets.'

'Well, Mrs Battley. Hardly typical.'

'I don't think you're being fair at all,' Lucy said. 'Just

because teachers are not married it doesn't mean they aren't women. They feel like everyone else, perhaps more intensely.'

Lucy wanted to be reasonable about the whole thing. Despite her experience the previous summer – now embellished out of all proportion in her memory, and not at all the way it had happened – she was not sure anyone would want to marry her. She thought she should be prepared for this contingency by being as charitable about it to others as she hoped they would be to her.

Of the three, Lucy had altered the most in the past year. The greenhouse episode had marked an emotional change in her life, and she never looked back from it. She was still devout, but no longer wanted to be a nun. She had never withdrawn again into herself and, although there was still shyness, there was a lack of that extreme uncertainty and timidity which had so stunted her early development. People had taken an interest in her, even if only on account of her notoriety, and this enabled her to give some value to her own personality. As she liked herself more, communication with others became easier; her reserve slowly disintegrated under the impact of concern and friendliness. Even her looks improved. She took more care with her hair, stopped slouching and went with her mother to the optician to select a more suitable and flattering frame for her spectacles.

And in all this Andrea had played a large part. At the beginning of the school year, she and Lucy had been transferred to the senior girls' dormitory, in the care of Mother Veronica. With the object of separating her from her fellow conspirator, Mother St John had kept Clare to succeed Mavis Myers, who had left the school, as head of the Immaculate Conception dormitory.

Lucy and Andrea were next to each other, and slowly they began to chat between their curtains, because of the relaxed discipline in this dormitory. Andrea still felt protective towards Lucy, but she was genuinely drawn to her because of a fey quality she detected in her – her devotion to her flowers and her practically unlimited capacity for doing the wrong thing. Andrea actually found her amusing, enjoyed her hurried breathless style of conversation, and saw that Lucy was not half so simple as everyone else thought. They began to exchange little confidences at night between the curtains, and Lucy became even more of a receptacle for Andrea's thoughts on life than Clare because Clare was a bad listener and she and Andrea frequently spoke at once when they were trying to tell each other something.

Clare was jealous at first of the intrusion of Lucy into her relationship with Andrea, and there had been a period of coolness between the two. However, Andrea had spent the Christmas holidays with the Bingleys, and in the spring term Clare decided to accept Lucy as part of her continuing friendship with Andrea.

Lucy was no match for the stars of the form, but she acted, as she once had with Clare, as a foil to their brilliance, a backdrop against which the others performed, as virtuosos or together. Mother St John approved of the influence of Lucy on Andrea and Clare, and theirs on her. She no longer seemed to attract those gigantic disasters, and if the other two continued to do as they liked they did so with less ostentation. They were all, she thought, much better behaved.

Mother St John failed to appreciate the fact that the Upper Fifth year demanded more from them in the way of application to studies, and they would probably have been much quieter anyway.

Miss Clark had played safe that year and had staged a nativity play. No part had been found for Andrea, because of the religious aspect, and Clare had a minor role as a prophet. It was a dismal little play, but the Bishop approved of it despite his nervousness, and the wary eye he kept on the curtain. Needless to say Lucy was not allowed on the stage at all, and her altar had been moved right out of the gym and into the corridor.

In the spring term old Mother Emanuel died, and her funeral took place in the chapel. The choir was rehearsed by Mother Mary Paul, and the Requiem Mass was dignified and sad. The night before, Mother Emanuel's body had been borne solemnly from the infirmary where she died to the chapel, where the coffin was placed in front of the sanctuary steps. The coffin was covered by a simple black cloth, and thick orange candles in tall brass holders stood on either side. The candlelight flickered gently throughout the night, to symbolize eternal life, and nuns took it in turn to keep vigil and pray for the repose of her soul. The Canon said the Mass assisted by Father Vincent, and the altar drapes and vestments were black.

Andrea never forgot the little procession of black-robed nuns and the priests following the plain wooden coffin, or the mournful chant of the choir and the sweet cloying scent of the incense. It seemed to typify for her everything that was good and uplifting about the religious life, because it was so lonely and majestic. This passing of a simple nun who had once been a young girl, but who in her old age used to grope her way feebly along the corridors, her one good eye looking at her feet to be sure she did not miss a step, moved Andrea deeply. Her life had been one of sacrifice, of obligation with one object: the service of God and the attainment of a higher place in heaven. She was so old that her family must have died over the years without her ever seeing them again. Her life had that one single purpose in front of it: the journey on which she had now embarked. 'Go in peace, Christian soul, out of this world,' the priest had said.

'Rest in peace, Mother Emanuel,' Andrea whispered, tears in her eyes, as the coffin passed her, and it was the first time she had ever consciously said a prayer for someone else, or prayed at all, and it seemed to mark a change in her own awareness of the religious life, which impelled her more and more towards it.

The first three days of Holy Week were always given over to a retreat at the school for the older girls. Those below the third form went home on the Friday before, and the rest composed themselves for this rather unwelcome exercise in the virtues of contemplation, meditation and, above all, silence.

From bedtime on the Saturday night to the same hour on the Tuesday silence was the absolute rule. It was never broken at all except for confession, discussion with the priest and the necessities of daily life. These necessities tended to multiply during the days of the retreat, just so that any opportunity could be seized to say something about anything.

Andrea, who was going to Clare's for the Easter holiday, decided to wait for her and observe the retreat in the privileged position of one who could participate or not, just as she pleased. Andrea thought it would be an opportunity to extend her knowledge of religion by engaging Father Vincent in some elevated conversation about God, the soul and hereafter.

Andrea continued to absorb religious atmosphere without stirring herself to do anything about it other than reading books. She liked novels with strong religious themes, and was attracted to the works of Owen Francis Dudley, which featured the Masterful Monk, and Robert Hugh Benson, who wrote vigorous tales about the persecution of Catholics under Elizabeth under such titles as *Come Rack, Come Rope*. Andrea had a very romantic notion of religion, and its appeal to her was strongly sensory and emotional.

The girls' retreat was usually conducted by a member of a religious order, many of which specialized in this kind of religious activity. But the war had also caused a shortage of priests and this year Father Vincent was to give the retreat on the subject of 'Worship: The Life of the Church'. It was a deliberately vague title so that he could include almost everything and get in those warnings about immodesty, impurity and materialism, which Reverend Mother always liked to be included in the retreat schedule.

In the morning the girls got up for Mass as usual, had breakfast, made their beds and then went to the first conference in the chapel at ten o'clock. After this there were walks round the garden, in silence, or reading of spiritual books in the study. In the afternoon the routine was repeated with another conference at three, more walks and more time for reading. Supper was early, for there was a final conference at seven after which, ostensibly imbued with holiness from the day's piety, the girls went to bed.

During the walk in the afternoon of the first day Andrea managed to overtake Father Vincent, who was saying his breviary along the Rosary Way.

'Do you think I could talk to you, Father?'

The priest stopped, clearly torn between duties.

Father Vincent was in his early forties, and had been chaplain to the convent for ten years. He was a careful and diligent man who did his job well, and was seldom troubled by deep feelings or crises of conscience. He had entered the seminary at the age of thirteen, and all his life had been spent in love and obedience to the Church of Christ. His only ambition was that one day he might have his own parish; but his attitude was one of perfect docility if this wish was not granted to him.

'I'm Andrea Mackintosh, the Protestant,' Andrea said with an air of importance. 'I am very interested, you know, in things.'

Father Vincent smiled and shut his breviary.

'Of course I know you, Andrea. And what "things" are you interested in?'

'I'm terribly interested in religion. I mean, I have none of my own, so it's natural. I am not actually supposed to do anything about it; but you can't really stop a determined soul, can you, Father? Not if God wants it?'

'Certainly,' Father Vincent said carefully, 'it is difficult to know what God wants. The great Cardinal Newman said that if only he knew the will of God, he would do it.'

Andrea thought that this just possibly might be a snub, the implication of which was that the great Cardinal might not know the will of God but she, Andrea Mackintosh aged sixteen, thought she did. She blushed.

'I didn't mean . . .'

'Oh, don't misunderstand me, my dear child. I just meant to say that the ways of God are mysterious, so that we don't always know how to interpret them. That is what the Church is for. To tell us what God has said.'

'And you really think it does?' Andrea got into step beside him.

'I do. Man by himself is so faltering and alone that he needs the support of the Church. He cannot really know for himself, without the divine guidance that Our Lord gave his Church.'

'But what about individuals like St Augustine or St Thomas Aquinas?'

'Ah, they were great people inspired by God to work through his Church. Other men, also great minds, did not listen to the Church and put themselves above it, like Luther, for example,' Father Vincent concluded censoriously. Andrea felt rather responsible for Luther. It was a name that one never uttered in the convent. She hung her head.

'Yes, I'm sorry about Luther. Do you think he went to hell?'

'One can never say who is in hell. Let us hope that in his last final moments he made peace with God.'

'And then he would just go to heaven?'

'He would have a *long* time in purgatory,' Father Vincent said cautiously. 'A very long time indeed.'

'He is probably still there?' Andrea offered helpfully, wanting to atone for the awful thing Luther had done.

'Probably. Was there something specific you wanted to ask me, or just a general chat? I saw you at both my conferences today.'

'What I really don't understand is Our Lady and the saints. I mean, they seem more important than God. Your first conference was all about God's mother as the protectress of the Church.' It had also been about her as a model of purity that all should imitate, but this was not the aspect that interested Andrea so much.

'Not at all. Our Lady and the saints mediate between man and God. Now take an example. Say you want something from your father. Who best to ask for it but your mother, on your behalf?'

'No,' Andrea said gravely. 'My mother always used to get

me to ask my father things. She was afraid of him and is now dead.'

Father Vincent winced at the abruptness of the reply. The trouble with Protestants was they were always so direct; only weeks of instruction got them to the required elasticity of mind where they were able to agree that they saw or understood something, when in fact they could not see or understand it at all.

'Well, that is different. But in general terms, God so loves His mother that He will listen to her when she intercedes for us. He did his first miracle for her, at Cana in Galilee when He turned the water into wine. For the same reason one prays to the saints and asks them to intercede for us because their lives have so exalted them above ordinary men. You will find that there are patron saints for all occasions – simply that we pay them this honour and they help us in return.'

'Like St Anthony for lost things?'

'Exactly. Or St Jude for hopeless cases. You see, Andrea, the Church is just like a family. We call it the communion of saints, and all its members help one another no matter where they are. We talk of the Church militant – that is, here on earth, we are still battling for Christ; the Church suffering – that is in purgatory where we expunge the effects of sin; and the Church triumphant, with God in heaven.'

'It's very beautiful.' Andrea was impressed. 'I rather like the whole idea.'

'There is this network of prayer.' Father Vincent pressed home his advantage. 'So you see how the saints and Our Lady and everyone fit in?'

'It's all to do with the world really, isn't it? I mean the further away from the world you get, the nearer to God?'

'I'm afraid it is. That is not to say that the world is a bad place, but it has distractions that can disturb the soul. That is why we priests and nuns wear black, so that even our clothes cannot distract us away from God. I must go now, Andrea, and prepare my conference for this evening. Tell me any time I can help you and I will do what I can.'

'Thank you very much.'

'Have you got a missal?'

'I just bought one, Father, to help me with the Mass.'

'If you study it you will understand the full meaning of the liturgy of the Church. It will help you, I'm sure.'

They had now reached the rose gardens, which began at the end of the Rosary Way. Andrea thanked Father Vincent for his help, and he gave a slight bow and went away. Andrea walked slowly down to tea, feeling glad that she was so special. There was certainly a lot to say for not being like everyone else, if it got one this kind of attention.

On the second day of the retreat Reverend Mother appeared in the study before lunch, and coughed in the way she did when she had anything important to say. 'Girls, I have observed you all making a very good retreat. It is an edifying sight, and Father Vincent is very pleased with you. Unfortunately, what I have to say will shatter a little the spirit of this quiet devotion; but it cannot be helped. An American general is visiting the schools in this area to tell us about the war effort. The visit has only been arranged at short notice. We cannot refuse, because we are asked by the Ministry of Education to cooperate. Besides, a general is a very important person. He will be here at three tomorrow afternoon and will talk to you for half an hour in the gym. I shall tell the day girls who are making the retreat after the conference this afternoon. There you will all meet in the gym and practise with Mother Mary Paul the singing of the American national anthem. That is all, girls.'

The immediate reaction on the part of the girls was to chatter. Such an event as the visit of an American general in the middle of a retreat was almost like a bonus from God for being so good. The first day of the retreat was always one on which everyone made a special effort; but by the second and third days strain had begun to take its toll on some of the less devout, who would chat quietly among themselves when no one was looking.

Among those suffering the most strain was a girl called Jocasta Younghusband, who had only come to the school the previous year and had quickly established herself as a trying personality. She had replaced Clare as Mother St John's cross and, although she shone in her lessons, she was never out of trouble. Mother St John positively stalked her in order to find out what piece of mischief she was up to next. Jocasta had come to the school when another of the Order, at which she had been a pupil, had been bombed during a raid on the south coast. She was a rebel and an outsider, and because of these qualities rapidly won the devotion of the fourth form. In her last school she had been found in bed with one of the junior girls, an incident that had caused a great deal of a stir in the boarding part and beyond. But she had been only twelve at the time, and said she was merely in the bed to comfort a weeping eight-year-old who had been told off by one of the nuns. The episode was passed over, and Jocasta was given a caution to keep out of other girls' beds and do her comforting from the side.

Jocasta did not take to the idea of a retreat at all, and had tried to avoid it by pleading a bad pain in the stomach. This was quickly cured by one visit to Sister Matilda, after which Jocasta preferred the retreat as the lesser of two evils. But she rebelled inwardly, resolved not to say one prayer, nodded off in the chapel when Father Vincent was in the middle of one of his uplifting sermons, and started reading the collected works of Sir Walter Scott because, in their buckram bindings, they most resembled books of devotion. She was halfway through *Rob Roy* on the second day when Mother St John stole up on her, and in her rage at such a blasphemy hit her over the head with it. Jocasta merely chalked this up as one of a series of incidents that she would one day have to settle with Mother St John.

Jocasta greeted the news about the American general with great delight and instantly recovered from her sulk at having been deprived of *Rob Roy* an hour before.

The person who had proved most vulnerable to Jocasta's techniques of corruption was Martha Oldwhistle, who, although a form higher, was Jocasta's slave if not her best friend. Martha was someone whom people found it difficult to love, because her marked capacity for obsequious behaviour invested her with a kind of slyness that made her seem untrustworthy. She had been an abject failure as the Ghost of Christmas Past in the school play, and, until resuscitated by Jocasta, her lot had been one of obscurity. Martha adored Jocasta in the way that Lucy had once adored Clare, and in her turn was accordingly despised.

Naturally Jocasta had not interrupted her nightly conversations between the dormitory curtains with Martha just because there was a retreat, and during the day the pair of them disappeared together into the trees at the far side of the lake where they lay on the ground and had a good talk instead of walking round the paths saying their rosaries or thinking edifying thoughts.

After the afternoon conference that day the girls went into the gym, where Mother Mary Paul was already engaged in practising 'The Star Spangled Banner' on her harmonium, which had been set on the stage. The Ministry of Education had rushed several thousand copies of sheet music to the schools in the area and some of these were now distributed among the girls.

Mother Mary Paul was definitely discomfited at having to add the American national anthem to her repertory, which was solely confined to church music, and she was punishing the keys of the harmonium with her long elegant fingers. Reverend Mother also led her nuns into the gym so that they could lend their mature voices in praise of the illustrious ally.

'First of all we shall say the words, and then I will play you the tune,' Mother Mary Paul said, standing in the middle of the platform and raising her hand. 'Now enunciate with me: "Oh say, can you see by the dawn's early light . . ."'

The girls seized the opportunity of this diversion for a good giggle, and generally the devout atmosphere of the retreat was dissipated. Then the music was added to the words, and there were one or two practices before the break for tea. Another half-hour afterwards perfected the performance, and then the day girls were sent home, and the boarders got on with their devotional reading in the study.

'I adore the words,' Jocasta said to Martha between the curtains that night. 'Perhaps not as good as the Marseillaise but much much better than "God Save the King". That's bunk.'

'Oh I wouldn't say that,' Martha said loyally.

'Who cares what you say?' Jocasta replied rudely; but Martha was by now so used to this kind of response to her every word that it is doubtful whether she even noticed. 'I have a very good idea about tomorrow. We should sieze the opportunity provided by the American general to go out and get a choc bar. I haven't had one for days.'

'In the middle of the retreat!' Martha looked shocked.

'What's wrong with a choc bar in the middle of the retreat? No, what I say is that everyone will be so busy with this general that we can easily slip out and get the ice cream. At least you can. I'll keep cave.'

'You mean during the singing?'

'Don't be silly. I like the singing. I don't want to miss that. No, I think just before, when lunch is over.'

'I don't want to do it at all.'

'No one asked you what you wanted. Don't be such a spoil-sport.'

Jocasta abruptly drew the curtain and fell back into bed, where she occupied herself for the next hour reading a Western novel by Zane Grey, which she had bribed one of the day girls to bring in for her.

The following morning, which was the last day of the retreat, the schedule was as usual except for a final rehearsal of 'The Star Spangled Banner' at twelve o'clock, just before lunch. Jocasta took the opportunity to impart her idea to a few sympathetic members of the form, so that by some mysterious process the plan soon got round and there were many orders for choc bars from the ice cream shop two streets away, which was strictly out of bounds to the girls. As the orders rolled in Martha was more and more appalled by her task and begged Jocasta for some help. Jocasta reluctantly canvassed around, but no one was willing to assist Martha. 'You'll just have to do it yourself,' she told her friend flatly.

'But where will I put them? How can I carry *fifteen* ice cream choc bars?'

Jocasta shrugged unhelpfully. 'That's up to you. Up your knicker leg or down your front. Only don't squash them.'

'How shall I go?'

'Really, Martha! You are hopeless. Out of the day girls' doors. No one will be on the lookout. It's ideal. We'll wait for you in the day girls' cloakroom, and then we can go straight into the gym for the talk.'

At lunch there was an atmosphere of suppressed excitement, and Mother St John kept on banging her gong to remind the girls that they were still in retreat. 'Do not, I beg of you, girls, use this interlude this afternoon to distract you. In future years you will remember these days when you had the time for quiet conversation with God, unhampered by the cares of the world. The retreat ends tonight, and to make full use of the indulgences you will get from it you must observe a strict silence, except for the singing of 'The Star Spangled Banner'. God will not mind about that at all. Now, after lunch there will be quiet reading in the study or you may make visits to the chapel or take a walk in the grounds. Assemble at two thirty in the gym for the talk by the American general.'

Jocasta gave Martha a little nudge. 'See. I said it would be easy.'

'I don't—' But Martha's protest was forestalled by a sharp kick on the ankle by the girl on the other side of her, who also had a vested interest in the choc ices.

After lunch Jocasta and Martha took advantage of the free time by going swiftly to the day girls' cloakroom. It was half past one and there was plenty of time before assembly at two thirty. What neither of them had anticipated was that the door of the day girls' entrance would be locked. Normally during school hours it was left open; but as making the retreat was voluntary for days girls and only a few took advantage of it, the door was kept locked and the day girls used the boarders' entrance.

'I can't go,' Martha said with relief.

'Of course you can. Use the garden entrance from the gym.'

This entrance was used by the day girls to get into the grounds. But it was a much longer way round and involved going up the drive and through the small door next to the large main gates.

'No, no,' Martha protested. 'It's much too dangerous.'

By way of answer Jocasta took Martha by the arm and propelled her along the passage to the gym door. They were met on their way by Mother Mary Paul, who was scuttling along to the gym to practise furtively. Her important part in the forthcoming ceremony was making her anxious.

'Girls, where are you going?' Her hands fluttered nervously in front of her.

'Just outside, Mother.'

'Then get your coats. It is cold. You know quite well you must not use the day girls' entrance. Go along now.'

She turned and watched as they went into the study, then she stood by the door for five minutes to ensure they did not come back. She knew quite well Jocasta's reputation, and she had not liked the sinister way she had been pulling Martha by the arm.

The girls dashed into their own cloakroom, which was in the basement, Martha wailing quietly the while.

'You mustn't put on your coat. Look, go out by the kitchen exit, where they put the dustbins. No one will see you now, they'll all be having their own lunch. I'll wait for you here and tell the others we shall have our ice cream in this cloakroom. I think it's better than the day girls'! Go on, scoot.'

The kitchen gate was past the greenhouse. It was a much, much longer way round, but perhaps not as obvious as the other plan, because the drive went up past the gym windows. Jocasta saw Martha on her way, made sure that the gate was open and then went to gather up the others and tell them of the change of plan.

Almost weeping with apprehension Martha ran round the back of the convent and then up the narrow little street that led to the ice cream shop. In fact it was a kind of small factory, employing half a dozen people.

Here a brave effort was made to manufacture ice cream from the synthetic ingredients, which were all that was available in war time: dried milk, powdered eggs, artificial colouring and inferior fats. The chocolate covering to the bars was plain and thick; but the girls, their memories of pre-war goodies dimmed, thought they were delicious.

When Martha reached the shop door it was shut. A notice pinned on to it read: CLOSED 1–2 p.m. Martha did not have a watch, so she waited, hoping that it would open soon. She waited and waited.

In the boarders' cloakroom fifteen eager girls were waiting too. They included Clare, who was also very bored with the retreat, and, although she did not care for Jocasta Younghusband, enjoyed an illicit ice cream from time to time. Lucy was in the chapel pouring out her devotions into the receptive ears of God, Our Lady, the saints or anyone who would listen. Andrea was closeted with Father Vincent, pursuing the subject he had chosen for that morning's conference.

'It's nearly two,' Clare said crossly. 'Where on earth is the girl? You should never have sent Martha. Why didn't you go, Jocasta?'

'Why didn't *you*?' Jocasta said coldly, reciprocating Clare's feelings for her. Just then the big bell near the nuns' refectory rang, which was used to summon the boarders and community for important occasions. One or two got up.

'We'll have to go.'

'What about the ice creams?'

'Can't be helped. We must be in the gym. There is to be a short run through of the anthem before the general comes.'

About six of the girls went and the rest stayed.

Ten minutes later the bell was rung again, this time more insistently, and Clare got up.

'We'll have to go. Rev was showing the general into the parlour when I came down. Everyone will be bang on time.'

Clare took a little party out with her, until only a nervous Jocasta and two others were left.

Meanwhile at the ice cream shop Martha had waited, not

daring to return without the booty. When the door opened a friendly faced man apologized and said he hadn't realized anyone was there.

'What's the time?' Martha said.

'It's just after two, love.'

'Can I have fifteen choc bars?'

'Fifteen? My, you are getting greedy.' The friendly man went into the store and pulled out a tray. 'I've only got ten, love; can you wait while we wrap t'others?'

'I'll have to,' Martha said. '*Please* be quick.'

Martha stood first on one foot and then on another as she waited. The man finally came back in a leisurely fashion.

'Just five minutes, love, and they'll be ready. Newly made and piping hot.'

He laughed, but Martha only looked at him. Besides having no sense of humour she was too frightened to take note of what he said.

At ten minutes past two Jocasta and the two others gave up and dashed for the gym. The final chorus of 'The Spar Spangled Banner' greeted them.

'Golly, he's here.' Jocasta opened the door and crept in. But it was only the end of the rehearsal, and the girls quickly stood in line. Mother Michael was on the platform, marshalling her cohorts.

Martha nearly wept when she returned to find the cloakroom empty. She had never run so hard in her life. Outside the gate she had taken the ice creams out of the bag and put them all down the front of her dress. Now, clutching her chilly burden, she wondered what to do. The clock in the cloakroom said twenty past two. Martha ran up the stairs and along the corridor. In front of her a party was solemnly processing in the direction of the gym. There was a tall khaki-clad figure with Reverend Mother next to him and one or two of the nuns capering along behind. Martha waited until they were out of sight before she followed them.

Inside the gym all eyes turned to the stage as the party entered to be greeted by Mother Michael. There was a table with chairs behind it and, tucked in the corner, Mother Mary Paul, her face quite pink, her hands poised above the harmonium. The crew-cut general clasped Mother Michael's hand, and then stood next to Reverend Mother behind the table. Mother Michael nodded to Mother Mary Paul, who thumped the opening chord on the harmonium.

> 'Oh say can you see by the dawn's early light
> What so proudly we hailed by the twilight's last
> gleaming . . .'

The general looked gratified, and lifted his hand in a smart salute. Reverend Mother and Mother Michael stood erect on either side of him.

Mother St John was at the back by the door, and gazed sharply at it as it slowly opened. She seized the handle and peered round.

'Martha, what . . .?' she hissed.

Martha stood on the threshold clutching at a bosom about five times its normal size, which rolled and heaved as the melting choc ices within jostled for position. She gazed round her in a puzzled kind of way, as though she had entered on the wrong cue. Having no idea of the time she was pleased when she heard the music, and did not think that the party would have reached the stage, so that she could sneak in and distribute a few limp choc bars about her.

> 'Oh say does that star spangled banner still wave . . .'

Mother St John made a grab at one of Martha's arms, which dislodged from its protective position across her chest caused a curious lopsidedness in her anatomy. She tried to bring it back again, but Mother St John hung on, staring in amazement at Martha's moving bust.

> 'O'er the land of the free and the home of the
> brave . . .?'

The general finished his salute. The whole room was silent, and Martha Oldwhistle let out an extended moan as a medley of dripping choc bars fell from beneath her skirt to cluster in a curious heap before her on the ground. It was as though she had brought forth; but brought forth what, everyone was too apprehensive to guess. She stood right in the middle of the aisle, facing the general, who was goggling at the spectacle before him. Reverend Mother stared too; then she nudged Mother Michael, who left the platform. Every eye in the room was turned upon Martha and the melting mass in front of her; cream starting to dribble from the ruptured packets of the choc bars. What was more, Martha had started to wriggle as one or two, not yet freed, completed their melting process next to her skin.

In a burst of inspiration Reverend Mother signalled frantically to Mother Mary Paul. The general turned, momentarily completely nonplussed. The opening chords sounded again:

Oh say can you see by the dawn's early light . . .'

began the chorus obediently. Martha Oldwhistle was yanked unceremoniously from the room by Mother Michael, and given a good hard slap on the face by this usually controlled and intelligent nun.

'Silly, foolish, *idiot* little girl!'

Slap, slap, went the hand, one cheek then the other. Inside the gym, with the help of a few of the girls, Mother St John was trying to camouflage the melting ice cream spreading in a large puddle on the floor; but to no avail until someone went to the day girls' cloakroom, fetched a cloth and a bucket and mopped the whole soggy mess up.

By the time the American national anthem had been sung twice more all traces of the debacle were removed, and the general, with a rather fixed smile, stepped forward and made a rousing, patriotic yet at times even amusing speech, as though nothing at all had happened. Then the national anthem was sung yet again, and the general went off to address the non-Catholic grammar school at the other side of the town,

175

obviously none the wiser as to the cause of the peculiar fracas inside the hall.

Jocasta never owned up about the ice cream and, of course, Martha never told on her. Clare thought it beneath her dignity even to refer to the incident. But there was such a furore in the study afterwards, with denials and counter denials, that all attempts to renew the retreat were abandoned. Father Vincent nevertheless gave the closing conference that night with quiet desperation to a largely inattentive audience. He chose obedience to one's superiors as his subject, and was particularly severe on those who brought attention to themselves by flouting the wishes of authority.

The only person not there to hear him was Martha Oldwhistle, who was having prolonged hysterics in the infirmary. Sister Matilda had tried four aspirins, and was now on her second dose of castor oil to try and stop them. But Martha wept all night, and when, next day, her father came to collect her for the holidays he was interviewed by Reverend Mother. As a result of this little talk Martha had a few more slaps on the way home.

Jocasta never renewed her relationship with Martha, because of her stupidity. Even those who were sorry for her could not think why she had brought the ice cream into the gym, instead of leaving it in the cloakroom. But it was easy for them to be so reasonable, because none of them had experienced the kind of blind panic that Martha had suffered at the moment of decision, to say nothing of her fear of Jocasta.

Anyway, Martha left the school at the end of the summer term, and got a job in a shop in the town. She married quite early, had a lot of children and soon forgot all about the convent.

Before the end of the summer term occurred the most important feast of the year, Corpus Christi, in June. There was a great procession on this day, and parents and even townspeople streamed into the grounds to watch or take part. There was a proliferation of shrubs and flowers, many of which had to be brought from the country by Sister Benedict's father, who kept a large nursery on his farm outside the town. Huge baskets of rose petals were carried by the junior girls and strewn in front of the Bishop as he carried the Blessed Sacrament through the grounds. A canopy over his head was carried on poles by four men in tail-coats and striped trousers; before them a dozen altar boys wafted their censers high in the air and the incense rose in a thick white cloud. In front of and behind the Bishop the procession, singing the Corpus Christi hymns, moved at a solemn pace. All the girls in the school, dressed in white frocks and veils, walked in the procession, and they were followed by the nuns, with their long formal veils over their black habits, the priests of the diocese in surplices, the altar boys, and the choir. Then at the end any parents who cared to walked with sons or with daughters who were not at the school.

The procession formed on the tarmac in front of the convent, and then wove through the grounds, along the path past the lake and across the playgrounds to where a magnificent altar had been constructed in the boathouse. After Benediction there, the procession turned and went back via the far side of the lake and up the path to the front of the convent once more, where another altar had been erected on the porch. There the Bishop, rather tired and panting a little with the effort of holding the monstrance over his head, celebrated Benediction again.

After that the assembly split up. The girls went to the dormitories and removed their white veils but kept on their dresses, which were worn all day for Corpus Christi, and looked very smart and pretty with the freshly ironed ribbons of the sodalities pinned to them. The Bishop and priests had a splendid tea in the two parlours; the parents were entertained in the gym, and the boarders had their tea in their own refectory and then rushed upstairs to see their parents, or played rounders in the playground with the altar boys, strictly supervised by nuns and priests.

Andrea was not allowed to take part in the procession, because it was such a public avowal of faith. She watched from the chapel window, which gave her a panoramic view of the grounds. The thick foliage of the trees sometimes obscured her view, but she could see the procession weaving in and out, and the singing reached her quite clearly. The swans on the lake almost seemed to be taking part themselves, forming their own little procession with the big ones at the head and the smaller ones behind, sailing importantly along the lake to accompany the concourse at the side.

As the Bishop passed, those who were lining the path without taking part themselves knelt for the blessing, and Andrea was reminded of a field of tall grass which undulated with the wind ready for cutting.

It was a very beautiful sight on that hot summer's day in June 1944, and confirmed Andrea's feelings about the satisfactory nature of a religion that had such a full-blooded, emotional impact.

Late in the evening, before they went to bed, she and Lucy crept into the chapel, which was next to their dormitory. Lucy gazed with pride at her flower display – the whites of the lilies and lupins, the yellow of the roses, the blues of the irises, and the bright burning red of the special display of hibiscus, which were arrayed on either side of the tabernacle, with its curtain of cloth of gold.

'They are really perfect this year,' she said. 'It's almost like they are talking to God.' The cupped hibiscus with their protruding yellow antennae leaned in the direction of the tabernacle.

'They are lovely,' Andrea agreed.

'But tomorrow they will die; they just curl up and die.'

'But the buds come out; look, there is a bud just beginning to open.'

'But I hate for them to curl up and die.'

'I think it is very symbolic. Somehow it is fitting that something so gorgeous should die so quickly, as though it were too perfect to live.'

Lucy, kneeling at the altar rail, looked appreciatively at Andrea.

'What a lovely idea. I have never thought of it like that.'

'And as one dies, another opens as perfect as the last one. It is very mystical.'

'It is *very* mystical,' Lucy whispered.

'And it is also like life; we blaze briefly and we die, and others follow us, just like the flowers on the hibiscus tree.'

The red sanctuary lamp in the gold vessel flickered in front of the altar, and on either side in the alcoves containing the statues of Our Lady and St Joseph blue and white altar lights winked and flickered. The massed flowers were hazily outlined in the shadows cast by the lights, and no other movement or sound disturbed the girls. Then Lucy crossed herself and genuflected, and they went quickly from the chapel because, despite its grandeur, the symbolism of the hibiscus flower was disturbing, and neither of them wanted to think of death on that splendid day of the feast of the Body of Christ.

Now it was the end of Andrea's second year in the convent. The School Certificate had been sat for, but the results would not be known until the holidays were half over. She was going to London to see her father, who was home on leave. The news of the war was more cheerful, the D-Day landings had taken place and the allies had started the second front. The Germans were being pushed back in Europe; but the concentration camps were still burning Jewish boys and girls with their mothers and fathers. Andrea and Lucy had not liked being reminded of death, and had scuttled out of the chapel at the thought. But, although they did not know it then, the symbolism of the hibiscus flower did signify something that briefly blazed and died: those small Jewish children, who, unlike Lucy and Andrea, would never grow up.

# Eight

Miss Clark, whose passion for Andrea was on the wane, had transferred her affections to Jocasta Younghusband, and had cast her in the role of Eleanor of Aquitaine in a rather sentimental interpretation of the court of love, which she had written with Mother David, that admirable history scholar. There was a lot of jealousy about the casting of Jocasta because, although she was undeniably beautiful, she was only in the fourth form, and those who coveted the part did not think she was mature enough for the role of such a celebrated woman, who had been queen both of France and England. Mother David would have liked Andrea in the role because she had more presence, as well as the looks for the part; but Miss Clark had insisted on passing her over for her new favourite.

The reason for Andrea's relegation was that she had a got a distinction for English Literature in School Certificate, and assured Miss Clark that this was because she had brought out the real nature of the passion of Antony and Cleopatra in the three questions she had been able to answer on the play; and that she had used the word "sexual" no less than ten times. It was the end, so far as Miss Clark was concerned. Besides, she liked a little reciprocity where affection was concerned, and Andrea had never really responded to her devotion, preferring to give herself to Clare.

Mother St John and Miss Clark had quite a row about the casting of Jocasta, because it had been done without consultation. Mother St John would have opposed it vigorously, as it would offer Jocasta so much more leeway for trouble than she enjoyed already. Mother David intervened first on one side and then on the other, in order to try and please both. But she pleased neither, each considering her weak willed.

Clare was given the role of Henry II, which was a very small part, as the courts of love were in Poitiers at the time of Eleanor's separation from Henry, who only appeared in one scene of the play. Andrea was also fobbed off with a small part, as one of Eleanor's ladies, and was so disgusted that she refused to give it any attention, preferring her sessions in religious doctrine, which she had started in earnest with Mother Veronica, instead. During the summer her father, in his joy at seeing his daughter once again, had agreed to anything provided that she did not actually enter the Catholic Church until she was old enough to know her mind. Judith Lynch played the Countess Marie, Eleanor's daughter, who ran the court of love while her mother was tripping round her estates. She was displeased, too, at being in a role so junior to a girl three forms below her.

Thus there was a great deal of dissatisfaction at the casting, which took place in the autumn term, when Andrea, Lucy and Clare were in the Lower Sixth. To everyone's astonishment, not least her own, Lucy had done quite well in the School Certificate; or to be more accurate, she had passed when she was expected to fail. It was decided that instead of leaving at the end of the Upper Fifth, and finding a place in a flower nursery or a shop, she should go on to the Sixth to see how she made out. She might even consider being a teacher of infants. Andrea and Clare had, of course, done very well and Mother Michael was determined to prepare them for university. Mother Michael did not care at all what happened to Lucy, whom she still could not forgive for the dishonour she had brought on the school in the episodes involving the Bishop and the greenhouse, even though they now seemed so long ago.

It was Mother David who finally did achieve a kind of peace, by suggesting that Jocasta might reform if she were invested with some responsibility. But Eleanor was a very big and important role indeed, and she dominated the play, so few were mollified. A small part was even found for Lucy, as fourth troubadour, because she had never been in a school play and there were a lot of crowd scenes.

Miss Clark was very excited about the production, which she had written with little regard for historical accuracy, from source material provided by Mother David. Her enthusiasm for her new play was born largely out of the boring little effort of the year before; besides, she had to have some outlet for her frustrated literary skills. She was also thrilled at all the opportunities she would have to be closeted with Jocasta, to rehearse her in her big role. What was more, instead of Andrea's polite remoteness towards her, Jocasta responded to Miss Clark in a very gratifying way by snuggling up to her when Miss Clark put an arm round her the better to demonstrate some gesture or action. There was a cuddly quality about Jocasta, a term one certainly could not apply to Andrea. Jocasta had a small, finely structured face, which came to a delightful little point at the chin, and a long and elegant body without bust or hips. She really had not the fullness or maturity for Eleanor, who was not a young woman during the period of the events recorded in the play. But Miss Clark, with her author's licence, had made her shed twenty years or so, thus making her probably younger than her daughter; and for this Jocasta did have the most astonishing thick auburn hair, which she wore in one large plait with little curly bits at her forehead and temples. For the part she would wear it loose and flowing, with a thin gold band. Miss Clark had it all planned. She also had, in Miss Clark's opinion, the most thrilling dark eyes, which could burn with a fierce intensity, or become remote and disdainful.

Jocasta and Clare shared a mutual antipathy, perhaps because they were so alike, though Clare now considered herself a very grand person, being in the sixth form, and she wanted no truck with this little squirt in form four. But, alas, there it was; she had to play Henry to her Eleanor. It was, however, a very forceful role, though small, and required much swaggering about, hand on sword, and a heavy beard and moustache. Clare was quite willing to cooperate with Mother St John in keeping an eye on Jocasta. This had the effect of bringing these two protagonists together, and Clare began her climb up the ladder of favouritism.

Besides, Clare had undoubtedly matured. She was very aware of her responsibilities as a sixth former, and had become haughty with age. But some of Andrea's former remoteness seemed to have rubbed off on Clare, and she had grown bookish and rather introverted. Whereas Andrea had blossomed outwards, Clare had closed in upon herself. She thought she might like to be a doctor like her father, and applied herself to mathematics and science, subjects that the school was hard pressed to teach adequately in the sixth form. So Mother Veronica gave her special coaching, and a new science mistress was engaged because of the expansion of the sixth form.

This was Miss Ottershaw, who had just graduated from Cambridge, and took herself and her subject very seriously. She had wanted to go into the scientific branch of the Civil Service to help with the war effort, but had decided to teach for a while to be near her old father, who lived in retirement at St Anne's-on-Sea. Miss Ottershaw had become aware at Cambridge of the dangers that beset academic women, and so she cultivated a deliberate air of frivolity, which did not really suit her austere personality, and dressed herself with a lot of frills and fiddly bits to show how feminine she really was.

She had a gaunt spiky face and frizzy mouse-coloured hair, which she curled frantically every night. She could hardly lie comfortably on her pillow, because of all the rollers and pins. But she thought it was worth it because in her third year she had acquired a boyfriend, a scientist like herself, who had gone straight into the army and was now with the advancing allied forces in France. She wrote to him every day, and kept his letters tied up with a blue ribbon under her pillow. The most recent she kept in her handbag to produce at the morning staff break, just to show the other mistresses how unlike them she was. The day before her boyfriend had gone to the war they had slept together. She was sure this was not a mortal sin, on account of his need and the comfort her body had given him, because he was very afraid. She kept the experience as a precious memory, and wove little fantasies round it as she lay at night in her lonely bed in her digs on the far side of the town.

Miss Ottershaw despised Miss Parker, the other science mistress, because of her ignorance about life, and the cautious way she taught biology – tadpoles and flowers and the like. She would have gone straight into the subject, if asked, based on her studies and supplemented by her own rich, if limited, experience. She immediately singled out Clare as the brightest of her pupils, and decided to make her her interest until Arnold came back from the war, which was sure to be over soon. They would get married and live a very fruitful and rapturous life together.

Clare found Miss Ottershaw a very exciting person, not only because she actually knew a lot about her subject, but because of the way she hinted at her knowledge of life, and the frank way she was prepared to discuss biological subjects. Clare was still not quite *sure* about sex, and she thought one day, when they had got to know each other better, she would ask Miss Ottershaw exactly what was *what*.

Twice a week Andrea met Mother Veronica in the sixth form classroom after tea to study religious doctrine. Mother Veronica, impressed by her obvious sincerity and piety had gradually overcome her former antipathy towards Andrea, had grown quite fond of her and felt it was a privilege to instruct her. Andrea dutifully went to daily Mass, and took part in all the religious services. She even sang in the choir, and Mother Mary Paul put her in the front row, because the sight of a Protestant singing with such rapture was so sublime. Andrea could not go to communion or confession, but otherwise she was as Catholic as the rest: well versed in the lives of the saints, and familiar with the basic tenets of Catholicism – the mysteries of redemption, resurrection and salvation. She was an eager and adept pupil and Mother Veronica was delighted with her; all the nuns prayed daily for her conversion.

There was no need to pray, however – though prayer in

itself is good whatever the object – because Andrea would have converted on the spot. Those of the nuns who knew how she felt thought her conduct very edifying, and saw in her obedience to her father's wishes a parallel with Isaac's docility to his father, Abraham.

'One day it will be all right. I know that,' Reverend Mother would say on the long walks she sometimes took with Andrea among the formal gardens, or along the Rosary Way. The rapport they had established at the beginning had developed into a harmony, a unity of mind that was spiritual and very human too. Reverend Mother never had obvious favourites or pets as the lesser nuns did. But she had always been particularly fond of Andrea because of the special responsibility she had towards her, in place of a parent. 'But pray that your father lets you be received before you leave us, because, once out in the world you will forget.'

'Never, Reverend Mother.'

'You are young, Andrea, and you have no mother. You have been sheltered and protected here, and you have come to love the faith in this atmosphere. The world is a very hard place. When it takes you from us you will be caught up in a stream of other things: new people and advanced ideas. But if you have the Faith it will make you stronger. Remember, Andrea, that the community here will always love you and pray for you.'

Andrea felt almost tearful.

'Oh, Reverend Mother, I will remember. I will never be tempted.'

'My dear, no one can help temptation, as Our Lord showed us during his forty days in the wilderness. But he also showed us how to resist, and to emerge stronger for having been tempted.' She turned and looked at Andrea. 'You are a pretty girl, my child, and men will want you. But until you have selected your partner for life, you must never let them near you.'

Andrea was not at all sure about this one, and remained silent as they walked quite briskly round the lake because it was late November and cold. Andrea had been thinking a lot about men and women and that interesting phenomenon called passion; even her preoccupation with religion had not absorbed it completely. She knew that to experience passion fully one definitely had to let men come near one, or one would end up like Miss Clark with all her theories. Andrea was thus convinced that in order to know, one could not be sidetracked by an obsession with guilt, as so many Catholics were.

She really could see no conflict between love of God and obedience to His will, and a normal human life. Reading *Antony and Cleopatra* gave her the same kind of exultation of the spirit as hearing Palestrina or singing during Benediction. She was sure that human love and divine love were very closely linked.

Andrea decided it was best not to tell Reverend Mother her thoughts, and as they walked back to the house she changed the subject.

Now that she was seventeen Lucy had almost lost her spots, her greasy nose was more controlled and restricted to patches at the side, and more suitable spectacle frames made her if not attractive, at least not unappealing. Only girls in the sixth form were allowed to curl their hair, and with the advent of pins and curlers and a good cut each holiday Lucy managed to keep her stringy locks in some sort of shape, so that they did not straggle on either side of her face like spaniel's ears. The three now were an established trio and went everywhere together, so far as this could be fitted in with their duties. They were each in charge of separate tables in the refectory, and sat at the end of different pews in the chapel in order to keep an eye on the junior girls. Clare had her own dormitory, and was a house captain, and Andrea and Lucy were both prefects. It was funny to see Lucy change from one who fell about all over the place, in trouble and out, to this rather nondescript but dignified older girl. They sat next to one another in class, and in their free moments kept together as the nucleus of the small court which surrounded them with homage.

The one person the three were united against was Jocasta Younghusband, who pleased no one except Miss Clark. Yet she did elicit some kind of response from everyone else, because she was so prominent. She was perpetually standing as punishment by the bookcase in the study, going early to bed or being sent to the playroom next to the refectory to have her meals alone. She flouted her role in the school play and her special relationship with Miss Clark in a quite flagrant fashion. She said her prayers with ostentation, rattled her rosary on the bench in front of her in the chapel, giggled and looked about as she came back from communion and sang loudest in the choir, to which she had been promoted because of her clear soprano voice. Like Andrea and Clare before her, she was exceptional, except that she employed none of their subtlety and her conduct was openly execrable.

She was vain and spent hours in front of the mirror in the Immaculate Conception dormitory. She curled her hair in secret and she never covered herself with a towel when she washed, until Mother St John was forced to banish her to her cubicle with a basin and a jug of hot water.

The downfall of Jocasta Younghusband came about like this.

One night just before Christmas Jocasta was found in one of the upstairs classrooms giving two of the school cleaners and several of her classmates hysterics by her imitation of some of the staff. She was imitating Miss Parker giving a guarded account of the reproduction of frogs when Mother David came in, having been sent to find her for rehearsal. Mother David was a very tolerant person but she had to report Jocasta because of the obviously nasty way she had been impersonating Miss Parker. Also, she was giving a very bad example to her classmates, as usual; but this was nothing to the indecorum of conversing so loosely with the cleaners. Jocasta was sent early to bed together with those of her cronies who had been found with her.

The thing that annoyed Jocasta so much was that this was the night when the choir gave a performance of Christmas carols for the nuns. She tried to get Mother Mary Paul to take her side; but that good nun, who found her as trying as the rest did, refused by saying that the choir could sing very nicely without her.

The dormitory was deserted, except for these few, who were supposed to be on their 'honour'. This was rather a ludicrous thing to expect from someone like Jocasta, who did not know the meaning of the word.

Jocasta washed in the bathroom with the others, showing her very small bosoms quite flagrantly. In fact, she improved on this and stripped off altogether. The others were at once shocked and amused. But this was not enough for Jocasta, who enjoyed carol singing and was seething at her deprivation. When they were washed and in their pyjamas, she made a mysterious little beckoning motion to the others and summoned them to her cubicle.

'Sit on the bed,' she told them, 'and I will tell you what we are going to do.'

'What are we going to do, Jocasta?' said a rather timid little girl who was easily led, but still doubtful about the moral implications of the display of nudity they had just witnessed. The others were shivering with awful and delicious expectation.

'We are going to play at confessions,' Jocasta said. 'I will be the priest and you will tell me your sins.'

The anticipatory faces lost some of their glow.

'I don't think that is a very nice thing to do.'

'It is a nice thing to do, and we shall do it,' Jocasta said firmly. 'It will just show them.' She put her dressing gown on back to front to resemble a cassock, tucked a white handkerchief folded at her throat to look like a clerical collar and strung her dressing cord round her neck as if it were a stole. Then she drew her chair up to the curtain and sat in front of this. 'Now you others must go into the cubicle next to me, and then come through the curtain one by one. Those who are waiting, go into the cubicle at the other side in case anyone comes in. You must kneel and cross yourselves just as you do for confession. I want this to be very realistic. And I also want the truth. No made-up sins, please.'

The others looked at one another, but there was no question of a refusal. Jocasta was already sitting in her chair, her hand cupping an ear as if she really were a priest behind the grille. The first penitent came in and knelt humbly down.

'In the name of the Father and of the Son and of the Holy Ghost . . .'

Halfway through the carol service Clare, who was not in the choir, decided she had a headache. She crept up to Mother St John, who was sitting at the back listening with a very edified expression on her face, and asked to be excused. Mother St John grimaced and nodded. Clare went upstairs and opened the dormitory door very quietly. At first she heard nothing, which surprised her, knowing who had been sent to bed; and then coming from the left she heard whisperings, interrupted by a firmer monotone. She thought they were saying their prayers. She crept along the aisle and listened.

'Bless me, Father, for I have sinned.'

'What have you done, my child?' came a gruff female voice.

'I have been cheeky to Mother St John, and I have had sinful thoughts.'

'What sort of sinful thoughts, my child?' enquired the voice with interest.

'Very sinful, Father.'

'How sinful? What were they about? I must know the details.'

'That I would eat meat on Fridays, Father.'

The deeper voice gave an exclamation of impatience.

'That is not a sinful thought at all, you silly child. You're making it up. Now I want a real good sin.'

'I can't think of one, Father.'

'Then go away and try. But in the meantime I will give you a penance and absolution. Say a decade of the rosary and the De Profundis, six times.' Jocasta was enjoying herself enormously, even though the sins were rather disappointing. She should have been on the other side of the curtain. She drew her hand up in blessing, and recited approximately the words of absolution, because she didn't know them all. Then she said in a loud voice: 'Next.'

Clare whipped inside a cubicle as the sinner emerged, and then went very quietly back along the dormitory. When the next penitent had gone in, Clare crept towards the door, leaving it ajar so as to make no noise. She ran down the stairs to the gym, where the carols were being sung, and whispered to Mother St John, whose features were immediately transformed into an expression of shock, indignation and delight. She went stealthily from the gym with Clare, after whispering to Mother David, who was sitting next to her.

'I felt very evil about Mother St John, Father. I felt I would like to kill her.'

Jocasta sighed with relief. The news had got round to the others that she expected good sins.

'That is a very terrible sin, my child. Why did you wish to kill this good nun?'

'Because she tells lies. She told Mother Veronica that I had copied my maths prep.'

'And had you my child?'

'No, Father.'

'Well that is very odd, because you usually do.'

'Not this time, Father.' The little voice was shaky. Jocasta had managed to instil a real feeling of terror in the hearts of her cronies.

'Well, my child, as we all know, Mother St John does tell the most awful lies, like the rest of the nuns, and I will only give you a light penance, because you were so provoked. Say—'

And with that the curtain of Jocasta's cubicle was roughly drawn back to reveal Mother St John and Clare. Clare whisked the intervening curtain aside and exposed a small child on her knees, almost in tears, before Jocasta.

Jocasta looked at first astonished and then afraid. She got quickly off the chair and tried to take the gown off. Mother St John stared at her, and that gaze was almost more awful than words.

'Explain this, miss,' she said at length. 'What *is* the meaning of it?'

Jocasta shrugged. 'I was trying to make them better at confession. It was for their spiritual improvement.'

Clare was collecting from various parts of the dormitory other putative sinners, who had scuttled for cover. They came back to hear Jocasta arguing her cause.

'But I was, Mother. It was only pretending. I thought it would be a good thing to do instead of night prayers.'

'It was a very, very wicked thing to do. You were imitating a priest. I think what you were doing is sacrilege. How many confessions did you hear?'

The others were quick to condemn their leader in order to try and make things easier for themselves.

'Mine, Mother.'

'Mine.'

'And mine.'

'Mine, Mother.'

'She made me come back *twice*, Mother St John,' said a virtuous little voice.

Jocasta looked at them with scorn. 'It was just for their own good.'

'What nonsense,' Clare said. 'They looked scared to death.'

'You have terrorized these girls, Jocasta. It is a very severe mortal sin you have committed. The gravest possible.'

'Gravest possible,' Clare echoed. 'I have never heard of anything like it in my life, Mother.'

Clare had forgotten very quickly the days of her youthful enterprises.

'And all you have to explain yourself, miss, is that you were trying to aid their spiritual betterment?'

'Yes, Mother.'

'But I heard what you said, miss. I heard every word. *I* tell lies like all the nuns.' Mother St John's expression was almost triumphant.

Jocasta, who had hoped that her words had not been heard, experienced a sense of defeat. She lifted her chin, stared boldly at Mother St John and said nothing more.

Mother St John tugged the made-up collar away from Jocasta's throat, stripped her of her stole and shoved her on to the bed.

'Get dressed, miss. I am going to take you straight to Reverend Mother. I cannot possibly deal with something as naughty, as grave and as sinful as this.'

*1945*

Jocasta's father was a captain in the army. Her mother worked as a welfare officer in a munitions factory. Jocasta was only saved from expulsion because there was no one really to look after her. But she was stripped of all privileges, any that she had left, and her part in the school play was taken from her.

Andrea declined it, because she refused to be second choice, and it was given to an indifferent performer in the Lower Fifth who forgot her lines all the way through, having had to learn them in a hurry over the Christmas holidays.

The play, Miss Clark's most ambitious work to date, was a flop because of its uneven execution, the ineptitude of Eleanor and the fact that the Bishop was shocked by the subject. Even though Miss Clark and Mother David had been at pains to emphasize the spiritual nature of courtly love the Bishop stayed awake all the way through – always a bad sign – and told Reverend Mother that the play should be put on the Index because one of the scenes had shown Eleanor being courted by a troubadour, and she was a married woman. Besides, didn't Reverend Mother recall that Henry II had been responsible for the death of St Thomas à Becket, and spent most of his life fighting the Pope and being excommunicated? Reverend Mother was deeply ashamed, and had quite a stormy scene with Mother David and Miss Clark, reprimanding them severely for the indelicacy of the subject they had chosen. Miss Clark was told in future to submit any script to Reverend Mother beforehand, and to stick to classical or spiritual themes that would edify the Bishop.

In a sense, then, Jocasta was vindicated, because she had known her lines perfectly, and would have given distinction to the role. Her very winsomeness on the stage might even have distracted the Bishop – who was susceptible to female beauty – from a consideration of the moral implications, which he had only dwelled upon because he was so bored. The final performance of the play was cancelled, following the Bishop's reaction, and the beautiful costumes were sent back to London. Miss Greene wept that her splendid sets based on prints of the period were so unappreciated.

Mother David was very firmly relegated to her role as sports mistress, and was told never to try her hand at historical writing again. It also damaged her career by confirming Mother Michael's suspicion that her unorthodox ideas made her unfit to teach history to the upper forms.

Clare was not at all ashamed of her part in the downfall of Jocasta, because she was at the age when righteousness is all, and vengeance is vindictive rather than loftily inspired. She unreasonably thought it served Jocasta right, for taking the part Andrea should have had.

Andrea thought the whole fuss was silly, and secretly sympathized with Jocasta. She knew how she must feel at having forfeited her role in the play. But she did think Miss Clark was suitably punished for not choosing her, and she was glad about this. Miss Clark was quite crushed for the rest of the term; but took comfort from the works of Thomas Hardy, who was the subject of the Lower Sixth's study for the term, who wrote so compellingly about the injustices and iniquities of life.

As for Jocasta, she continued with her bad ways until in her last term in the Lower Fifth, the following year, she was expelled for being found behind the boathouse with a bewildered altar boy on the feast of Corpus Christi, tugging violently at his trousers, with her own white knickers round her ankles. No one had any doubts that time as to who was responsible, and the altar boy emerged with honour and subsequently became a dignitary of the church.

Jocasta didn't care. The war had ended and her father, corrupted no doubt by his time in the army, thought the whole thing very funny and sent her to RADA to work off her dramatic impulses. Subsequently she was to achieve fame as an actress whose loose morals were a continuing source of copy for the front pages of the more sensational Sunday papers. Not surprisingly, long before then she had given up her Faith.

In the end, the one to whom Jocasta caused most suffering was Miss Clark, who had thought she had a disciple in Jocasta in every sense of the word, and had defended her to the end. The episode with the altar boy upset her so because she considered that it betrayed the beautiful nature of their own relationship. Which just shows how easy it is for the human heart to be crushed and deceived by those it has loved and trusted most.

Anne Wedgewood had had little to do with Andrea, Lucy and Clare since she had played Mrs Cratchit in the school play two years before. She had been referred a year in the Lower Fifth, because she was younger and, on the whole, dimmer than anybody else. So now she was in the Upper Fifth, and planned to leave school as soon as she had taken her School Certificate, and do a secretarial course at the local college of commerce. She hoped she would marry quite soon, and have a large family.

Anne's was a contained, narrow view of the world, which was not singular. She had grown up in the country in a devout Catholic family and gone to school in a nearby town. The sum of her ambition was to get a job there and find a nice boy with whom to settle down. She had never been further south than Manchester, and had no inclination to do so. The fact that she had a number of brothers and sisters in no way diminished her enthusiasm for the further proliferation of the human race.

Anne had remained best friends with Judith Lynch, who, though very pious, had acquired a clandestine boyfriend during the Christmas holidays. He was a sailor called Pat, and he wrote her rather formal, short and semi-illiterate letters, into which she nevertheless managed to read a good number of passionate double entendres – whether they were there or not.

Mother St John, who opened all the boarders' letters, and read them eagerly for contents that were even slightly amiss, was assured that Pat was a girl. She believed this lie, because Judith was a quiet and unremarkable girl, and Mother St John could not imagine her doing anything so wicked as writing to a man. She unwisely neglected the element of fantasy in Judith's emotional make-up, and the daydreams she constructed on very little substance.

Only sixth form girls did not have their letters censored; those of all the other boarders were read coming in and going out. The very junior girls had a letter-writing session after lunch on Sundays, which had used to be run by that half-blind nun Mother Emanuel, who collected the letters at the end and took them away so that she could peruse them at leisure through her large magnifying glass. Frequently she had to be reminded to give them back. The session was now taken by one of the nuns who taught outside at one of the council schools, Mother Lawrence. She was very ruthless, and frequently scored the letters through and made the girls write them again to correct points of grammar or spelling errors.

Mother St John saw the incoming letters and, according to mood or how much she had to do, either read them carefully and with enjoyment or just opened them with a paper knife and gave them out unread, especially if she knew they were from parents. Depending on mood, too, she would either give the letters straight to the girls or keep them prominently on her desk for hours, gazing sulkily at the expectant throng trying to work in front of her. If a girl had been naughty she would not give her her letters until she had improved, which might take days. Another of her disarming little tricks was to announce the contents of a letter to a girl as she gave it to her. 'Your mother is in bed with a cold, Patricia, and your brother has got a boil on his neck. Your Aunt Polly has come on a visit, and your father has started to dig up the back garden to get out of her way. Doesn't your family *like* Aunt Polly, Patricia?' She did this in full voice, so that any passer-by could hear just what was going on in the girl's household.

Mother St John accordingly did not, could not, fail to notice the sudden influx of letters from Pat to Judith, and was at first suspicious. She asked carefully about the friendship, and was told it had started in the holidays and that Pat was a good Catholic girl. The news about Pat's gender soon got round, and Judith for the first time in her unremarkable school career found herself the object of some surreptitious envy.

Anne, however, thought Judith was being dishonest, deceiving the nuns in this way. She said the lies worried her; but, more truthfully, she was jealous of Pat, as Judith spent the free time she had formerly passed with Anne curled up in a corner composing letters to Pat in her large girlish hand. The more remote Judith became from her, the more wrong did Anne consider Judith's deceit. And to have a boyfriend at all, at her age, was surely wrong? What had begun as a joke had now got beyond one.

Apart from Judith, Anne had no close friend and, as she would be leaving at the end of the summer term, she thought it too late to acquire a new one. Andrea and Clare had never really had much time for her since she had made such a fool of herself, and incriminated them all, at the seance.

Lucy was quite pleasant to Anne but she had little time for her either, because of her own involvement with Clare and Andrea. Thus Anne grew very lonely watching her former great friend write all those letters. She started to brood.

The day before the school broke up for Easter, Mother St John pulled Anne from the line of girls who were coming up from their tea. Mother St John had developed this quite threatening clutching action, and although she had never actively succeeded in detaching an arm from the body sometimes she appeared to come close to it. The girl was usually almost swung off her feet, and then twisted into position to face her persecutor. It was always a sign that Mother was very cross when she grabbed one in this vigorous fashion. This time she kept hold of Anne's arm and took her into the junior classroom nearby, shaking her violently as she went.

Anne had already begun to tremble at the sheer force of

196

the clutch, and the threatening expression on the face of Mother St John made her feel even worse. When she considered that she had sufficiently jellified her victim, Mother St John spoke.

'Anne, who is Pat?'

'Pat, Mother?'

'You know *which* Pat. The Pat who writes to Judith Lynch.'

'A f-friend, Mother.'

'It's a man, isn't it? A man, I say. Stand straight, miss, and look at me.'

Anne looked at her feet.

'Well? It is a man, isn't it? Don't tell me a lie!'

'Yes, Mother.'

'Ah. He's a sailor isn't he?'

'Yes, Mother.'

Mother St John's face shone with blissful pleasure at the success of her detective work.

'The hussy. A man. A *sailor*!'

'There's nothing wrong, Mother.'

'Wrong? Of course it's wrong. The thought that Judith should be so wicked appals me. To lie to a nun; and so often. It is a mortal sin. And you have helped her. Do her parents know?'

'I think so, Mother. She met Pat in the Christmas holidays, at a dance.'

'A *dance*? What is Judith doing going to dances? She is much too young for that kind of thing. I must say I am surprised at Mrs Lynch. I am sure that she would not approve of her daughter continuing this relationship. I trusted Judith. Yes, I trusted her. She has always been so honest. And now this morning there is a letter from Pat, and the address is "On board HMS . . . somewhere at sea."'

'Yes, Mother. He was on land before. He's just gone back to sea.'

Mother St John drew the crumpled, well-read letter from the folds of her habit, and waved it around like a flag. Little tears trickled from Anne's eyes, and she dabbed at them with a grubby handkerchief.

'Mother, please don't say I told you. Judith will hate me.'

'Go back to the study, miss. I cannot forgive you for conniving at Judith's wickedness. You must both go to confession. Do any of the other girls know?'

'I think they might have guessed, Mother.'

In the study Judith looked at Anne as she slunk to her desk, carefully avoiding Judith's eyes, which were sharp with worry.

'Psst! What did she want?'

Anne still didn't look at her, and got her books out of her desk, keeping her head concealed for as long as she could. A nasty little feeling of foreboding clutched at Judith's heart. With reason.

The fuss that followed later that evening was a typical convent commotion. Judith was allowed to speculate and suffer for a bit, and was then shown the latest letter in front of the whole study. It was parked under her nose, and she had to stare at it for seconds before Mother St John drew paper from envelope and dramatically read out the address, as though it was a missive from the Devil himself. In a moment of inspiration Judith weakly tried to protest that Pat was a Wren but then Mother St John played her trump card and said 'someone' had told her. Judith and everyone in the study turned solemnly to gaze at Anne Wedgewood.

The letter was then torn up before everyone, like the public burning of seditious literature, and Judith was ordered to open her desk and produce the rest. These Mother St John tucked into her habit, and said she would show them to Reverend Mother. Judith was then made to stand out against the bookcase so that everyone could see this Jezabel until supper time, after which she and Anne were sent straight to bed.

Anne tried to get ahead of Judith but found her way into the dormitory blocked.

'Judas!' Judith hissed. 'Judas, Judas, Judas.' Then she went to her cubicle without another sound. Mother Euphrasia was already in the dormitory, so Anne had no opportunity to speak to her that night. It was not until the next morning when they were packing their trunks in the box room that Anne got near her.

'She knew. I didn't tell her.'

'Judas!' Judith spat at her.

'She knew, she knew. Oh, Judy, *please* understand.'

'Understand? You are a petty, jealous little cat. I never want to speak to you ever again.' Then she closed the lid of the trunk, locked it and strode away.

Anne tearfully packed her things, and then her father came for her. Away she went without a word to anyone, hoping that the holidays would put things right and all would be well next term.

However, it was not to be. On the morning of Easter Saturday Anne was taking her young brothers and sisters to the service at the local church. In those days the final liturgy of Lent was held on Saturday morning. For three days since the school had broken up she had grieved all the time, thinking of Judith, and how unjust everyone had been to her, refusing to speak because she told tales. On Maundy Thursday and Good Friday the family had spent a lot of time in church, and the penitential season seemed to Anne to reflect the very nadir of her unhappiness.

So perhaps she was brooding and reflective, and careless too, as she shepherded her younger brothers and sisters across the busy main road. She certainly could not have seen the lorry that came racing round the corner, braked as it saw the group crossing and swerved to avoid them. Anne, who was the last and halfway across the road, was caught up by the bumper and carried a hundred yards before it mounted the pavement and crushed Anne, in all finality, against the front of a newsagent's shop.

The school heard the news with shock on the first day back for the summer term. Judith had been told during the holidays and had gone to the funeral with Mother St John, placing a large wreath of spring flowers on the grave of her friend with a sentimental little note, bordered in black, to go with it.

Andrea and Clare were among the most shocked, because, with Judith and Lucy, they remembered the seance and the words that had so upset Anne and caused her to fall on the floor.

They were sitting on the bench in the sun outside the cloak-room, the four of them, Lucy, Judith, Clare and Andrea, who had been intimately concerned with the seance. It was quite traumatic, quite horrific the way someone's life could be snuffed out. One moment they were there, and the next moment gone. It was their first real experience of death, except for Andrea, who remembered her mother dying, because the terrors of the war had passed them by. Anyway, death on that scale could never be such a personal thing as the death of one's companion at school; not even Mother Emanuel's death had affected them like this. It couldn't.

'She was just sixteen,' Judith said in a far-off voice. 'Sixteen.'

'Stop saying that!' Clare declared crossly. 'It's about the fourth time you've said it.'

'Sixteen.' Judith started to cry. 'And we had fallen out,'

'You couldn't *help* it.' Lucy tried to comfort her. 'It was nothing to do with you. We all thought she was a sneak.'

'But she didn't tell Mother St John,' Andrea said, having spent some time the night before with a very disturbed and contrite nun, whom she hardly recognized as the terror of the boarders. Even more than Judith Mother St John had seemed to reproach herself for what had happened to Anne. 'Mother St John had guessed it was a man, and because Anne was so timid knew she would get it out of her more easily than Judith. She said she already knew, and Anne just had to agree.'

'Typical,' Clare said. 'If only we'd known. Johnny was such a sneak. Not poor Anne.'

'I was so cross, so unreasonable,' Judith remonstrated with herself. 'And I didn't even like him very much. Pat, you know. It was just rather a terrific thing to do, write to a man. He was a bit of a lout really. Anyway, it's all over now. I shall never write to him again. *He* really killed Anne. I hold him directly responsible.'

'Don't be silly,' Lucy said. 'You can't say that. It was her time. "A time to be born, and a time to die." Reverend Mother would say that. It's in God's plan.'

'But how mean of God.' Andrea experienced a moment of severe religious doubt. 'To take Anne. Why poor Anne? I can't understand it.'

'God takes His chosen ones to Him,' Lucy said piously. 'She is with Him now in heaven.'

'Well, I just can't see it. It simply doesn't make sense. And such a horrible death; to be crushed.'

'I'm sure she didn't feel anything.' Lucy was trying hard to give God a chance.

'How do you know?'

'God is very merciful, and Anne was a very good girl. Perhaps she might have changed when she got older, and He wanted her now. We can't question what God does.'

Clare, because of her scientific studies, was sceptical too. 'Well, He does it in a funny way.'

'Clare!'

'Oh all right.'

'Pat had terrible spots all over his face. He hadn't even started to shave.' Judith was still brooding over cause and effect. The others nodded in sympathy. 'A lout.' They groaned.

'It makes you think about the seance,' Clare said. 'I mean, it was terrible the way the glass went over to Anne. How could *anyone* know?'

'The Devil,' Lucy said. 'It was the Devil, like Reverend Mother said.'

'Oh, that's nonsense,' Andrea protested. 'It was just a silly game.'

'It was your idea.' Accusingly from Judith.

'Don't be beastly,' Clare said protectively. 'Are you now trying to blame Andrea for Anne's death? What about you? You were so nasty to her; wouldn't even listen to her explanation.'

Judith bent her head towards her lap and began to sob bitterly. Lucy put an arm round her and murmured 'there, there'.

'But it was odd,' Andrea said when Judith had become more composed, 'because I'm sure no one pushed the glass. I didn't. I know I didn't. And everyone else said so too. It would be such a cruel thing to do.'

'Yet it came true,' Clare said gravely. 'Anne did die first. I am pretty sure, you know, that there are spirits at work in the world. It was like a warning for Anne.'

'How do you reconcile this with religion?'

'I don't know. Perhaps God wanted to warn her.'

'Why?'

'I don't know that either.'

'There is a lot I don't know. I must ask Mother Veronica. I have instruction with her later on.'

Clare jumped up, looking at her watch. 'Golly, I have a lesson with her now. We're doing advanced maths. See you.'

The girls looked after her as she went indoors.

'Clare has changed,' Judith said. 'Remember how madcap she used to be? Now she's so serious. Advanced maths, if you please.'

'She's growing up,' Andrea said thoughtfully. 'We all are.'

'I think she's unhappy,' Lucy said. 'Why is she unhappy, Andrea?'

'I don't think she is unhappy. But she doesn't really know what she wants to do. I don't either, really. I think we are all entering a difficult time. But everyone does change. Look at Lucy, and how awkward she used to be. Why, now she's almost a woman of the world.'

Lucy gave a shy smile, and flicked her hair back from her face. 'Am I? It's funny. I was so nervous before. That made me clumsy. I never actually meant to do any harm.'

'It was all those altar boys in the greenhouse,' Andrea said slyly. 'They made you mature. Did you ever tell the truth about that, Lucy?'

'In a way.'

'What way?'

'I forget. It was so long ago. I know I embroidered a bit.'

'I bet you did. Anyway, I've forgotten too. Girls, we're all getting old.'

Lucy looked at her watch and got up, smoothing her dress. 'Anyway, I must go to the greenhouse. I want a really fine display for Corpus Christi. The hibiscus are at their best this year.'

Andrea laughed. 'You and your hibiscus. I think when people ask me in later life what were my memories of the convent, I will say, "Lucy Potts and her hibiscus flower."'

'They are significant,' Lucy said gravely. 'You told me that yourself.'

'About death.'

They remembered how the flower blazed and died so swiftly; and they were silent as they thought of the short insignificant life of Anne Wedgewood, and the mystery of why it should have been so.

# Nine

But before the feast of Corpus Christi that year, the war in Europe came to an end. The girls, who had been so unaware of the struggle going on during their schooldays, celebrated with as much joy as their elders, who knew what they had been spared. They had two days off, and those who could went home to attend bonfire parties where some of them saw fireworks for the first time.

Andrea went briefly to London with her aunt to see her father, who was being sent on a mission to New York. Lucy went to her family, who marked the occasion by eating a lot, and she saw her father drunk for the first time. She remembered VE Day because of that, and how ashamed her mother was of having to get her elder brother to put Father to bed.

The nuns celebrated by having specially nice meals. But they also spent a lot of time in the chapel, saying prayers of thanksgiving and singing the *Te Deum*.

In the village where the Bingleys lived there was a big dance in the parish hall, and Clare put on lipstick for the first time and a very pretty party dress, and went to the dance with her elder brother. Clare had never been to a dance before. Now she discovered how inadequate the dancing was that the girls had done in the gym, and she fell all over her partners' feet. What she hated most was the way the women stood at one end of the floor and the men at the other. Then when the music began the men would swoop down on the women they had selected from the other side of the hall. It reminded Clare of a cattle market, where the farmers would go very carefully round the stock before making their selection. However, few swooped down on her, or if they did she was not asked again because of her clumsy steps. She danced a few times with her brother, but he was a rather randy eighteen-year-old and had his eye on the local talent, which was all dressed to kill. Most of the time Clare stood talking to a few of the lumpish and highly made-up local girls, who thought she was stuck-up and superior.

The worst time came at something called the supper dance. In the room next to the main hall were tables, and the men were expected to choose their partners and take them off for supper. The throng of women round her dwindled as the sedate waltz started, and they were claimed by the husky local youths. Clare looked round desperately, hoping that her brother would turn up and rescue her. But he was locked in the arms of one of the local belles, and had no time for his subdued little sister from the convent.

Just as she was about to despair, and was looking for some way to escape and go home, a hefty young man with a red face and almost bald head appeared and asked her for the dance. Her feet were immediately imprisoned beneath his, and they tried to sort themselves out and get going. He smelled of beer and kept giving her a frothy, and she thought unpleasant, grin. He was devoid of conversation, but kept squeezing her in a way that nearly winded her. Then, as the music ended, he lurched off and left her feeling very hot and unhappy in the middle of the floor.

Now all the couples were going into the supper room, or some of the men were bringing tables out and setting them on the dance floor. There were plenty of shrieks, and much gaiety all round. Except for Clare, who felt lonely and inadequate. There was no sign of her partner returning, so she just sat at a table near her with a spare seat. It was occupied by two couples who Clare thought must be deeply in love because they were cuddling and squeezing a lot and paying no attention at all to their food. This was obviously the passion at work that Andrea was always on about. She thought it looked disgusting.

At the far side she could see her brother with this tarty-looking girl on his knee, his arms tight round her. Clare looked away in dismay. Her brother was head boy at the local Catholic grammar school, as well as chief altar boy, and she thought his behaviour most unedifying.

Clare got up and stepped past the couples and the tables on her way to the cloakroom. No one seemed to care about her going. She was getting her school coat and panama hat when there was a shout behind her, and her partner of the supper dance appeared at the door.

'Thur'y'are, luv,' he slurred. 'I've been looking for ye.'

He had a trickle of beer on his chin, and Clare was sure he had been looking for something else.

'I'm going home,' she said primly. 'I am not enjoying myself at all. Why did you rush off like that?'

'I was looking for a table, love, and some food. Come on.'

'No thank you,' Clare said and put her hat on her head, tucking the elastic under her chin.

'My, hoity-toity,' the youth said, and stumbled towards her. He grasped her face in his thick red hands and planted a warm, wet and smelly mouth on hers. Clare tried to scream, but the more she struggled the harder he held her. His nasty hot body was clamped against hers, and he was writhing about in an unpleasant way. Clare – cool headed despite her panic – grasped the elastic under her chin and tugged at it hard until it snapped and flashed up into his face. He gave a cry of pain, and staggered away, reeling.

Clare rushed for the door and ran all the way home. She sobbed the story to her mother, who gave her two aspirin and a glass of milk. When her father, who had been to see a patient, came home and heard the story he laughed, and said her brother was a young scoundrel. Clare went to bed without pity from anyone, and lay in the dark listening to the fireworks and screams coming from the village. She thought how awful and ridiculous people were, losing control of themselves in this way. However, by the time Clare went back to school the next day she had thought sufficiently about her experience to try and make capital out of it, the way Lucy once had.

Everyone else seemed to have had a marvellous time.

Andrea had been to a victory ball at a large central London hotel, and had danced with a handsome lieutenant who, she said, had pronounced himself captivated by her. All the girls couldn't stop talking about the good times they had had, so that Clare, during recreation after supper, waited until they had talked themselves out, and then said very loftily:

'As a matter of fact, I had an experience myself.'

The way she mouthed 'experience' made everyone look at her.

'What kind of experience?' Andrea enquired.

'A very intimate and personal one. This man, very handsome, danced with me all evening. Then he said he was in love with me, and he kissed me.'

'He *kissed* you?' They were all most impressed, no one, even Andrea, having owned to have gone that far.

'On the mouth.'

There was a gratified silence.

'Was it nice?'

'Marvellous. I was swept away completely, and forgot myself.'

'In the arms of passion? Like Antony and Cleopatra?' asked Andrea, thinking how correct and boring the lieutenant brought by Daddy, and forced to dance with her, had been.

'Exactly that. That is the way they must have felt.'

'Goodness.'

'I always knew I had it in me.' Clare was a little abashed by the interest she had caused. 'To be passionate, you know.'

'Quite.'

'I shouldn't let Mother St John hear about it,' Judith said, remembering Pat. 'I don't know what kind of mortal sin that is.'

'Oh, I shall have to confess it,' Clare said gravely. 'I know I let my emotions run away with me and felt all sorts of things I shouldn't have.'

'Like?'

'Well, passionate things.'

'To do with the body?'

'Of course.'

'In what way?'

'I can't really tell you. Just that it was definitely sinful. I shall tell Father Vincent all about it.'

Andrea giggled. 'You might give him a thrill.'

Clare looked at her sternly. 'Don't be coarse, Andrea. You just don't understand.'

Andrea was hurt by this rebuff, and left the circle, where the others continued to ask Clare to elaborate on her experience. Then Lucy broke away and followed Andrea.

'Don't be hurt,' she said. 'I don't believe a word of it.'

'That's funny. That's just what Clare said about you in the greenhouse. You Catholics do tell a lot of lies.'

Andrea, having passed her hurt on and hurt Lucy in turn, went up to bed where she had a long chat in the dormitory with Mother Veronica, with whom Andrea was now a firm favourite.

Mother Veronica was a tall beautiful nun, who kept herself a little apart from the community. Mother Veronica was aware of her beauty, but saddened by it too, because, as the years of her religious life passed, she felt that she had misplaced her vocation. She was nudged by a continual feeling of discontent that her devotion to her work or to her charges did not completely sublimate. The rules were irksome and childish, and the intelligence of the majority of the nuns was inferior to hers. She never felt completely that she belonged, but always wished she were someone else, like one of the parents of the children. She was always sad when they went home for the holidays, and longed for them to come back again. She lived her life in other people.

This was in no way connected with a denial of religion. Mother Veronica was a considerable theological scholar, and engaged in correspondence with eminent clergymen on matters requiring interpretation, like the age at which the soul enters the body or the salvation of the unbaptised. Her mathematics would easily have gained her a teaching place at a university.

Perhaps had she been given more scope for her talents she would have been more fulfilled, and more contented with her vocation as a servant of God. But Mother Veronica would never think of leaving the convent; her acceptance of the situation was as perfect as her obedience. Twenty years later, when the climate in the Church changed so much, she might have done something about it, such as seeking a dispensation from her vows. But by then she was too old and the idea would never have occurred to her.

But when she sat talking that night to Andrea in the dormitory those days were many years away. Andrea had renewed doubts about her religious beliefs, and she did think that Catholics told a lot of lies. Then there were the awful atrocities that the allies had discovered in Europe: the living cadavers in the concentration camps, and the mountains of human bones piled like slag heaps outside. How could God permit it all?

Mother Veronica composedly folded her arms in the sleeves of her habit. Her beautiful and disturbingly tranquil face, behind which she concealed the conflict inside her, gazed at Andrea as though she were propounding to her one of the ineffable mysteries of the divine law. It was how she taught Andrea doctrine, gazing at her with those very calm and thoughtful eyes burning with the light of a fine intelligence.

'It is true we don't know the answer to many things. The ways of God are inscrutable and His way is interpreted for us by Holy Mother Church. But you see, the Church, though divinely founded, is a very human institution. And because more is expected of it, more is required, as we see from our gospel: "Everyone to whom much is given, of him will much be required; and of him to whom men commit much, they will demand the more". To be a good Catholic one must be better than anyone else; and if we fall, then we fall further than others. The Devil is at work among those whom God has chosen, and he makes them seem sometimes even less worthy than their fellows. God is always calling us to Him, and we are always pulling back. Do you see that, dear child?' She lightly took Andrea's hand in her own very long white one, with the beautifully rounded, shiny nails, which she buffed frequently.

'The question of suffering is one of the great mysteries. Few people who are honest will say they know why God, who is goodness itself, will permit it. This is what you also asked me when poor little Anne Wedgewood died. But the ways of God are not the ways of men; and much that we do not understand now we shall see at the time of the divine revelation, when all things shall be made known.

'Above all, Andrea, faith is a mystery. We believe by faith, as St Paul says; and this helps us to love God through things that would seem impossible to other people.'

'Yes. Yes, I see.'

The gentle, inspirational way Mother Veronica explained the mysterious workings of faith always affected Andrea strongly. It seemed to cement her own resolution, and clear a way through matters that had been puzzling her. This again was an emotional response to something that might not have convinced her had she read it in a book. Mother Veronica had a beautiful voice, low keyed and melodious; and listening to it expounding the mysteries of the Faith was in itself an experience.

'God is calling you, Andrea, is he not?'

'I think so, Mother. I mean, I feel very strongly about it.'

'I think so myself. I have noticed it grow stronger in you. Do you think your father . . .'

'I am seeing him again in the holiday. I will ask him then. But I want to be perfect when I am a Catholic. I never want to tell lies or hurt other people.'

'Then you must pray very hard for grace, and God will give it to you. My dear Andrea.'

A momentary glow of beatitude, of warm affection drew them together, and Mother Veronica kissed Andrea very lightly on the forehead. Then the noisy clamour of the girls coming up from recreation intervened, and Mother Veronica glided away, ready to receive any other confidences that might come her way that night.

Clare was very troubled by the stupid lie she had told. She knew she was trying to fight this creeping sense of coldness, and to make herself as warm and responsive to people as Andrea was. Clare did not suffer from religious scruples, and as a contrast to Andrea she was, by reason of her devotion to science, beginning to question many of the premises of religious belief. But at this time her religion was an objective response to what she still considered were the realities of heaven and hell: salvation or burning. After being so long at the convent, she was very clear about good being rewarded and bad punished. Her lie troubled her not only because it had been so silly – she had been trying to impress people who did not really matter to her – but because it had been so deliberate. It was despicable, and made her ashamed of herself, which increased the sense of sin.

The next time that Father Vincent came to hear the girls' confessions, she spent a lot of time with him in the confessional. This intrigued the others waiting outside, because usually confession was a case of whip in and whip out; two minutes per penitent. They speculated about what was keeping Clare so long, and whether she had perhaps gone further than *just* a kiss at the dance.

It was Father Vincent's custom to say his office while in the box. He had heard thousands of little girlish confessions during his years as chaplain, supplemented by thousands more on Saturdays at his parish church. The nuns' confessions were heard by a monsignor who came from another part of the diocese. The Bishop always appointed the nuns' confessors, just anybody wouldn't do.

Father Vincent knew most of the girls by their names; he had heard Clare's first confession when she made her first communion soon after he came to the convent.

Clare went into great detail about her lie to Father Vincent, and he stopped reading his breviary and listened carefully because she was usually one of the very quick ones. He sensed in Clare a new kind of disturbance.

'Are you very worried about it, Clare?'

'Well, not so worried. I just feel a bit stupid about it all. I hate myself for going to all the trouble of telling such a silly fat lie.'

'In fact you're worried about yourself, not about offending God?'

'Do you think God is very offended?'

'That's not the point. It was a deliberate lie. It was certainly sinful. You are not really aware enough of sin, are you, Clare? What you are suffering from now is disappointment with yourself. You feel you should be above this kind of thing. Hardly a religious attitude, is it?'

'No. I suppose not.'

'And you went so far because you wanted to shock them. You wanted them to think you had kissed and enjoyed it.'

Father Vincent was usually not so stern, and Clare was rather upset.

Through the grille he could see the girl's profile. He could remember her as a small nervous junior, and now she was almost a woman, with thick black hair, unfastened by a ribbon, and an aesthetically pale face. He suddenly felt very close to this girl he had known for so long. In fact, he had not felt like this with anyone since Virginia Clearwater had left. But Virginia Clearwater had been very scrupulous, and had spent ages going over the details of the smallest sin.

Father Vincent had been aware of something that was not wholly priestly in his attitude towards Virginia Clearwater; in fact, he had even asked the Canon if this was a danger signal and if he should be removed from the convent. But the Canon, that bibulous and jolly man, was also rather wise, because he had been at his job a long time. He had said that this kind of temptation came to every young priest, perhaps many times, because they were normal men and ordination did not make them any less human. He said Father Vincent must pray about the feeling, resist it, and not keep Virginia Clearwater so long in the confessional.

'You have been rather a silly girl, wanting to get attention for yourself,' the priest continued. 'You might also regard it as a danger signal that you should want to dwell on matters of the flesh, which are the easiest ways to sin; the hardest paths to leave. You can remember this when you go into the

212

world. Now pray to Our Lady for purity, and say a decade of the Rosary for your penance. *Ego te absolve . . .* '

Clare left the confessional feeling rather annoyed. The old twerp, ticking her off like that. Next time she wouldn't be so scrupulous. She felt resentful rather than strengthened, because she objected to this kind of woolly homily, which missed the point. As for thinking she was on the road to ruin . . .

What Clare wanted was advice about herself. It was silly warning her about fleshly matters, because they did not frankly appeal to her. The earlier musings on procreation were a thing of the past, and she knew exactly how it was done. At her request, Miss Ottershaw had put their study of Darwin aside one morning, and had taken up pencil and a clean sheet of paper instead. It was all quite clear now. But what was not clear was the feeling; the response that she and Andrea used always to be wondering about. You didn't just 'do' it, Miss Ottershaw had tried to explain, you felt something at the time that made you want to. She made no secret of the fact that she knew what this was. But Clare didn't like to ask her; she was also a bit shocked to think she would know.

Clare's experience at the dance had only reinforced her suspicion that sex was actually unpleasant. The only things about which Clare was certain were inside the covers of her scientific books; facts appealed to her more than feelings. They were, anyway, much more reliable.

And then it was time for the summer holidays once more, and once more the girls packed and went home.

That August the first atomic bomb killed a lot of people in Japan, injured thousands more, and affected the lives of many who were not even born. But, anyway, World War II came to an end, and a new age, the Nuclear, had begun.

Many people's lives had been ended by the war, and many had been changed. But the girls of the Convent of the Blessed Apostles faced the future as though nothing had happened, although the world they now faced was very different from the one they had grown up in. There would be changes in attitudes, morals, behaviour, politics, fashions and standards of living. There might be nothing very fundamental in some of these, or there might be: because all life is change.

There would be a gigantic upheaval in the Church that had seemed so unchanging in their childhood. This really would be fundamental, and some would say it was as important as the Reformation only not so bloody.

The new society would present more opportunities, and yet impose more limitations: because conscience would become a matter of determining truth for oneself, rather than obeying without question strict laws decreed from above. But some people would always want to do what they were told; and others would prefer to refuse. There would be nothing very new about this.

But this is still the summer of 1945. The convent had its long summer rest, and then prepared to receive new pupils, as well as to welcome back the old. And among this group were Lucy, Andrea and Clare, who faced their last year at school.

# Ten

The pale autumn sun shining through the chapel windows played on the white chasuble of the priest, picking out the heavy gold embroidery on the back as he held aloft the host, genuflected and raised it again. It was a moment of breathtaking splendour and Andrea felt her heart swell with a strange, almost violent emotion. Once more the bell tinkled and this time the chalice was held aloft and all heads were bowed again. On either side of the tabernacle the huge white and yellow chrysanthemums seemed to sway very slightly, and beside them the tall candles in their burnished brass candlesticks flickered as though disturbed by a soft breeze. The measured, almost mysterious movements of the priest continued, and as he faced the congregation, holding the host above the chalice, and began to descend the altar steps, Reverend Mother lead the congregation to Holy Communion in celebration of her feast day.

As usual Andrea remained in her place watching them, wishing that she could be among them, still aware of that strange, strong, soaring emotion that seemed to gather in intensity as it passed right through her. She thought Reverend Mother raised her head and glanced intently at her as she passed on her way back to her pew. It was a sign. Andrea knew it was a sign, and taking up her Roman missal she read the postcommunion prayer in the proper of the Mass for St Teresa:

*May the heavenly Mystery, Oh Lord, inflame us with the fire of that love by which Saint Teresa, thy Virgin, offered herself to Thee as a victim of charity*

*for mankind, through our Lord Jesus Christ who
liveth and reigneth world without end.*

Reverend Mother had taken in religion the name of Teresa
after the young girl who entered the Carmel of Lisieux in
1888 at the age of fifteen. She died there only nine years
later in the odour of sanctity, vowing to spend her heaven
doing good on earth. Such was the exemplary nature of her
life that she was beatified in 1923 and canonised as St Teresa
of Lisieux only two years later. She became known as the
Little Flower of Jesus.

St Teresa, known for her piety and humility, for the humble
tasks she chose to do around her convent, seemed very
different from Reverend Mother, who, despite her diminutive stature, was a strong and forceful personality. One would
have imagined that she might have chosen as a model the
great St Teresa of Avila, eminent theologian, doctor of the
Church, reformer of the Carmelites. But no, she chose to
attempt to emulate the person least like her, maybe to
encourage a sense of humility that had rather been lacking
in her life.

Soon afterwards Mass ended and the children gathered
round Reverend Mother as she came down the stairs on her
way to the nuns' refectory, pressing on her small presents,
usually a medal or a holy picture. She received them all with
smiles, a little pat, sometimes a hug. In this peaceful domestic
setting Reverend Mother was seen at her best, almost like a
mother of the children she had never had.

It was known in the Order that Reverend Mother came
from an old titled Catholic family, that she was one of a large
number of brothers and sisters and that she had been educated
at the best houses of the Order in France and England before
entering and bringing a substantial dowry with her. What was
not known was if she had ever regretted her decision or ques-
tioned her calling, because she was a woman who, once her
mind was made up, seldom allowed herself even to consider
an alternative or think that she might have been mistaken.
She was an enlightened nun, thoughtful and intelligent, and

kept abreast of all the news, particularly to do with the war as she had several nephews in the armed services.

Once she had received all her gifts and passed them on to Mother David, standing behind her like a dutiful lady-in-waiting, she extended her hands in a collective embrace, her face illuminated by a warm, happy smile.

'Thank you all, my dears,' she said, her voice betraying strong emotion. 'Thank you all very much for your gifts, above all your prayers.' She paused. 'Try and always have before you, as a model of virtue and obedience, the beautiful saint whose feast we are celebrating.

'She was only a young girl when she entered Carmel, younger than some of you here today, but her life was one of perfect obedience, small tasks done in the service of God. An unremarkable life, one might have thought, yet she has been raised to the altar as one of our greatest saints. You might remember, as you pass through life, that small things are sometimes more important than big ones.' She glanced round her at the eager thoughtful faces so intently watching her. 'As for you, you are all my little flowers, my precious little flowers, and I treasure you.'

And almost as though she thought she had gone too far, Reverend Mother, who was not as a rule a sentimental woman, gave a little cough and went quickly on her way while the little flowers, as if gratified as well as uplifted by the dignity she had in a sense bestowed on them, tripped eagerly down to breakfast, which that day was full of special treats in honour of Reverend Mother's feast.

Later that day Andrea knocked on Reverend Mother's door and after a moment she received the command to enter. Reverend Mother was sitting by the window looking out on to the park. There was a book on her lap and she looked as though she might have been napping.

'Happy feast day, Reverend Mother,' Andrea said, shyly holding out a card that she'd bought that morning from the holy shop.

'Oh, thank you, Andrea.' Reverend Mother slit open the

217

envelope, withdrew the card and sat back, admiring a pretty posy of flowers.

'I couldn't find one with St Teresa on. I thought that, as it had flowers. . .' Andrea trailed off lamely.

Reverend Mother nodded appreciatively. 'It is very beautiful.' She sat back with a sigh of satisfaction. 'What a lovely day it it is for my feast.' She gazed again at the garden. 'And how lucky we are to live in such a beautiful place.'

'It is beautiful.'

'And are you really happy here?' Reverend Mother looked at her searchingly.

'Very.' Andrea had an expression of ill-concealed excitement on her face, as if she could hardly contain herself. 'I have been very, very happy here. Oh, and, Reverend Mother, I would like to be received,' she concluded in a rush. 'I feel I am ready, I really do. Mother Veronica thinks I am too.'

Reverend Mother hastily put aside the card and leaned towards Andrea, taking her hands in hers. 'This is the most wonderful news. Are you sure?'

'Quite quite sure,' Andrea said. 'I knew this morning in the chapel I was sure. Everything looked so beautiful. It is just as I want it and as I think it should be. *Things*, you know . . .' she finished awkwardly. 'It seems the right thing to do.'

'And your father won't object?'

'Oh no. He said I could do what I liked. I asked him during the holiday.'

'It must be the intercession of the Little Flower,' Reverend Mother said with awe in her voice. 'Having prayed so much for this you must take her name for your confirmation.'

'Oh yes I will.' Andrea nodded fervently. 'And after you too, Reverend Mother.'

Reverend Mother leaned back, Andrea's hands still clasped tightly in hers. 'It is the best, the very best present for my feast day I could ever have had. You are to be one of us, at last.'


Two months after her conversation with Reverend Mother Andrea achieved her ambition and was received by Father

Vincent into the Church on the Feast of the Immaculate Conception. The ceremony took place before the assembled boarders and nuns in the chapel before the nine o'clock Mass. She received conditional baptism, and the water was sprinkled on her head. She resolved to renounce the Devil and all his works, and be true to the Catholic Church founded by Christ. Her sponsors were Reverend Mother and Clare. All the nuns and some of the girls were tearful as Andrea, looking the perfect picture of a saint, preceded Father Vincent down the aisle and went into the box at the end to make her confession to him.

The choir sang a hymn very slowly, as Andrea recalled the sins in her eighteen years of life, and Mother Mary Paul was greatly moved as she gently wafted her hands with unusual emphasis back and forth, welcoming, as it were, Andrea to the fold.

Then Andrea emerged from the confessional and Clare and Reverend Mother escorted her back to her pew. She knelt a long time with her head in her hands; but she was too confused to pray. A kind of rapture possessed her that she would only know again when she combined this kind of emotion with physical passion. The original moment, then as now, would be ecstatic because she was responding to the deep inner feelings of her sensuous nature: the need to be loved.

Father Vincent came up the aisle again for the Mass in his white vestments, the magnificently embroidered chasuble, the chalice and paten in his hands. The choir had never sung better, and the Mass had a mystical quality for Andrea that continued when she went up the communion rails with the others, and received for the first time the host on her tongue.

That afternoon she took part in the procession through the school, singing and saying the Rosary at the altars, which had been gorgeously bedecked with flowers by Lucy. She remembered looking down on the procession three years before; but now her white veil was there too, and at last she belonged.

That night as a special mark of favour Reverend Mother invested her with the blue ribbon and the silver medal of Child of Mary. She never lost the medal showing the Virgin in glory, even much later when she had ceased to practice her faith and thoughts of her days in the convent and of the Church were only a nostalgic memory.

Andrea and Clare were eighteen within a month of each other, in the November of the Upper Sixth year. Lucy was the eldest, and had her birthday the day the second atomic bomb fell on Nagasaki.

The three were the only ones to go into the Upper Sixth; Judith had left at the end of the summer to go to the teacher training college near Manchester. She too would start to look for a man, but she would have more success than Virginia Clearwater, who had only one date in her two years' training, and was now teaching infants in a tiny village in North Yorkshire. Judith would marry quite soon, and lead rather a normal uneventful life.

Clare became head girl. Mother Michael would have preferred Andrea, but Clare had been in the school from the age of seven and everyone thought it would have been very unfair to have overlooked her. Lucy had decided she wanted to be a nurse. Stories she had read about the war had stirred her; and she felt this would be something practical as well as altruistic, to appeal to that side of her nature. But she would not take the Higher School Certificate, and would only stay in the Upper Sixth until she could get into a hospital.

Clare was studying maths and science, and Andrea arts. They had both applied to the universities of Oxford and Cambridge, and several of the colleges in London. They were determined to go south and, if possible, to be together. Dear Lucy, with her clumsy ways and obsession with flowers, her sentimentality and her lack of tact – they had become very fond of her and hoped she would be near them too.

The girls were now very grand. Stacks of younger ones had crushes on them. They had moved out of the large study, and worked in their small classroom next to the staff room. They were all three in the dormitory of the Holy Ghost, and stayed up half the night chattering in the bathroom with Mother Veronica. The very awareness of their lofty station in life seemed to fit them for it, and the change from this supremacy to their freshman year at the university or Lucy's year as a probationer nurse was to prove quite shattering.

These grand girls now did nothing wrong. They became the confidents of the lay mistresses, and the pets of the nuns. Mother St John toadied up to them all the time, forever seeking their advice about some erring junior.

All the little faults they had had while growing up were now seen as intolerable in others; they were strict disciplinarians and stern leaders of the young. They would tolerate no talking in forbidden places, no falling out of line, no jinks in the dormitory, no unscheduled excursions to the playground or the ice cream shop two streets away. When they were young it had been a great feat to get there and back with a choc bar without being caught.

Andrea had grown into a beautiful girl, and had cut her long fair hair short so that it curled softly round her head. She had a very fine figure indeed with long shapely legs, a trim bosom and a nicely rounded bottom. Unlike Clare, who was doubtful, Andrea was excited about the future and continually adjusted herself to its possibilities. Her father wrote her long letters from New York, and kept her in touch with the sophistications and opportunities of the world. As she had got older and begun to resemble her mother, she and her father had grown closer.

Aunt still kept up her platonic liaison with Mr Clearwater, but she had given up hope of it becoming anything more profound and considered him just a good friend. Besides, he very kindly helped her with financial matters, and invested her money for her. In time he would take it away completely, leaving her with nothing, because of misplaced investments in a shifting post-war market.

Lucy had not grown much beyond her fifteenth year. She was the smallest of the three but, from having been skinny, was turning plump. She moved awkwardly and if there was something to fall over she would fall over it, because she was so short sighted and her spectacles needed changing. A sight in the school was Lucy charging – she always charged – along, pushing her glasses up her nose, her feet pounding

221

on the floor. Her hair was now straight, because she had never been able to curl it very successfully; it had usually been dead straight on one side and a seething mass of curls the other. So she stopped, and just let it hang, securing it with a large grip on the right-hand side of her head. Lucy would always compromise with life because she would never feel sufficiently sure about a thing to stick to it. She was an extrovert, simple girl and had never lost her naïve piety or her devotion to flowers. She would always think that life was as uncomplicated as she was, and would be distressed and saddened by its intricacies. She would never marry but would have a satisfying career as a nursing sister and eventually retire to a pretty cottage in Devon with a large garden. Her best friend among the nuns was still Sister Benedict, and she remained scared of Mother St John and in awe of Reverend Mother.

Clare. Clare was the most complicated. She was even taller than Andrea, but her figure was relatively undeveloped and rather like a boy's, with a small, almost non-existent bosom and very slim hips. She was aware of herself as head girl, and often displayed her nasty temper to those under her.

Clare was beset by inner problems that she did not understand, and that would take her years to work out. Relationships with people also bothered her, and always would, but she never wavered in her affection for Andrea, who, with her family, was the one understandable solid thing in her life. She also envied Andrea's gaiety, and her charm, her ability to communicate. But nothing about Andrea ever made Clare jealous; she loved her because she almost felt she was part of her, that their personalities were twin aspects of the same person. They would, with several breaks because of being separated by distance, remain friends for the rest of their lives.

*1946*

That winter Andrea watched her beloved trees in the grounds turn yellow and brown, and knew she would never see them like this again, not slowly changing their colours from day to day. The leaves gathered on the ground and were swept into piles and burned by the handyman. But before she left she would see them again in their splendour; and the memory she would keep would be of that green expanse that one looked out on to from the rooms at the top of the convent, which seemed to obscure the world outside in a symbolic way.

In January young Miss Ottershaw's fiancé Arnold was killed in an air crash on the way home from the Far East, where he had been on military duty. He was about to be demobbed and had asked Miss Ottershaw to marry him just as soon as it could be arranged. Clare, who was almost her closest friend, as well as being near to her in age, did all she could to console her; although the tragedy appalled her – another of those cruel, meaningless acts. She could sense also Miss Ottershaw's fear that she would spend the rest of her life as a member of the convent's staff, becoming almost a part of the fabric of the building, like the others. They talked often in those sad days about life, because of its close links with death; and she almost forgot her own problems as she urged Miss Ottershaw to look forward, because hope would return again. Sometimes Andrea and Lucy would join them, and they felt the stirrings of a premonition of that ultimate mortality that was altogether absent from their younger days, even when Mother Emanuel had died, or Anne Wedgewood.

One or two of the younger mistresses had left, and been replaced by others. But the atmosphere of forced girlish gaiety in the staff room never changed, nor did the furnishings or the bright floral paper on the walls. Personalities changed from time to time, but on the whole they stuck, becoming more resigned to the reality of their situation, and assuring themselves of its advantages.

Miss Clark had by now completely abandoned thoughts of marriage and devoted herself to her work. She would go home at night and write short stories, which she tried to sell, but usually published for nothing in the parish or school magazines. She wore her hair in a tight little braid round her head, as though to symbolize the closing in of herself, and the colours of her clothes became more subdued, though in design they still tended towards the eccentric.

Miss Greene had not many years to live, but she had no premonition of her premature end. She expressed herself solely in her art, which was patterned and coloured, while the world outside her work was grey, grey.

Miss Goldie and Miss Moppatt were nearly due for retirement. They planned to buy a little bungalow near Lytham when their parents died, and live there contentedly together. Unfortunately, Miss Goldie would die quite soon, leaving her mother to see her hundredth birthday all by herself in a nursing home, bitterly resentful of the thoughtless way her daughter had left her. Miss Moppatt spent her final years alone in the little house her parents had left her, devoting herself to good works.

Mrs Battley watched her sons grow up, and hoped that at least one would become a priest. She now only spoke to her husband when it was necessary to communicate, and the rest of her free time she devoted to work in the pious associations attached to the Church.

Another mistress had joined the school who was newly married and very happy, and this rather put paid to the superiority of Mrs Battley's position, so that she retired into obscurity while the new staff member made broad and rather vulgar hints about the delights of married life, and the others were envious or disgusted according to temperament.

Miss Larkin continued to sing 'Cherry Ripe' or 'Where E'er Ye Walk' in her thrilling contralto at school concerts, and even the accustomed applause never seemed to grow stale or diminish her enthusiasm. Miss Parker went on relying on tadpoles for her lessons on reproduction, but Miss Ottershaw took a firm hand when the girls reached the senior forms, so that at least some of the convent products had a more realistic view of the process of human propagation when they left, and did not expect their husbands to behave like frogs.

After the end of the war the standards of the school were to improve considerably, and by the 1950s there would be quite a large sixth form. It would not be so uncommon to send girls to university, and the great stream of infant teachers that the convent produced would gradually diminish. One or two girls ultimately entered the Order; but not many. None did so at the time of this story, and the nuns started a novena of prayer, which resulted in triumph four years later when one sixth former actually did enter.

And the nuns? The nuns remained the same, or they would until this breed who had joined the Order in the twenties and thirties died out, and a more broad-minded and racier generation replaced them under the influence of the reforms in the Church inspired by the Second Vatican Council. Everywhere, though, vocations went down because religion was neither such a necessary or attractive alternative to life in the world. It was more acceptable for women to have careers, and they could participate much more in their own destinies than had been possible before. One of the great changes in the postwar era was that it gave to women a place that was honourable, sometimes exciting, and often to equal that of men.

Mother St John was to stay on for a number of years as mistress of the boarders, and then she was abruptly translated to be Reverend Mother at a small convent of the Order in Ireland. She was glad to be home at last, and her old age was mellow and happy.

The Bishop would die soon and be replaced by a younger and more vigorous man, who would be receptive to new ideas and, in time, would replace his gleaming gold cross with a wooden one, and put aside the magnificent purple-stoned ring for a plain gold band.

Reverend Mother was soon to go, to be deputy provincial of the Order. She would be followed in the convent by a nun who was almost her exact replica, except that her background was not a noble one. But she kept her community firmly on the path they had trodden since they had made their vows, and consecrated themselves to God in perpetuity.

For change was not part of the convent mentality, and

when it came it came so slowly that one hardly noticed it. Convent life would go on, and so would the breed of convent girls who almost always, and in any age, had to adapt themselves, often in a traumatic way, to life outside the walls.

But this is to go forward. For the rest of that academic year life was as it ever had been. The school play took place, and work proceeded as usual. Neither Andrea nor Clare was cast in the play, because Miss Clark had lost heart after the fiasco of the previous year and, in a spirit of defeat, staged another nativity play because it was the only safe thing she could think of. She didn't even write it herself, but used an accepted text. It was mostly performed by the juniors, except for Jocasta Younghusband, who played the Archangel Gabriel and lost her wings in the middle of the Annunciation, which was just what the Bishop, on the look-out for heresy after his previous experiences, had expected her to do. The Archangel Gabriel would never have pranced about and proclaimed in such a melodramatic, sensational manner, first at one side of the stage and then at the other. Everyone knew from pictures that he had stayed quite still at the time. Jocasta shook a lot and her wings dropped off and lay on the ground, much to the confusion of the child who played Our Lady and burst into tears as the curtain fell.

At the end of the spring term Lucy left the school and went to London to begin her career as a probationer nurse in a large teaching hospital. There was a sad little party in the parlour for her, and a few tears were shed, except by Clare and Andrea, who knew they would see her again, and Reverend Mother, who had to set an example to everyone else.

Lucy took leave of Sister Benedict and her greenhouse. The plants were ready after their Lenten rest, when they were not much required, for a good summer season, and the hibiscus looked superb. Sister Benedict said she would take good care of them, and have them at their best for the Feast of Corpus Christi. She would arrange them on either side of the tabernacle in the chapel, and Our Lord, she promised, would think kindly of Lucy and all she had done in her years in the convent for him.

In the summer term the grounds of the convent gradually took on once again their lovely colours: the merging of the various inflexions of green, and the sharp, bright contrast of the flowers. Andrea watched the fat sticky buds turn into leaves, as she studied in the classroom for her Higher School Certificate with Clare by her side working at her maths. She gazed for hours out of the window, because she knew she would do well in her exam, and the unchanging variety of nature fascinated her more. She was already beginning to experience a nostalgia for this part of her life so soon to be over.

In the warm evenings before bed Andrea and Clare would walk through the grounds, talking about the future and some-times about the past. Then they would go upstairs to the dormitory for a good long chat with Mother Veronica, who was already subdued at the thought of losing her favourite girls.

They both walked for the first and the last time together in the Corpus Christi procession, Andrea at last as a Catholic, and Clare as head girl. The Bishop was more feeble now and kept having to stop and rest, though he always held the monstrance aloft above his head. It was the last procession too for the Bishop. The following year the monstrance would be carried by the Canon, and soon after that the Bishop would die after a meal of pork cooked in red wine, rich cheeses and a bottle of claret to drink.

So this year the procession wound round the grounds, and the swans sailed up and down in harmony, for they didn't change much. There seemed more greenery and blossom every year, and the grounds had never looked so good. The smell of rose petals mingling with incense was pungent and sweet. Afterwards, as usual, the children had their tea and met their parents, or went to play rounders with the altar boys in the playground. This was the year when Jocasta Younghusband managed to lure a poor innocent youth to go with her behind the boathouse, for experimental purposes; only she told him it was to carry plants. There was a great old fuss that night, with Clare and Andrea intervening in various ways. It was the usual kind of convent upheaval, with a lot of enjoyment for everyone, including Jocasta, who was dying to leave school and was glad she could go with panache.

At the end of the term in July, having sat their final exams, Andrea and Clare packed their trunks, cleared their desks and left everything ready for the new generation.

On the last evening they walked together slowly round the grounds after the others had gone to bed. They would pause to look at a place that reminded them of something – Clare at the trees where she long ago used to hold her secret society meetings, and Andrea the Rosary Way where she had had so many uplifting talks with Reverend Mother. They tried to be trivial, but they could not help being solemn; and they stopped for a long while by the lake to watch the swans, and resolved they would always be friends no matter what happened.

They went up towards the house, and stood at the top watching the sun going down slowly behind the houses outside the convent wall. They said that this place would never change; the trees and the flowers, the swans and the lake would always be there, as well as the community of nuns who had brought them up.

They were grateful, then, for the singular atmosphere of the convent, for the sense of peace and belonging it had given them, and for the experience of those years. The time of their youth.